You Weren't Mine Then

A Riviera View Novel

Lily Baines

she had earned the nickname Plain Jane in high school.

She was so engrossed that she almost missed Hope's exit from the bakery with a confused expression on her face. She waved at her with a hand that felt like clay.

The voices of the other customers and her parents, who were busy serving sticky buns and cupcakes, along with kind smiles as they had been doing for the last twenty-five years, resurfaced, as if a volume button had suddenly been turned back up and reality burst back into her Finn-centric vision.

"What can I get you?" she asked as if he was just another customer when he finally stood in front of her with nothing but the counter separating them. She knew it was only her imagination that made her smell a whiff of pool water. She wanted him out of there before her parents noticed him and would be all familial with him, or before Avery—her cousin and his ex-wife—would follow him into the bakery with their son.

He gave her a soft, understanding smile, knowing why she was sticking to business-as-usual mode. With their history and convoluted family ties, there was no other choice. "I'll take one of each of these, please." He pointed at the red velvet and hummingbird cupcakes. "I'm in town for Max, and I know he loves these. You make them?"

Anne placed the cupcakes in a box carrying the Breading Dreams logo. "Sometimes," she replied. Laconic replies were all he ever got from her, all she ever could offer him or afford in the family get-togethers that forced them to share space.

When she handed him the box with the sweets for his and Avery's son and reached for the credit card that he handed over, Finn caught her fingers for one drawn-out moment that peeled layers of years from her heart. She snatched her hand back and turned to the register, promising herself to get a contactless payment device as soon as possible.

"Can we talk sometime, Jane?" Finn asked in a lowered voice, a voice that had once whispered, "*Fuck, I can't ever unlove you*," with lips that kissed every inch of her body.

"Thank you for your purchase. Have a great day," she said, plastering on a customer-friendly smile. She then turned it to the lady who stood behind Finn and, with a gesture of her chin, added, "Hi, Mrs. Kim. How are you enjoying the fair so far, and what can I get you today?"

"Hi, Anne, dear," the woman replied enthusiastically. "It's lovely and crowded outside! So many people. Can you please get me ...?"

Anne hardly heard her. Though her gaze wasn't on him, her attention, unwittingly, was. In her periphery, she saw how he steeled his lips and hardly budged, even when Mrs. Kim shouldered her way past him to the front of the line.

"I'm sorry. It's a bit noisy today. What will it be again?" Anne asked the older lady as soon as Finn finally turned and strutted his wide shoulders and swimmer's build out to the street. The door that opened every few minutes swept in waves of music, chatter of a large crowd, and ocean breeze.

She wished she could hate him, be mad at him, or at least unlove him. God knew she had tried. But she never did. She never could. Not even when he had married her cousin, the woman whom she had been raised to think of as the sister she'd never had. Not even when she had to keep secret everything that had happened between them before. Not even when she'd had to attend their wedding and decorate their wedding cake.

Chapter 2

With an ashen heart, Finn squinted under the glare of the sun and ran a hand through his hair that was always a bit stiff from the chlorine of the pool water that he spent so many hours in. He skimmed his eyes over the crowd that strolled the closed-for-traffic Ocean Avenue, the main street of his hometown. Color and sound burst over him from every angle, but he didn't see any of it. All he could see was the tall woman who had turned as pale as the tiny white flowers on her wine-red summer wrap dress at the sight of him. The woman he had promised himself that he wouldn't go near, even after his divorce from her cousin. He had kept his promise for three years.

Even after she had moved back to California.

Until he broke.

Until today.

"Sorry."

"Excuse me."

"Pardon."

He stood in people's way, and after a few bumped into him, Finn moved to the side and tried detecting his son among the food stands, gift booths, and the balloon arches that decorated the sidewalks. Max wasn't near the T-shirts booth where he'd left him with his mother when an unkillable urge gripped him and catapulted him into the bakeshop.

For two years, knowing Anne had been back in town to work with her parents after years spent on the other side of the country, he had avoided going near the bakery, even when he had to be in Riviera View.

Unfortunately for him, Avery had moved back there, too, soon after, following her promotion to vice principal at the local school. Whenever he drove from Blueshore, the town he and Max still lived in, to drop Max off or pick him up from his ex's, he was grateful that Avery's house was close to the town's entrance, so he could avoid driving farther down Ocean Avenue where Bert and Linda Drecher's bakery was located. He had no other reason to come to Riviera View—his mother had moved to Florida years ago.

"Do you want one of those red velvet cupcakes you love from Grandma Linda's bakery?" he'd asked his son a few minutes before, using the family terminology that coined Linda Drecher, Anne's mother, as Max's grandmother, although she was only his grandmother's sister. He felt like shit using his son as an excuse to finally succumb to the urge he had resisted for so long—to go near the woman he hadn't stopped loving all these years, even when he had forced himself to do the right thing, even when he had forced himself to stop loving her, even when he had convinced himself that he had succeeded despite constantly dreaming of her only to wake with his mouth dry and his chest empty.

He spotted Avery first. With her back to him, standing at a booth that carried a sign announcing it to be a "Real-Life Etsy Shop," his ex-wife was unmistakable. Her hair, which was dark brown even at the age of forty-one, was the only similarity she bore to her cousin, who was four years younger. While Avery's hair was long, wavy, and highlighted, Anne's rested just above her shoulders, smooth and unburnished, just like it had been in her junior year in high school when she had tutored a senior year swimmer so he could get into the college with the swim team of his dreams.

The two cousins looked like their fathers and unlike the twin sisters who were their mothers. Sisters who couldn't be closer; the exact opposite of their daughters. This closeness had made everything so unbearable. And it would have been even more painful if Anne—his *Jane*—hadn't moved to the other side of the country soon after his marriage. For years, he had prayed for some relative to get married, baptized, christened, or even buried, so he'd have an excuse to see her, just so he could stand next to her, exchange a few public niceties, and whisper a private, "Jane," her old name, which he hoped she could decode to mean *I love you*. The guilt that ate at him for failing to let go of her was almost the size of his love for her.

"There you are! Brought you these," he said, placing an arm over his son's shoulders and handing him the box that Jane had packed.

"Thanks, Dad!" At twelve years old, Max's voice was still childish, and his face hadn't lost the boyish roundness, though he was as tall as his mother and tall enough to reach his dad's shoulders. No common feat, given that Finn was six-foot-three.

"Didn't find anything at the T-shirt stand?" Finn asked, unable to stop himself from patting his son's hair, though Max had begun shunning PDAs. As an only child himself, Finn knew that his son had probably been wanting to dodge these uncool parental affections earlier but had kept quiet for his parents' sakes. If the pregnancy that had forced Finn to marry Avery had survived, Max would have had an older brother or sister.

"Everything was about surfing, not swimming," Max said. He had recently joined his school's swim team in Blueshore, in addition to the club team that Finn coached.

"Surfing is big in beach towns," Finn said with a smile. "You and I should do more of that."

"And it was all either too large or too small," Max added, opening the cupcake box.

"Keep on practicing, and you'll grow into the larger ones, I promise," Finn replied, ruffling his son's light brown hair, a mix of his and Avery's colors.

"Eli's mom says we'll develop swimmers' bodies like yours," Max said, taking a healthy bite from one cupcake.

Finn let out a silent scoff. He was aware of the way some of the mothers eyed him, even some of the college girls when he joined his alma mater's practices twice a week. But he couldn't care less. He wasn't looking for attention, or meaningless hookups, or even love. He'd had enough of the first two when he had been much younger, which had landed him where he was now, ironically making the latter impossible, though it still gripped his heart.

"You're already better than I was at your age. And smarter. So, stick with it but don't forget your grades." He spoke from experience. By the time he had reached his senior year in high school, his grades hadn't been enough to land him at Cal Poly— California Polytech—whose swim team, one of the best in the nation, he'd aimed for. And, as the son of an older single mother, he had needed a scholarship. That had led to the hard decision to repeat his senior year. He had been assigned a tutor. A seemingly quiet and shy girl from junior year by the name of Jane Anne Drecher.

"Yeah, I know, Dad. Academic and athletic excellence both start with an A," Max chanted over another mouthful of cupcake, rolling his eyes with a smile.

Having never known his own father, Finn reeled in the fact that his son remembered the things he'd taught him and wanted to engage in the same activities. Since he had learned he was going to be a father, he had read every parenting book that he could get his hands on. While his mother was amazing, he didn't know what having a father was like and had wanted to make sure he did it right. He had a year of book reading before Max was born.

"That's right, buddy." He made sure to let his son know, not only of his wins but of his losses, too, the hard work it had taken to win, as well as the failure to sustain the career he had dreamed of. He hadn't told him about the biggest loss of his life, because that was directly connected to Max's mother. And if there was anything he knew without any book telling him, it was that he should never ever show any regret about marrying her. If he hadn't, he wouldn't have had Max, and Max was the best thing in his life.

"So, did you see anything you like here?" he added, one hand on his son's shoulder, the other pointing at the selection of gifts in the Real-Life Etsy booth—whatever that meant.

"These are nice. They have these swimmers painted on them, and there are enough of them for everyone." Max pointed at laminated swim bag tags and shower kit pouches.

"They are. We can get those. I think your friends will love this." Finn knew he was stretching the term "friends" a bit. Max was still finding his way socially in middle school. Buying gifts for his new swim team members at the fair had been Max's idea, and Finn had promised that when he would bring him to Avery's for the weekend, he'd stay for the fair and help him pick.

He had inwardly promised himself that, although he would be at the town center, he wouldn't go near Jane, but the pull to see her had proven to be more than he could bear. The last time he had laid eyes on her was before his divorce, at a family Christmas dinner, and she had arrived with her then-boyfriend.

Finn pulled his wallet from the back pocket of his jeans as Max politely asked the woman at the booth to pack eight tags and pouches.

"What's an Etsy shop?" Finn whispered, leaning his head closer to his son after paying.

"I don't know. I think it's some arts and crafts website," Max whispered back.

Just then, Avery, who had been trying on earrings at another table, approached them, noticing the pastry box in Max's hands. "Didn't you get me one, too?" she asked, looking at Finn.

"I asked if you wanted anything, and you said you didn't." Knowing her, Finn had planned on getting her something, anyway, but seeing Jane had banished any thought from his head.

"Never mind," she said irately. "I'll take a bite from Max's." She smiled at their son.

"I can go get you something now. Which one do you want?" Finn offered, handing the payment for his son's gifts to the lady. They'd had a peaceful day until now, and he didn't want to give her a reason to ruin it. Like a Nintendo Donkey Kong game, it had been their pattern—she'd find reasons to fight, throw them in the air as baits, and he would try to catch and pacify them for his son's sake before they'd turn into an argument. He'd become an expert in identifying the first signs before her mood turned combative. He had kept at it for years, driven by scorching guilt, even after she had managed to see a full-term pregnancy a year after their marriage. He had kept at it even after realizing, through witnessing her relationships with others, that she had always been like that, regardless of the miscarriages. He had kept at it, especially so Max would grow up in a peaceful atmosphere. But, at some point, his guilt alone couldn't carry the weight of a marriage that had begun loveless and had grown more so every year. And, at some point, he had realized that living in an imminent explosive atmosphere wasn't the same as being peaceful, and as much as he wanted his son to grow up with two parents and not like how he had grown, Max was better off with them apart.

He had been relieved when, two years ago—one year after their divorce—she had announced she had gotten a promotion and was moving back to their hometown. At first, they had chauffeured Max back and forth three times a week, but with time, it dropped to Max spending just the weekends with her. They had all gotten used to it, and Finn had a feeling they all preferred it that way, not just him.

"Should I go get you one?" he repeated. He had no intention of fighting with her and ruining Max's day.

Waiting for Avery's reply, he couldn't help but admit to himself that going back could also be his chance to see Jane again, though, unsurprisingly, she had made it clear she didn't want him there.

"Don't bother now," Avery snapped, her tone indicating the imminent blow-up. "How's my dear cousin and aunt?" She directed her venom elsewhere all of a sudden. "I assume they were all there today? It looks pretty busy." Avery glanced at the bakery on the other side of the packed main street.

"Yes," he replied laconically, choosing to answer only her second question. He had never told her about Jane, just that she had once tutored him. The unforgettable kiss that they had shared in college, or the week that had owned and ruined his heart, had been kept his secret all these years. He never let her drag him into conversations about her.

Avery was in a constant, one-sided competition with the world, and especially with her younger cousin since the two had been kids. With the way his heart pounded in his chest in the rare times that Jane's name had been mentioned between them, it wasn't a safe topic for him to discuss with Avery.

"Want some, Dad?" Max asked, handing over the hummingbird cupcake.

"Maybe just that frosting, though it's too beautiful to eat." Finn scooped a finger over the frosting, put it in his mouth, and sucked. *Jane made it*, he thought. He swallowed. Or maybe it was actually her dad, the gentle giant, Bert Drecher, whose dream to own a bakery and bakeshop had been fulfilled when he had bought Breading Dreams from Connie Latimer when she had been compelled to sell due to financial issues. He had kept the name, the logo, and Connie herself as an equal member of the small staff.

"It *is* beautiful," Avery said, granting a rare compliment. "That's the only art my artistic cousin gets to do these days," she added in true Avery form. "Remember her wedding cakes?" she unknowingly added a gut-punch. "Wedding cakes and birthday cakes. Oh, and cupcakes." She jutted her chin toward the cupcake he held.

She used to put him down for sticking with the closest thing to his shattered dream of professional swimming after his NCAA Division 1 days, too.

He took a deep breath then muttered, "It's art, too."

It was. He sometimes looked at the bakery's Facebook page just for a glimpse of Jane's life. Her mother uploaded pictures of the cakes. They were art.

"D'you know that I offered her to substitute for the art teacher at school one time, and she declined? Said it didn't fit her schedule. What schedule? It's her parents' bakery; she can do whatever she wants. My aunt said they were going to retire soon and hand it over to Anne."

Like a thirsty man in a desert, he had always gulped any drop of third-hand information about Jane. The information flow had slowed to a trickle after his divorce, but that was how he had learned that she had returned from Cincinnati, that she was single, worked at the bakery, and lived at the old house that used to belong to her grandparents. The house he had known every corner of.

But her parents' retirement and her taking over the bakery was news. And he couldn't blame Jane for not wanting Avery to be her boss, even temporarily. Unlike him, who had married a woman he had hardly known, Jane had known Avery forever.

"You did your best," he said, trying to avoid the topic. Avery couldn't stand anyone having, becoming, or doing something better than her.

"She taught art in Cincinnati," Avery muttered to herself, as if Jane had bested her by refusing the substitute job.

With his hand on Max's shoulder, they continued to stroll to other booths, and Finn tried to enjoy his son's company, the ocean breeze, and the sun for the next hour until Avery said, "We should get going, Max. Grandma Darian and Grandpa Fernando are waiting for us." She then turned to Finn. "I'll drive him to you tomorrow evening."

Finn hugged his son goodbye then watched them walk away. The mention of Avery's mother made him think of her tall niece.

Familiar guilt gnawed at him. God knew he had tried, but years of marriage to Avery couldn't obliterate the love he felt for the woman he had spent one glorious week with before his world had turned upside down with a single phone call. The woman he was now carving his way through the crowd toward.

Chapter 3

"Thank you. Have a great afternoon." Anne waved at the last customer leaving the bakery and continued rearranging the bread baskets on the display tables. The sun was still high in the sky outside, and she expected another wave of customers to arrive shortly now that the fair outside was being dismantled.

"I'll see you at home, Bert." Linda appeared from the storage room and placed a hand on her husband's shoulder. She then stepped from behind the counter and stopped next to Anne on her way to the door. "Are you doing rounds tonight, dear?"

"Yes. I hope there's enough left when this day is over." It was her turn to distribute the food donations that used the bakery's and other shops' daily unsold goods.

"The Mean Bean had a lot of traffic, too. I hope they'll have spares," Linda said, brushing a hand over her daughter's arm. "Treat yourself to a hot bath and a glass of wine after you're done. That's what I intend on doing, Jane sweetie."

Her mother, a Jane Austen enthusiast, had named her after her favorite author and her favorite heroine by that author, and she had always switched between the two names when addressing her. That was how

Anne had gotten the idea to go by her middle name. Linda didn't mind, probably because Anne had never told her about the Plain Jane nickname.

"Don't worry, Mom. I have plans." Anne kissed her mother's cheek. She planned to work on some paintings instead.

"Remember, we have to work on the job description tomorrow," Linda added, shouldering her bag.

In preparation for her parents' retirement at seventy-two, they had to hire a baker who would replace her father and join Connie Latimer, the original owner and baker, in that capacity. Though Anne had pretty much grown up at the bakery, she was no baker. She could bake, but she lacked her dad's and Connie's magic touch. Her department was the decorations and the specially ordered cakes. Connie's children weren't in the business either— Gabe was a graphic designer in L.A., and Libby worked in Riviera View's Social Services department and, as such, was involved in the food donations initiative.

"If you're home before ten, they'll be airing *Miss Austen Regrets* on *Masterpiece*." Linda stopped at the door.

"I'll catch it another time." She had enough regrets of her own; she didn't need Jane Austen's, too, namesake or no namesake.

"Okay, sweetie, drive carefully, and I'll see you tomorrow."

Working at the bakery six days a week, Anne tried to take some of the load off her parents. That was why she had left Cincinnati. She withdrew as little salary as possible, enough to pay for the green Kia that she had bought especially for the food project, and the mortgage for buying off her aunt's half of the little house that she lived in, which was the twin sisters' inheritance. To satisfy the restless artist in her and save for the second reason that stood behind her decision to return home, she sold her paintings on Etsy, mainly to other sellers who used them in their products. In Cincinnati, she had taught art in community centers and small group private lessons, but here, she painted at home and sold her work online.

"I'll be in the back, Annie," Bert announced, ducking his head at the doorframe that led there.

She had taken his height but, thankfully, not his bulkiness. As much as she ate from their pastries, she remained slender, which was ironic because, growing up, her gangly stature used to bother her and make her the target of jokes. As she had matured, people had commented on it and perceived it as an advantage. Jane wasn't so plain anymore, she thought.

After the bustle of the morning and early afternoon, which were great not just for business but as safeguards for unwanted thoughts and feelings, she didn't welcome the silence that now enveloped the bakeshop.

As she sorted the table with the boxed cookies, someone blocked the sunlight that washed in through the glass door. Her gaze caught the shade slanting on the floor next to the display shelves just as the bell above the door behind her rang.

"Jane."

She closed her eyes for a moment then turned.

"It's Anne now, Finn, as you know."

"You're always Jane to me. Even when you're Anne," he said, reminding her of similar words he had once said and had later written on that first sunflower card that he had left in her mailbox on November eleventh. Her mother had sent it to her in Cincinnati without knowing who it was from.

Sometimes her mother had waited to send her those unsigned annual birthday cards along with Avery's Christmas cards. The latter contained thinly-veiled braggings for select family members and friends that Avery thought should know about her successes. The recent one had pronounced her as the fastest adjusting to promotion to vice principal in their school district and Max's grades as the top sixth of his class.

He was the only one, except for her parents or sometimes her aunt, who still used that name. It was the name spoken softly so only she could hear it in family gatherings, as if he couldn't hold their unspoken past alone anymore, the secret undercurrent that bled between them, carved into their hearts, threatening to turn into something more every time they saw each other.

It had the same effect now.

"Where are Avery and Max?" she asked, purposefully bringing reality back into the picture.

"Went home. He's with her this weekend. I only came because he asked me to be here for the fair. He wanted to buy gifts for his new swim team."

It was the longest private conversation they'd had in years. If they had found themselves separated from the rest in an event, one of them would walk away, knowing instinctively it wasn't a good idea.

"That's kind of him. He's a good kid," she said. She was impressed with Max whenever she did see him, which wasn't too often. She liked him. He was different than both his parents—he seemed introverted. "Can I get you anything?" She waved a hand across the display.

"You know why I'm here," he said, piercing her with eyes the color of a summer storm.

"No, I don't." She knew, but it was a desperate attempt to defy something that was perhaps inevitable.

"Because I had to see—"

"You have no reason to," she interjected. "And you shouldn't—"

"Annie, this is the last batch of the fair-themed cookies." Her father's resonant voice preempted his entry into the shop from the back.

They both jumped back, as if caught red-handed, though they weren't even close to each other.

Bert appeared, carrying a tray of sun-shaped, yellow icing cookies. "Finn?" he called as soon as he entered. "How are you, son? We haven't seen you in a long time. It's great to see you." He placed the tray on the counter then came out from behind it to join them.

"Hello, Mr. Drecher." A muscle danced in Finn's jaw, straining his neck muscles.

Anne looked away, remembering what it had felt like to trace her fingers over them and imagining what they looked like under his open-collared, dark gray, buttoned-down shirt.

"What is this *Mr. Drecher* nonsense?" Bert drummed his voice in a chuckle. "It's Bert. Always has been. I know it's been a while—I think it was three years ago—but with Max and everything, you'll always be family. So, there's no need for Mr. Anything. Just Bert, plain and simple."

While her father had meant it as a welcoming speech, he had no idea that he had just reiterated everything they grappled with.

"You're right, Bert," Finn said with a tight smile and a quick nod. "Great seeing you again. And plain and simple is my absolute favorite."

"I hope we can see more of you. You're here for the fair, or are things warming up with Avery?" Bert smirked and lifted his eyebrows in a cheeky innuendo.

Anne guessed that the sinking feeling she experienced coursed through Finn, too.

"We've been divorced three years; nothing left to warm up, Bert. Even before," Finn said, his last two words almost half-whispered. He shot a quick look at her. "There's just Max," he said louder, looking at her dad again.

"That's a pity. And with everything you two went through that first year … well, you know."

"Dad, I think Finn was just leaving and—"

"Oh, yes, yes, I know, sweetie. I always embarrass you, sticking my nose where it doesn't belong, talking about things that aren't any of my business. Anyway, don't be a stranger, Finn. Now that both Avery and Anne live here, we'll have more opportunities to spend time together. We've always considered these two as sisters, and you as Anne's brother. Brother-in-law, ex-brother-in-law, it doesn't matter. Family is everything, it's forever, especially in a small family like ours, and even an ex-brother-in-law is better than the brother she never had. You see, Anne was an only child, and we always wished—"

"Dad! Can you please, pretty please with frosting on top, start packing for the evening rounds for me?" she hurried to say, coming up with the first thing she could think of.

She wanted to die. Her *brother*. Brother-in-law was bad enough.

She wondered how loud the thud of her father fainting on the floor would sound if he knew that these "siblings" had fallen madly and irrevocably in love and fucked each other senseless for an entire week … until Finn had found out that the woman he had forgotten he had casually hooked up with two months before was pregnant and that she was none other than Anne's cousin. A woman Anne was raised to consider and expected to think of as a sister.

Bert chuckled. "You got it, Annie." He waved a *don't-mention-it*, then patted Finn on the shoulder. "See you, son," he said before turning toward the back of the bakery.

The silence that ensued felt as if they had been tossed into the deepest part of a pool where all sound was muffled. It trapped them, and all that was left for them to do was give each other a little head tilt and tight-lipped smile of two people who had been brutally reminded of the difference between right and wrong, dream and reality, desire and duty.

Finn's voice, his words, being close to him, alone with him for the first time in so long—she had almost let her guard slip. She had to remember what he was to her now, despite yearning for what he had been to her then.

Building on her father's words, Anne settled Finn back in her mind as her cousin's ex-husband, the father of her aunt's grandson, and added a reminder that Max was her first cousin once removed and that she could never be with his father.

From day one, she had been taught how important family was. "You can live without anyone else as long as you have your family, Janey. Family is everything. You should fight and sacrifice for your family, to keep it together," they said. Her dad was an only child to parents who had lost everyone in the camps. Her mother and her twin had lived as if they were joined at the hip. And she was an only child to parents who adopted everyone into their family. Including Finn.

As if he was silently admitting defeat, Finn turned to leave. He took one step then halted.

Anne followed his gaze. It landed on the stack of brochures that her proud mother had placed at the end of the table for people to pick up with their sourdough rolls.

Finn took one brochure and skimmed through it. "You're still painting?"

Her hand involuntarily gestured toward him, wanting to snatch the paper from him. "A little."

"And participating in an exhibition," he stated what he'd just read, raising his eyes to her.

"It's nothing." While it wasn't what she had dreamed of coming out of art school, it was the first exhibition she would be a part of in years. Her impressionist watercolor style wasn't as popular in the art world and had made her an outsider even in college, but it was her favorite style.

Impressionist paintings always made her want to leap into the canvas and live inside it. She loved the quiet sceneries, everyday scenes capturing fleeting moments, revived by the right use of color and light. Crafters on Etsy loved her work, even if art galleries didn't. So, while she couldn't say she was a renowned artist, she did what she loved and managed to pay the bills. An Etsy painter by night and a cake decorator by day. She was too introverted to deal with fame, anyway.

"At Eddie Melton's gallery," Finn half-mumbled, still perusing the brochure.

She knew what memories that name evoked for them both. Eddie was an acquaintance, and when she had returned to Riviera View after a short, failed artistic career following her graduation in Chicago, he had offered for her to exhibit a few paintings in the art gallery that he had opened with his boyfriend.

"It's nothing major," she repeated, just as she had back then when Finn had persuaded her to attend the opening. That evening had been part of the time she was still trying to repress for her own sake.

"Eddie's gallery is what my dreams are made of," he expelled, taking them back to before her father's intrusion, and even farther back—fourteen years back. And, as if he realized it, he immediately added, "I'm happy for you, Ja—Anne. And proud of you." He then placed the brochure back on the stack, gave her a tight-lipped smile, and exited the bakery in a few long steps.

All the noise, bustle, and warmth swelled in through the door that he opened, along with a group of shoppers who came in before it closed behind him.

She wished she had never allowed herself to fall for him. She wished she could *stop* loving him.

~~~~~~~~~~~~~~~~~

After collecting the donations from the shops that participated in the food project, Anne went to her last stop, The Mean Bean Café, to meet Amy Locke, the owner, at the café's kitchen, where they distributed the pastries, produce, groceries, and other unsold products into neatly and elegantly packed boxes. From there, Anne called Libby, Connie Latimer's daughter, to ensure there were no changes to the address list that Social Services had provided.

Their conversation was polite but stilted, as usual. Libby was one of the nicest people Anne knew and Hope's best friend. Growing up in the same town, same class, then the same bakery where their parents were still working together, Anne always wished she could shake off feeling like a usurper. At fourteen, it had been strange seeing Libby every day in school, knowing her parents now owned what used to be Libby's mother's bakery. Maybe someday, through Hope, they could get closer. She sincerely wished it.

She left the boxes by the front doors of the houses and apartments that Social Services indicated, knowing the residents expected to find them there.

Taking the longer route home, she drove along the beach promenade, which gave the town its name. She drove slowly, so slowly that if Aaron or one of his officers from the local police station had driven behind her, they'd ask her to speed up. She had taken this road thousands of times in her lifetime and could probably do it with a blindfold on.

Passing by the families' beach, as locals referred to the one with the lifeguard tower, she remembered going there in the summers with her mother and aunt, with Avery and Noah, Avery's younger brother.

Avery had played with them only until she had found someone else to play with, leaving Anne and Noah alone to finish their sandcastle. As an only child to older parents who had problems conceiving until she had been born, Anne hadn't attended pre-school. Though four years older than her, Avery, and later Noah, had been her main playmates. But, if Anne or Noah had won at something, Avery would become sour, angry, and taunting.

"Who told you that you were adopted?" her mother had gasped when a tearful Anne had asked if she looked different—tall and pale—because she wasn't really theirs. "Look at this. You look just like your grandma Ada—she was very tall and fair." Linda had pointed at an old picture. "I never met her because she died when your dad was small, but you look just like her. She and your grandfather escaped Europe right before the war. Oh, honey, we wanted you so very much; it just took time until God made you perfect and put you in my belly. You're not adopted," her mother had said.

"You should talk to your sister," Bert had told his wife when he'd heard about it.

"They're just kids, and Avery is like a sister to her. Siblings can be like that sometimes, but I'll talk to Darian."

By the time she was six, Anne had been as tall as ten-year-old Avery. She used to think that this unwanted victory was what had made Avery ignore her when she had started first grade and had sat alone on the swings during recess, inexperienced and fearful of approaching the other girls. Avery, who had stood with a bunch of her friends not far from her, hadn't even gazed in her direction. At least their four-year difference meant she had been spared from attending middle and high school at the same time as Avery.

Despite their parents' ingrained beliefs, efforts, and expectations, they weren't even close to being close as adults. After facing two miscarriages before Max, Avery must have mellowed out. Or so Anne had thought. The family had wrapped her in cotton wool and kept it a secret at her demand. Anne had just reached Cincinnati then, deciding to make it her home, giving her parents her non-existent art career as an excuse for her leaving. Though the situation had been unbearable for her, given that the father of that baby had been the love of her life, and though she had never received the same kindness from Avery, she had called to console her and sent her flowers.

Anne opened the car window to let the night breeze in. The part of the promenade that she passed now looked like a teenagers' after-party. They flocked to Surfer's Point, cars beeping, music blasting through open windows, the illuminated beach showing more people were down on the sand.

As a teenager, she hadn't been part of the crowd that partied there. Now she didn't envy Aaron and his officers, whom she saw checking cars to make sure everyone behaved. She just wanted to get home, get off her aching feet, take a long shower, paint, and think about the email she had received.

Her mother's difficulties conceiving, and Avery's miscarriages, had prompted her to test in a fertility clinic, where she had been assured it wasn't hereditary. Being single at thirty-seven, she had asked them to check her fit for a natural cycle IUI sperm donor process, just in case. They had emailed the results earlier that day. She was found fit.

She preferred it the natural way but didn't see herself having children or growing old with any of the men whom she had dated since her return, or the one she had lived with on and off in Cincinnati.

"I always wanted siblings," she had said in the interview at the clinic. "And my parents are dying for grandkids."

They'd advised her to hurry if she wanted more than one child. "You always want more for your child than you had."

This was why she understood Finn, why she couldn't blame him for deciding as he had all those years ago—he was an only child who didn't know his father. Besides, she hadn't given him much choice. "*There's no way we can be together, not with my cousin having your child,*" she had told him back then, pushing him to seal their fate, though he begged her not to.

Finn again. She couldn't escape this. Somehow, it was all related. Him. Her. Children. Tough decisions. Related. Family connections.

Finn.

~~~~~~~~~~~~~~~

"Is this one of those horns? A clarinet?" A head taller than her, he picked up the black case from the floor and carried it for her as he walked her to the library door.

"A trumpet," she said.

"Why did you choose trumpet? You like playing it?"

She side-eyed him, wondering if he was playing a joke on her. Why would Finn Brennen be interested in her band choices? "I was demoted from the oboe."

His laughter surprised her.

"Why did you take band?" He pushed the library door open and held it for her.

"I'm on a secret mission to ruin them from within by getting them to play hardcore punk."

He chuckled, his left arm brushing against her as she passed by him on her way out. A whiff of soap, deodorant, and remnants of chlorine drifted toward her from his skin.

"Seriously, though, why?" he asked, walking next to her in the hall.

"Okay. It's the uniform. I love the uniform." As if anybody could love that ugly, green synthetic horror.

He laughed again. A short, husky, deep sound. She noticed his gaze sliding down her body as if he was looking for the uniform, though she was in her regular jeans and tee. She returned his gaze, and their eyes met.

"I am trying to get them to play more pop songs," she said more seriously. "Maybe we'd be laughed at less if we stopped playing only uncool, old march tunes."

"You like pop?"

"Don't you?"

He just looked at her and smiled. She felt the smile spreading wider on her lips too.

She had never talked to a guy like that, especially not a guy who belonged in Finn Brennen's league.

During that first tutoring session, she found it hard to look straight into those unbelievably blue eyes, and was unprepared for how comfortable he had made her feel, and how easy it had been to talk to him, especially given that she didn't talk with many people in general. All the girls from freshman year to senior knew Finn, the star of the swim team, with a swimmer's body to top off his dark blond hair and ocean blue eyes that were set in a wonderfully male-proportioned face.

"Pearl Jam is my favorite band, so ..." He shrugged.

"So, no pop?" Her smile hid her surprise. Finn Brennen. Pearl Jam. Interesting. There was something raw in their music.

She scrutinized his face.

"I do pop, too. Who's your favorite?"

"All sorts. These days, I'm into Abba," she replied.

"Timeless," he said. "Can I give you a ride home? My car is ... Unless you came with yours?"

She scoffed. "I don't have a car. I walk." She walked every day, seeing others like Eric Hays, who lived on her street and drove alone in his car, or in groups like Libby Latimer and her friends, Luke and Roni, who drove to school together. The latter didn't live near her, and she wouldn't get into a car with the former, even if her legs stopped working.

"So, can I give you a ride home?" They had reached the exit.

"Sure. Thanks."

He opened the car door for her. She was impressed by the chivalry and by the non-flashy model he drove. How different than Eric Hays' new red BMW.

"Sorry, my friends left it all messy last night," he said, picking up an empty paper cup and napkins from the front seat and throwing them into the back before she got in.

She buckled up as he started the engine. Sucking in her lips, she had just realized she had never ridden a car with a boy before. She had never been on a date either. While this wasn't a date, it was still exciting.

"You can move the seat back a bit, so you'll have more legroom there," he said.

She looked at him. He was backing up from the parking spot, his arm on the back of her seat, his head turned backward, the posture highlighting the magnificence of his well-built, wide torso.

Her denim-covered legs were a bit cramped in the space. She felt heat rising from her shirt to her neck and throat. Afraid she'd break into a sweat, she rolled the window down a bit. She was used to comments on her height, but he was taller than her. Maybe he spoke from experience. She was pretty sure that, even with heels, she still wouldn't be at eye level with him.

"So, who makes fun of you and the band?" he suddenly asked.

"What?" She looked at him again. "Um ... No one." Eric Hays.

"You said before that ..."

"Oh, I was just kidding." She wasn't. But she was trying to shrug these things off, having learned from an early age that not everyone liked her or her choices. Nevertheless, she had no intention of telling Finn Brennen about it. She'd just met him.

They began meeting twice weekly in the library after school hours to go over the material, his homework, plan his papers, and prepare for exams. He drove her home after. In the second semester, they took Elective English together.

"I'm named after her," she told him when they read Pride And Prejudice. *Or, more accurately, she read and he studied from her notes.*

"Oh, wow! Jane for Jane Austen. Cool."

"I'm glad you think so." She chuckled. Eric Hays had started calling her "Plain Jane" just weeks before, and a few others had adopted it. "My middle name is after my mom's favorite Austen heroine, Anne." Ironically, Anne in Persuasion *was considered rather plain.* Great job, Mom, *she thought.*

"Anne's great, too, but I love Jane more. I don't have a middle name."

She faked a gasp. "And you lived to tell?"

Finn laughed. "Barely."

A few weeks later, when they reached that part of the curriculum, he said, "I like Dorothy Parker. She reminds me of you." He looked at her. They were sitting at what had become "their table" at the library.

She looked at Dorothy Parker's picture in her textbook. Dorothy, who wasn't known for her beauty but her wit. "Remind you how?"

"Her sarcasm, how she says things as they are, and you both make me laugh."

"Me? Sarcastic?" Maybe she was. Earlier that morning, she had told Eric Hays, who had hurled another Plain Jane at her, "I guess we both earned our nicknames, Douchebag Eric." Looking in the mirror, she couldn't deny she was rather plain. She had the type of face that would be lost in a crowd, if only she didn't tower over most girls and some of the boys.

Now she just smiled at Finn.

He smiled back then looked at the textbook. "Men seldom make passes at girls who wear glasses," *he read aloud. "I don't think it's hard to analyze this one."*

"But you do have to provide your opinion about it," she said, reading from their paper instructions.

"My opinion is that they're idiots." He raised his eyes from the book and looked at her.

She wasn't sure if he was trying to make a pass at her or what. She wasn't wearing glasses. Besides, this was Finn Brennen and, while he didn't have a girlfriend at the moment, he had had one for a few months and was surrounded by clamoring candidates.

"Very eloquent. Let's write that and see if it gets us an A," she said with a smile.

Before one of the bigger exams, they studied until the library closed. He then drove them to his house to continue.

That night, after they had finished, he walked her back home. They both needed to breathe, and the ocean breeze was perfect after hours of cramming. He told her then that he never knew who his father was. His mother had never married and had him when she had worked as an administrator in a hospital in Los Angeles. She never talked about it, and he suspected he was the result of an extramarital affair on his father's side. "I've never told this to anyone. I trust you to not say anything to anyone."

"Of course," she replied. "Your secret will die with me. Probably from exhaustion."

Finn laughed. "You're a good friend, Jane."

It was the first time he had termed her his friend. She was glad. While he had many, she had few.

"Don't worry about the exam tomorrow," she said when they parted. "You'll do swimmingly."

She loved the sound of his laughter.

Sometime after, they studied at her house. It was the first time he had been in her room. She was aware of how envious some girls would be to know that Finn Brennen was in her bedroom. She had developed a little crush on him—it was hard not to—but they were so different and belonged to completely different spheres that she refused to fall in love with him. Like her, he had solid dreams, plans, and took his studies seriously, but their lives were going in different directions. Besides, he knew everyone, got along with everyone, had many friends, while she kept mostly to herself. If she fell for him, it'd be almost like falling for a Hollywood star, and she was too level-headed for that.

Her room was decorated with reproductions of Van Gogh and Claude Monet, not movie stars. If she fell in love with someone like him, after a while, she'd be just a torn page in his book, while he could be an entire chapter in hers. She didn't want that.

That evening, when she went to make them sandwiches, she returned to find Finn sitting on her bed and not on the chair by her desk. He shot his head up and threw something on the cover. It was the white, oversized Jane from Daria *T-shirt that she used to sleep in. She loved that show, identified with the characters, and wished she had a friend like Daria or Jane. Maybe he was reading the quote that was printed on it—*"I actually accomplished something. I mean, other than getting up.*"*

"Thanks for dinner," he said, taking a plate from her.

After she saw Finn to the door later that night, her mother asked, "That was Marie Brennen's son, right? He's very handsome."

"Yes," she replied, her foot already on the carpeted first step, intending to go back to her room.

"The type of boys that break hearts," her mother sighed out.

"Not mine," she said then went upstairs.

A few weeks later, he solved her internal debate about asking him to her junior prom when he told her about the two-day swim meet that fell on the same date. She wondered what his answer would have been if she had asked him.

"Plain Jane's a wallflower much?" she heard a guy mutter quietly to his girlfriend as they passed by her on junior prom night.

She stood with her back to the wall, not far from the entrance, looking for familiar faces. One of the girls from band, who she was supposed to go with, had called in sick at the last moment, but she had decided to go anyway. Admittedly, wearing a yellow dress with her pale skin might not have been the smartest choice, but comments like that had become rare and usually whispered these days.

She ended up enjoying the evening as soon as she had found a few friends to hang out with, and when the news of the swim team's victory made its way through the prom crowd, she was even happier.

She was walking down the hall one day, toward the end of the year, when a pat on her shoulder surprised her from behind. As soon as she swung around, she was met with the happiest smile that she had ever seen. And the bluest eyes.

"I got in, Jane! I got in!" Finn called then scooped her up in his arms and hugged her, her feet dangling above the floor.

She was dazzled by his mix of soap, deodorant, and chlorine, and the way his body was as hard and solid as it looked.

"In?"

"Cal Poly! I'm in!"

"Oh my God! I'm so happy for you! Finn!" she yelled, wrapping her arms around his neck.

Kids who passed by looked at them.

He put her back on her feet then reached for his backpack. "I got you something as a thank you," he said.

"You didn't have to."

"I wanted to. You really made a difference, you know?" He smiled as he handed her a gift-wrapped box.

"Thanks." She opened it, trying to keep her fingers from trembling.

"I didn't know if these were the best ones, so I asked my friend, who's also taking Art, and she said they were. I hope you like them," he hurried to say.

She swallowed, her heart expanding in her chest. "They are. I love them. Thank you," she managed to half-whisper. They were the watercolors and brushes she had wanted. She bit her lips and looked up into his eyes. "Finn, thank you." It was the first time she felt, beyond a shred of a doubt, that she could not just fall—but collapse in love with him.

"You're welcome. Don't be a stranger, okay? I hope you have a great senior year."

"Thanks. Me a senior, you a freshman. Just like nature intended it."

Finn laughed. It had become her favorite sound.

Her senior year was eventless and boring, but in a good way. The remnants of the Plain Jane nickname had died out, though she began introducing herself to new people as Anne. She became a bit closer with Bella, the girl from band who had skipped their junior prom, and a boy from band had asked her to their senior prom. A head taller than him, she wore flats, along with a navy collar dress, and was excited when, at the end of the night, he rose to his toes and kissed her. Only later, she had the wisdom to recognize that, if she had made a difference for Finn, he had done the same for her, showing her that she wasn't really a wallflower.

She followed news of his success through the town's rumor mill, the school's newspaper, and his mother, who sometimes shopped at the bakery.

~~~~~~~~~~~~~~~~

It would be two and a half years before she would see Finn again and accidentally share a life-changing kiss. And it would be another four years before they would lose themselves in each other so completely that it would be hard to imagine they could ever be severed from one another.

Chapter 4

He didn't expect there to be this much traffic on a Saturday. With so much time behind the wheel, Finn blasted his favorite Pearl Jam album, *Ten*. Songs about bitter hands cradling broken glass of what was everything fit his mood to a tee.

"Do you think they'll like the gifts? I won't look … stupid? Or like I'm trying too hard?" Max had whispered to him right before they'd parted.

"They will, and you won't. Usually, team captains do that, you know? Bring everyone something nice to get the team spirit going. I know that role is not your aim, but you're positioning yourself, even though you're the newest and youngest. The older kids will appreciate it, and the younger ones will copy them."

"Promise?"

"Promise."

"See you tomorrow, Dad." Max had thrown his arms around him.

He had leaned in and sniffed his son's hair.

Max was at that age when he was still mostly sweet and not yet a full-on grumpy teen. He loved that Max took to swimming enough to want to be on a team and compete, but that he had other dreams, as well. He didn't want his son to be a replica of him.

While Avery had her issues, and he was far from perfect, as well, unlike his childhood, at least Max had both of them. If his job wasn't in Blueshore, he would have moved to Riviera View, too, so Max wouldn't have to travel between his two homes. But his job wasn't the only hindrance. He knew Jane's presence there posed a complication, a risk.

Finn shut off the air conditioning and cracked the window open, letting in the salty September ocean breeze.

That long-legged, former trumpet player was his drug. He couldn't be near her without needing a dose. And whenever he had a dose, he yearned for more. That was why he had stayed away, even after his divorce. In the handful of times that he had seen her in the past fourteen years, he'd paid the price for weeks after, trying to wean himself from thoughts, dreams, and fantasies of her; from blowing his sham of a marriage to hell, from calling her, from getting into his car and driving all the way to fucking Ohio just to hold her in his arms and breathe her in—something he couldn't do in whatever family event she had attended, even if she had let him. He wanted to hold her, promising himself it would suffice but knowing that he would only yearn for a bigger dose after. Yet today, he had caved in to the need, and even the safety valve of his son's and Avery's presence hadn't stopped him until her father's words had.

Her *brother*, Bert had referred to him. It had almost killed him to hear it. That family still thought of him as Avery's husband, and they'd always considered Avery and Anne as sisters. *And sisters don't date each other's exes.* A recipe for disaster, especially when one had treated the other as competition her entire life.

He was divorced, but he knew they couldn't really be together without stirring up an uproar and causing an explosion that would tear that small family apart. It would devastate her, crush her under a ton of guilt. Not to mention confuse his son.

He didn't even know if her love for him had survived. It'd been years. A fucking lifetime. And, after all, he had let her down in the worst way possible. It didn't matter that it was all a result of fateful timing. She had never blamed him and had even said that she understood, that she wouldn't have expected him to do any different, that he had no other choice, and that they couldn't be together, anyway. Yet, he couldn't expect her to forgive him.

He wished he could turn back time.

~~~~~~~~~~~~~~~~

'Who art thou,' he silently read the words printed on the T-shirt of the tall girl who approached him. She seemed vaguely familiar—thin, with smooth brown hair cut to her shoulders, and dark brown eyes that were in sharp contrast to her fair complexion. He stood at the entrance to the library, looking for the tutor that he had been assigned.

"Finn?" Her almond-shaped eyes reflected the light that came through the large windows.

"Jane Drecher?"

"Yes. Hi!"

"You're the daughter of the Breading Dreams owners, right? I've seen you around."

"Couldn't bake a damn thing even if my life depended on it, but yes," she said.

He chuckled, surprised. She seemed the quiet, mousy type. Sort of a wallflower. And yet, she had thorns. He liked it. Now he had hope that the tutoring sessions wouldn't be as boring as he'd expected them to be.

The more time they spent together, the more he liked her and looked forward to their meetings. She made him laugh and didn't go easy on him with his studies. She managed to make art history and English interesting, and he found himself striving for good grades, not just to be accepted into Cal Poly, but for her sake, too, so she'd see that her efforts paid off.

He even went to watch the band play in a pep rally, something he'd never done before unless he had to.

"You did great out there," he said when they met at the library after the performance.

"You managed to see me behind the cheerleaders?" She chuckled.

"I came to see you. And the band."

She didn't reply, busying herself with taking books out of her backpack. He wasn't sure if she blushed or not. It was the week she had gotten sunburned while trying to get a tan, and her nose was peeling.

"What's the one tune you wish the band would agree to play?" he asked.

"Abba's 'Dancing Queen'." Before he had a chance to reply, she added, "You thought I was going to say, 'Whiter Shade of Pale', right?" She pointed at her peeling skin.

He laughed. Her sarcasm was one of his favorite things about her. The way her eyes sparkled, too.

"I never understood the lyrics of that one," he said, still chuckling.

"Me neither. Sixteen vestal virgins*?"*

"Who are doing cartwheels across the floor?"

She burst out laughing.

"Shh ..." the librarian hissed, giving them a death glare.

They muffled their laughter and leaned closer across the two sides of the table that they were occupying. She had a fresh, lemony smell.

"For years, I wondered why they crawled under the night train until I realized they called out for another drink," he whispered. "Though both sentences make zero sense. We should invent new lyrics, ones that actually mean something."

She laughed. "This song makes sense without really making sense, you know?"

He looked at her. "Somehow, when you say it, it does."

She drew herself back, away from him.

He straightened and opened his books.

In the second semester, they studied for longer hours. At her house, he met her parents. They knew his mother, but it was the first time he'd spoken to them.

"I never see you with Libby Latimer," he said later when they were in her room. "Both your parents work at the bakery. And your dad bought it from her mom."

"That's why," she replied. "She's nice, but ... I don't know ... She has her friends, and I always feel

kinda bad that her mother was forced to sell because of her dad, and then my parents bought it and ... I guess I think she'd resent me for it or something."

"Do you think she does?"

"I don't know."

Later, when she went to make them sandwiches, he roamed around her room and looked at the various books, pictures, and girly knick-knacks she had around. On one easel, there was an unfinished painting, and several others leaned against the wall next to it. In an open sketchpad that sat on one of the shelves, he saw a self-portrait that she had made of herself. She hadn't done herself justice in it, he thought. In the sketch, Jane held a long-stemmed sunflower, the kind he had seen in Van Gogh's reproduction that hung on her wall. He wondered if she had sketched him or anyone he knew but didn't want to pry. Though, later, sitting on her bed, he absentmindedly picked up the T-shirt that was thrown on it. Without knowing what he was doing, he brought it to his face and inhaled. It smelled like Jane—lemony and fresh. The unmistakable stirring in his jeans took him by surprise.

He suddenly wondered what those long legs and slender back of hers looked like naked, what her breasts looked and felt like, what color were her nipples. When she entered the room, holding two plates, he quickly threw the shirt back on the bedcover, grabbed a plate, and, right before getting up, he realized he couldn't stand without a visible tent in his jeans. He started rambling about the material that they were studying until it was safe enough for him to go back to the desk.

Jane was too good for him to mess around with. He was nineteen, and she was seventeen. He was bound for college, and he wouldn't casually date her like he had with one of the senior-year girls.

Sometime after, he was coming out of class and, thanks to both their heights, he spotted her at the other end of the hall. He was about to wave at her when he heard a male voice calling from within the half a billion people that poured into the hall, "Hey, Plain Jane."

Finn looked at her face from across the crowd. She turned red.

"Plain Jane. Yes, you. I'm talking to you. Do you have the homework in Math?" the voice repeated just when Finn saw its owner's face. Eric Hays from junior year.

Without thinking, he pushed aside the students who stood between him and Eric. With his palm on his shoulder, he made Eric turn around. The moment the blond, shorter guy faced him, Finn grabbed him by the collar of his Quicksilver T-shirt and pinned him to the nearest locker.

"What did you call her?" he hissed into Eric's face.

"Plain Jane. Because, you know, she's ... plain and ... she's ... Jane," Eric mumbled, stuttering the more he continued speaking, the expression on his face revealing that he was realizing his mistake while he spoke.

"I didn't hear that. What did you call her again?" He brought his face closer to Eric's, further twisting his collar.

"Um—"

"What. Did. You. Call. Her?" He fisted Eric's collar under his chin while pushing him harder against the locker until the metal began to dent. With Eric being seventeen and him nineteen, and Eric's parents being the fierce protectors of their entitled son, he knew he could get in trouble, but he didn't care.

"Nothing. I didn't call her anything," Eric mumbled, his bright blond hair falling onto his flushed forehead.

"That's better. I thought so. I knew you wouldn't call her something other than Jane, right? Am I right?" He was in Eric's face, ignoring the spectators who had stilled around them.

"You're right. You're right," Eric hurried to say breathlessly.

"Good. I love being right. So, don't get me wrong, Hays."

"Okay."

He loosened his grip and let go of him.

Eric remained leaning against the locker to catch his breath and rearrange the rumpled collar of his T-shirt.

When he walked away, looking for Jane's face in the crowd, she wasn't there. The kids he passed by just moved aside, letting him through, and since Eric was a general douchebag, many of them smiled and a few patted his shoulder.

"I heard you went all Mr. T on Eric Hays," Jane commented when he walked into the study room and sat next to her a few hours later.

"Mr. What?"

"Mr. T. You know, from the A-Team?"

"Oh. If anyone ever—"

"Nah," she cut in and said over a breathy, embarrassed chuckle. "You didn't have to. I don't need saving." Her cheeks flushed, and she cast her eyes downward.

"I know. You're too busy saving my ass with this," he replied, tapping on the thick textbook that he had taken out of his backpack.

"But I appreciate the thought," she said, bringing her eyes up to meet his.

Those dark chestnut eyes and the genuine smile that spread on her lips plunged themselves right into the crux of his heart.

~~~~~~~~~~~~~~~

A car beeped behind him. There were at least twenty yards between him and the car in front. Finn stepped on the accelerator.

On the car stereo, Eddie Vedder sang about his memories, washed in black, knowing that his love would one day be a star in someone else's sky. "*But why, why can't it be in mine*," Pearl Jam's lead sang, his voice splintering to pieces, like his heart, and Finn knew exactly how deep and painful those wreckages cut.

Jane.

He hadn't known back then that, one day, he would hurt her more than Eric ever had. He also hadn't known when she had first approached him at the library that she would become the love of his life and that he would have to live without her.

Chapter 5

The professional voice on the other end of the line implied she'd be in good hands. Anne stood on the sidewalk, outside the bakery, under a large Elm tree, concentrating on the multitude of information that was being dispensed into her ear while gazing at both sides of Ocean Avenue. At this hour of the morning, all the shops were open, and she nodded and smiled at a few people who passed by.

"Uh-huh. Yes. I understand. Be careful with cats' litterboxes, buy home testing kits, and … What was the third one?" She looked back to see that no one from the bakery was behind her. "Oh, yes. No need to extricate my IUD until I'm ready. Um … Like I told you before, right now it's an *if and when*. I don't … I'm not ready to start."

She finished the call and peeked into the bakery. Connie was busy cleaning the display glasses.

"Connie, there's something I have to do. Is it—"

"Sure, hon. I'm good. Take your time," Connie replied, straightening up, her light brown hair waving in the breeze that came through the open door.

"Thanks."

She walked up the main street and into Sarah Latimer's warmly decorated pharmacy. The place looked like it belonged in a quaint English village.

Of all the things the woman from the clinic had told her, the only thing she could do without committing yet was to buy ovulation test kits. Only when she stepped into the pharmacy and the bell over the door announced her entry, Anne realized that buying these at Sarah's, who was Connie's former sister-in-law and best friend, and Libby's aunt, could be an issue. She hadn't told anyone about it, not even her parents, not wanting their pressure, concerns, and hopes in case it doesn't work out. Though she trusted Sarah's professionalism, it was an unnecessary risk when she could buy those kits in another town.

"Hey, Anne, sweetie. How can I help you?" Sarah asked. Her hair color, which she changed every few months, was light brown. Having rather smooth skin at sixty, she looked younger than she really was.

"Um, hi. I just came in for Tylenol. I ran out."

"Sure," Sarah said, already spinning on her heel to the medicine drawers and cabinets behind her. "Regular strength? Extra?"

"Regular. Thanks."

"Would that be all?" Sarah asked, tilting her head a bit as if she was examining her.

Anne hesitated for a moment. "No. I need these, too," she said, then went to a nearby shelf and picked up two kits.

"Sure thing, dear," Sarah said without a muscle moving in her face. She scanned the boxes and put them in a bag, along with the Tylenol. "Do you know how to use these?" she asked, her gaze focused on the computer as she processed the sale.

"Yes."

"There you go," Sarah said, handing her the bag. "Good luck."

"Thanks." She took two steps toward the exit, then turned. "Sarah—"

"All's well. I know my job, rest assured, dear. But if you need to consult, I'm here," Sarah cut in, raising her palm in front of her in a *don't-worry* gesture.

"Thanks," she repeated.

Back at the bakery, she had to work on two cake orders; one for a Bat Mitzvah and one for a Quinceañera.

That evening, it was her turn to do the food rounds again. When she had the evenings or mornings off, she worked on her Etsy commissioned paintings and cooked for herself with the TV in the background, playing a rom-com or a sitcom, nothing too heavy. Sometimes, she went down to the beach, wearing a ton of the highest SPF sunscreen, or drove to an art show if there was something good in the more touristic towns around. She didn't mind going alone, though she enjoyed going with Bella when she could find a babysitter.

Bella lived with her three children on the third floor in a condo that used to be a motel in the 80s. Its pool had been turned into a playground. Her husband was deployed in low-ranking military positions, and she preferred to stay in her hometown rather than move the kids around to follow him.

Anne had two food drops on Libby's list in that building. Though Bella had managed to keep her head above the water just enough to not make it into Social Services list, twice a week, when it was her turn,

Anne would leave her a box. "I always have extras," she had explained, knowing that Bella could use the help, though she worked a part-time job as a secretary in the local school.

Reaching her destination, Anne parked the car then got out to climb the stairs.

Both late-blooming wallflowers, even when she and Bella had become closer in their last year of high school, they weren't friends in the full sense of the word—telling each other their deepest secrets and sharing everything. However, they had kept in touch through most of Anne's college years and had renewed their friendship after her recent return to Riviera View.

Working at the same school as Avery and Hope, Bella sometimes divulged stories about Avery, which made Anne realize that her cousin hadn't changed much in all these years.

"Hey." Bella opened the door. "Come in. My sassy teenager is staying at a friend's tonight, and I managed to get the little ones to sleep. Coffee first?" Her kids were fourteen, ten, and six.

"You bet." Anne placed the box on the kitchen table.

"I already have the movie on," Bella said, pouring coffee and arranging cookies on a plate. "Brad Pitt at his hottest."

"Which one?" Anne kicked her shoes off then went to help Bella carry the mugs to the living room.

"*Legends Of The Fall*. All I remember is crying several times and how hot Brad is. Ever seen it?"

"Yep. A long time ago." Not a movie that would be good for her to watch at the moment. But, since

Bella wanted to see it, and since she had never told her the entire truth about Finn, she couldn't explain why she preferred watching something else.

"It's so freaking sad," Bella said, wiping a tear midway into the movie. "They loved each other, but she married his brother."

"I need to pee," Anne said.

"Speaking of relatives," Bella said when Anne came back from the bathroom. "Remember I told you that rumor from school that Avery was trying to snag that old crush of hers, Jordan Delaney, because she brought him to judge at our Model UN? Now they say he's with your friend, Hope."

She remembered. Knowing the Delaneys, she couldn't imagine Avery with him, but if Avery was dating, maybe, just maybe …

She extinguished that thought fast.

"Really? I just saw Hope recently. God, we need to expand the gene pool in this town," Anne muttered. Jordan Delaney was Luke Delaney's brother, and Luke was Libby's fiancé.

"I know, right?" Bella laughed like she had when Anne had told her years before outside the Echo nightclub, that she had just experienced the best kiss of her life with Finn.

"There are so many good kissers out there, Anne. Trust me. You've just begun. You need to kiss more people. Simple statistics," Bella had said back then.

"And who's *they*?" Anne said now. "It's always *they say*. This town is full of gossips. You can't do anything without someone knowing and talking about it."

That was why she had never confided in anyone, not even in Bella, about her and Finn beyond what Bella already knew.

~~~~~~~~~~~~~~~~~

"We're going out to the Echo club tonight and I don't want to hear a no," Bella announced as soon as she picked up the phone. "It's near Wayford."

"Will they let us in?" Anne asked. She had come back home from Chicago for spring break, and Bella had called her almost immediately.

"Yes. But they won't serve us. Do you have an I.D.?"

Anne chuckled. "Not a fake one."

"We'll manage." Bella laughed. "There are so many new faces since you left. We'll find you a boyfriend."

"What about you?"

"I'll find one for sure. Maybe more than one." Bella laughed again. Like a butterfly that only had a day to live after months of chrysalis, Bella grasped at her newfound social blooming after high school.

Anne had dated two guys in college, but it hadn't lasted long and hadn't even been close to Bella's stories.

Soon after they reached the Echo in a cab, Bella met a guy she had a crush on.

"I'm going for one dance," she said.

She soon disappeared, leaving Anne to stand alone on the sidelines. There were no seats available, and though she wore a pretty, little black dress, she felt like a fish out of water in this crowd. Most were older and hung out in groups.

After a while, she couldn't see Bella on the dance floor anymore. She pushed her way through herds of clubbers and bystanders, thinking she'd suffocate if she weren't tall.

She had no cell phone and neither did Bella.

Going to the foyer at the entrance and waiting there seemed like the best solution. Bella would have to pass through it at some point.

The foyer was a large, atmospherically-lit, carpeted space with a smaller bar than the one next to the dance floor. The music was loud out here, too, but it was less crowded. Sofas in various sizes, shapes, and colors were scattered around, creating a Mad Hatter's living room ambiance. Most of the seats were taken by groups of people; some sitting, some standing, drinks in hand, chatting and laughing.

The booming bass, the lights, and what felt like a million strangers surrounding her with no ability to disappear into the background because, with her height, she protruded like a sunflower, made her feel disoriented.

Though there were seats at the bar, she tried to find a spot where she could stand without attracting unwanted attention. Then, like someone who swam way too deep into the ocean, panicked, and suddenly saw a lifeguard tower to swim toward, she recognized a familiar face among a group seated on a long sofa not far from where she stood.

Finn Brennen.

Surrounded by people, as per usual, he looked as good as she remembered him. Even better. Manlier.

He was twenty-one and probably visiting for spring break, like her, though his college was much closer to their hometown.

She tried not to stare, but at some point, their gazes crossed paths. He recognized her and jerked his head back in surprise as a smile spread on his face.

"Jane," he called and waved.

She read his lips more than heard his voice in the noisy space.

She took a few steps toward the group. The others were busy talking amongst themselves. They were the older version of the cool, "just right" types from high school.

"Jane," he repeated when she was near enough. "Wow. It's so great to see you. Are you alone here?" he added when she stopped to stand in front of him. He sat at the end of a line of six. His left arm was wrapped around the shoulders of a pretty girl who was busy chatting to the short-haired girl sitting next to her. Finn's other side was vacant.

"No, I'm with a friend, but I can't find her and thought I'd wait out here."

"We're waiting for a few more to join us." He tapped on the narrow, vacant spot next to him on the ochre velvet sofa. "You can sit with me until you find your friend. Everyone gets here eventually."

Only her disorientation made her take him up on the offer.

"Thanks," she said, cursing her friend, cursing herself, and even her and Bella's parents for not getting them cellphones.

Her entire left side brushed against Finn as she sat down. She felt it acutely where her bare arm pressed against his swimmer's bicep that his short-sleeved tee exposed.

The group on his other side didn't seem to notice the addition to their sofa.

"You're home for the break?" he asked.

"Yes. You?"

"Just until the day after tomorrow. We're practicing for Nationals."

A clean scent of Davidoff Cool Water aftershave wafted toward her. She inhaled, hoping to find remnants of the familiar chlorine that she had come to associate with him.

"You took Art?" he asked with a smile.

"In Chicago, yes. How's it going with the swim team?"

"We just won the Big West Conference. You have no idea how much I appreciate you helping me get there."

She blushed, though he probably couldn't see it in the dim lighting. Feeling a bit uncomfortable when her dress hiked up her thighs, she pulled it down when the girl on Finn's other side called for his attention. He leaned toward her as she whispered something into his ear. Soon after he turned toward Anne again.

"So, Jane, no sign of your friend yet? Did she drive you here? You can ride back with me. I'm the designated driver, so even though I'm legal now, I can't drink tonight."

"Oh, I'm sorry. Why do bad things happen to good people?" she said, tsking and shaking her head.

Finn laughed. "I missed this."

She missed making him laugh. Not everyone understood her.

"Thanks for the offer. I'm sure she'll turn up soon," she replied to his question, though she wasn't sure Bella would turn up. It'd been thirty minutes.

"You can join us," he said.

"I think I'll wait."

"I can wait with you."

She just shook her head with a smile, feeling silly.

"Okay. But, Jane, if you need anything, and I'm inside, just come to me," he said, gesturing with his head toward the interior of the club.

She summoned her courage and said, "Thanks. I go by Anne now, by the way. My middle name."

"What?" he asked, tilting his head, almost leaning it against hers. He was suddenly so close. "I didn't catch that."

"Yeah, it's loud in here."

"Maybe we should tell them to skip to a light Fandango," he said with a smirk.

They looked at each other and started laughing in synch. Her heart skipped a beat. He remembered. The song.

"What were you saying before?" His forehead nearly rested against her temple, and this closeness became a new, unexpected torture. She felt her body softening, and hardening, and liquidating all at once in different places. They were so close that she could inhale his breath. It made her wonder what he'd taste like.

"I'm going by my middle name now—Anne."

"You mean, instead of Jane?" He perused her face with those blue eyes of his, suddenly all serious.

"Well, yes, kind of. My parents and some people ... forget sometimes, but everyone in college knows me as Anne."

"Is it because of ...?" He didn't have to finish the sentence.

"No. Well, it was a catalyst. But I've always liked Anne."

"I like Anne, too, but I love Jane, because that's how I think of you. Can I still call you Jane?"

Think of her?

"Um ... Sure." She was certain she'd never see him again after tonight anyway and thought it was cute of him, especially since he had faced off with Eric over it.

"You will always be Jane to me, even when you're Anne," he said, his voice dropping a decibel. She had to lean closer. "Jane. It's plain and simple, and I love it," he mumbled, almost to himself.

She bit her lower lip. Just then, the girl who he had his arm around pulled him to whisper into his ear again. Finn tilted his head down toward her, his upper body slanting away from Anne.

Anne stared at the random people and groups that passed before them when a group of three men approached them. They looked much older.

Finn was suddenly pushed against Anne, and the girl who had been whispering to him quickly got up from her seat and hurried in her tiny sequin dress toward one of the approaching men and threw herself into his arms.

The short-haired friend, who sat farther down from Finn with a new space between them said in a loud enough voice for Anne to hear, "Shit, that's her boyfriend. It worked, Finn. He came looking for her."

Anne's gaze was glued to the scene in front of her, so she noticed the surprise on Finn's face only when he said, "This is him? She didn't say he was ... that."

"Oh, it is. And he saw you."

The guy was eyeing them while whispering something to the sequin dress who was now kissing his neck. He glared at Finn.

"Quick, pretend like you're with that girl," the friend said, shoving her hand against Finn's shoulder and pushing him further into Anne.

Instinctively, he wrapped his right arm around Anne.

Anne looked at Finn's nape, holding back from leaning closer to inhale his skin while he spoke to the short-haired friend. She was thinking how much like a college movie his life was in comparison to hers, just when he turned to her, and she found herself face to face with him, with less than an inch between them. Her gaze dropped to his lips, then back up to his eyes, where she caught his gaze doing the same—dropping to her lips then back up to meet her eyes.

Before she knew why he said, "Jane, sorry, can we ...?" his breath intermixed with hers, the non-existent distance between them closed, and he crashed his lips against hers.

The sudden impact found them both with their lips parted. He brushed his tongue along her lips, and she exhaled a surprised breath against his mouth. It was confused and hurried. But, a second later, their lips closed around each other in synch, and their *tongues met. She tasted him, and her entire body hummed when Finn slipped his tongue into her mouth. She found herself devouring him with a passion she didn't know she had in her.*

Finn tightened his hold, nestling her head in the crook of his arm, and with his free hand, he cupped her face and neck, lacing his fingers into her hair as he deepened their kiss until she became lightheaded. Every stroke of their tongues throbbed between her legs.

The voices of the people around them, the presence of the short-haired girl, the sequin and her boyfriend, Finn's other friends, the music, and the ambient club lights were all gone. All that remained was the pulse of the bass that beat inside her body and the taste of Finn, and his smell, and the feel of his hands on her. He didn't break their kiss even as they shallowed it to draw air. He then deepened it again and roughened it, their lips bruising as if they were trying to consume one another.

She felt, more than heard, the groan that rose from deep in his chest where she placed her hand over the hard muscles that the cotton of his shirt covered. Hearing it, feeling it, made her moan into his mouth. Her body was liquid fire.

"Anne, Anne," someone called repeatedly from afar.

For one dreadful moment, she was certain it was her mother who had come to wake her up in the middle of a dream. But the unmistakable scent and taste of Finn were real, and so was his tongue in her mouth, and his palm that now nestled the back of her head, and his fingers that gripped a fistful of her hair as he melded her further to him.

"Anne." The voice was close, and it was Finn who broke their kiss, leaving them both heaving, their faces an inch apart, their lips raw, their eyes blazing into the other's in a mix of incredulity, surprise, and something else that she couldn't unravel.

"Anne." A hand now touched her shoulder as Finn released her hair and untangled his fingers from within it and his arm from around her.

She pivoted toward the voice. Bella.

"I was looking for you, but I see you've been busy," Bella said, moving a grinning face between her and Finn.

She was too lost for words to reply, so she just nodded as Bella said, "Come on; I called my dad from a payphone, and he's here to pick us up. I told him I couldn't find you, and he said he'd come up to help me look for you. We don't want that, so let's go before he gets here or calls your parents."

She turned to look at Finn. The sofa beyond him was empty. Two of his male friends were standing at a distance from them, speaking among themselves, as if used to waiting for one of theirs to finish his business.

Their eyes met again. His lips looked wet and swollen, and he was still slightly panting, like she was.

"Jane," he just said in a hoarse voice.

"I have to go."

He grabbed her hand as she got up. "Don't. I'm sorry. I ... I hope you're ... I'm ..." He didn't seem sorry or rueful; he seemed shocked, like her.

"It's okay," she said. She thought she was smiling but wasn't sure. Her body still felt like he *owned it, not her.*

His eyes looked like a mist had settled over the ocean. He got up, still holding her hand. "Jane."

"Come on; my dad's waiting." Bella grabbed her by the crook of her elbow and dragged her.

"I'll call you," he said, releasing her hand.

"What was that?" Bella asked as they walked away. "Finn Brennen? Oh my God!"

"I don't know," she mumbled, glad Bella had her arm linked with hers because her knees felt weak.

"I got the phone number of that guy I danced with, but I don't know if I'll be able to see him before he goes back to his base," Bella said.

She hardly slept that night. Her mother took her for a girls' fun day the next day, and the next, she helped at the bakery. Finn called her house twice and missed her both times, leaving messages. She returned his calls, but they didn't get to talk before he had to go back to his practices. She flew back to school a few days after.

~~~~~~~~~~~~~~~~~

She watched Brad Pitt kissing Julia Ormond on the screen. Bella, on the sofa next to her, wiped a few tears.

That kiss with Finn had become the standard by which she measured every other kiss. None came close.

She had been young then and too busy trying to excel in her field, knowing that he had been doing the same. Though she had thought of him with a racing heart for weeks after, it hadn't hurt in a searing way. It was an ache of a missed opportunity. Maybe they'd been too different to work out anyway, but she knew for certain that Finn had always made her feel special, cherished, cared for, even in that brief encounter after years.

The look in his eyes that she had seen that night—she'd discover an infinitely deeper version of it a few years later, when they'd fall so hard that they wouldn't have come out of it the same even if the sky hadn't tumbled down on them soon after.

Chapter 6

"Good practice today, everyone. Give each other a pat on the shoulder. We've had several SWOLF score improvements today, everyone worked hard, and you all behaved as a team," Finn said as the kids climbed out of the pool.

"Hey, Dad, after I shower, can I go to Eli's for a sleepover? His mom will pick us up." Max stopped in front of him, wrapped in a towel. With his hair and eyelashes wet, he looked much younger, reminding Finn of his son's toddler days when they used to cuddle together after Max's bath time until they both fell asleep. He spent more nights in his son's room or on the sofa than he had in his own bedroom.

"Is it okay with his parents?"

"Yes. He checked with them before he asked me."

"Fine. But, are you sure you're not too tired?" Though he had planned to take Max out to eat after practice instead of cooking dinner, as usual, he was glad the boy spent time with friends. Eli was his closest friend from elementary school, and though they didn't attend the same middle school, they kept in touch, thanks to the club.

"I'm not tired, and all we're gonna do is play X-box with Eli's sister."

Something about the blush that spread on Max's face, and the way his voice became a little hoarse, alerted Finn that the sister might be a point of interest.

"His sister, huh?"

"She's a year older than me … than us."

Finn nodded. "Okay. Be good and have fun. I'll call later to check in on you. I'll pick you up tomorrow morning for breakfast. We can go to Blue Jam Café."

"Thanks, Dad!"

He patted his son's shoulder then texted Eli's mother to ensure the sleepover on a Friday night was really okay with her.

Max was still young, but they'd already had "The Talk" earlier that year—physical changes, sex, consent, protection—the latter was a tender spot for Finn—being attracted to various people, exposure to porn.

Growing up without a dad, Finn had learned everything from his friends, and their information had been far from accurate. He didn't want Max to rely on such sources or, worse, on porn. Starting when Max had been ten, Finn began with age-appropriate information and, at twelve, had sat him down for a longer talk about the physical changes he was beginning to experience.

When Max had follow-up questions, Finn happily realized how much his son trusted him, even with things that had been difficult for him to utter at first.

"The size will change. Promise," he had answered one question.

"It might happen, but it's not the end of the world if it does," he had answered another.

"It's natural and as it should be. Nothing to worry about," he had answered yet another.

After Eli's mother picked the boys up, Finn called Avery to finalize their arrangement regarding the holidays. She was supposed to get Max for Halloween and Thanksgiving, and he for Christmas until noon. Max wanted to spend Halloween in Blueshore, like he had the year before, but it was Avery's turn.

On the one hand, he hated that his son's life was spread between two towns and two houses. On the other hand, there wasn't much he could do about it, except try to streamline it with Avery as much as possible.

When that uncomfortable phone call was over, Finn locked the pool area's front doors.

He had no more practices that evening, and Max's unexpected sleepover removed the safety belt that he relied on to keep him from doing something stupid. He knew exactly what date it was, because he couldn't get that date out of his mind ever since he had seen it on a brochure in a bakeshop. Maybe if he tired himself to the point of collapse, he wouldn't do what every atom in him craved since the Riviera View fair.

He flipped through the contacts on his phone. He couldn't think of anyone on that list as the type of friend that he could confide in, spend the evening with, and ask to keep him from doing something he wasn't supposed to do.

The sound of water lapping at the pool's edge echoed in the vast, silent space.

Finn threw the phone down on a towel and arrowed himself into the pool, determined to swim until he was too tired to think.

Two hours later, with burning muscles, he showered, knowing he'd pay the full price the next day. Although he still competed in his age group, his endurance wasn't the same as when he had been a pro. At almost forty, he wasn't in the same shape anymore, especially since he didn't dedicate every waking hour to his training and nutrition, nor did he have sports medical professionals available for him twenty-four-seven.

On the way home, he negotiated with himself, summoning logic, common sense, sense of duty, and even wardrobe don'ts—surely people didn't go to gallery exhibitions in Henley shirts and jeans they kept in their lockers. But, right before turning onto his street, Finn broke the wheel left and drove out of Blueshore, toward the highway that would take him to Wayford, to a gallery that he had been in once.

Once he had opened the floodgates, there was no escape from the deluge.

~~~~~~~~~~~~~~~~

He was about to finish his coffee and leave when he noticed the woman who stopped at the bar in Life's A Beach, her long, ashen pink, paisley dress cascading down her body. She spoke with Ben, the barman, and stood with her back to the room, but Finn immediately recognized that dark brown, smooth hair, cut above the shoulders, and the lean, long body. He hadn't seen her in four years, ever since she had nearly knocked him dead with a kiss, but he knew it was her just by that slender back and neck. He could still remember how they felt in his hands.

He left his table by the window and approached the bar. Ben was busy making a smoothie, and the sound of the industrial blender whirred in the half-empty café.

He stopped behind her. The rays of the afternoon sun kissed her bare nape. "Jane?"

She turned around. "Finn!" she called, looking as surprised as he was.

They looked at each other, hesitating for a brief moment, before they simultaneously reached for one another. She threw her arms around his neck, and he grabbed her waist, and they hugged like old friends.

He was bathed in her familiar, lemony smell. Her body in his arms felt soft yet strong, lithe and supple.

"Oh my God, what are you doing here?" she asked, her lips hovering close to his neck, just as he said into her hair, "I didn't know you were back in town."

She pulled herself back, and they stood, holding each other's hands, scanning the other's face as if looking for the familiar and noting the differences.

She looked mature, as if the features of her face had found their rightful place. Her eyes looked larger, and their almond shape lent a cat-like quality to her face, their dark brown highlighted by the contrast of her skin tone, as always. Her lips were Anne-Hathaway-like, and he remembered exactly what kissing them felt like. The kiss that had started as an almost-accident had become the standard by which he measured others. None came close.

If she wore makeup, he couldn't see it. He didn't know what others saw when they looked at her but, to him, she looked absolutely beautiful. Maybe because he knew that behind that quiet, fragile-looking, almost translucent façade, she was the complete opposite—a colorful, strong, lively woman with an artistic soul and a sarcastic streak that not many knew. And an ability to derail a man off his axis with a kiss.

"What are you doing here?" he repeated. "I thought you were in Chicago."

"After college, I moved to San Francisco," she said. "I could ask you the same." Her smile was wide, her eyes sparkled.

"Anne, your smoothie," Ben said from behind the bar, setting down a tall glass with mango-colored liquid.

"Thanks, Ben," she said, dropping her hands from Finn's to reach for her purse.

"Add it to my bill, Ben," he hurried to say. "I have a table over there," he added to her. "I was about to leave, but I'd rather stay if you join me."

"Oh. Sure. Thanks." She took her drink and followed him.

"Anne. Ben called you Anne. I keep thinking of you as Jane."

"That's okay," she said with a smile.

In ten minutes by the window overlooking the ocean, they were all caught up. She had come back from San Francisco two weeks before and had just been to a friend's gallery in Wayford to drop off a few paintings that he had offered to exhibit for her. Her dream to live off art hadn't materialized. When she couldn't afford to pay the San Francisco rent and her parents offered she use her grandparents' old house and just pay her aunt her part of the rent, and help at the bakery, she had decided to return home.

"Take a step back and reevaluate my options. So far, the decorated cakes line I started for them already sells better than any painting I ever tried selling at the gallery I worked for in San Francisco," she said with a chuckle. "So, I either had the wrong dream or used the wrong canvas to paint on."

He had to hold himself back from reaching over the corner of the table and smooth a hand down her cheek because her lips smiled but her eyes didn't.

"But enough about me. Tell me about you. Are things going swimmingly?" she asked.

He scoffed. "They were. But I didn't make it on the Olympic trials. I found a sponsor, and competed, and tried again, but I didn't improve my times, so ..." He shrugged.

She nodded. He knew she understood the swimmers' lingo from that day she had questioned him about it in the library. "Wow, the Olympics."

"It was a stretch, but I had to try. So, here I am, kinda like you," he said. "Came home to good old Riviera View to weigh my options."

From the sympathetic smile on her face, he knew she understood exactly how defeated he had felt at first and what it had taken to adjust. He had a feeling he didn't have to tell her how lost he had been, having to find a new focus, a new dream, a new goal. He could see that she was just at that place now.

He didn't add that realizing his dream had reached as far as it ever would, and being back home, living at his mother's again, without the routine he had been used to for a decade, had depressed him so much that he had spent the first two weeks doing nothing. Nothing, except sleeping in, going out with old friends, and hooking up with a woman or two. He couldn't even say for sure if it was one or two. That whole period was a gray cloud that he had been lost in. But once he got his act together, realizing it wasn't all or nothing, he focused on finding a job coaching a leading club, one that he could push forward and where he could still compete nationally on a semi-professional level.

"I got a job coaching a club in Blueshore. They're leading in several strokes and age groups. If it goes well, I might move there." Blueshore was an hour away. "I finished a meeting with one of their directors just before you came in."

"Congratulations!" She raised her smoothie glass and clinked it against his iced coffee. "A good way to continue living your dream even if it's not …" She raised her shoulders in a you-know *gesture. "That's kinda what I'm aiming at. We should drink to that!"*

"Speaking of," he said after taking a sip, "that exhibition of yours, will there be a grand opening or something?"

"Nah. It's not my exhibition. Eddie is a friend, and he did me a favor. I didn't even tell my parents about it. What's the opposite of grand opening? Unimpressive finale?" She chuckled, her lips hovering over the straw in her drink. Never in his life had Finn been so jealous of a straw.

"You should tell them, and you should attend; see your work presented, talk to people. You should be proud."

"I don't know. Maybe. I kinda lost the nerve."

"You? The girl who eventually convinced the band to play 'Dancing Queen'?"

She laughed and buried her face in her palms. "Ah, don't remind me."

But he loved that memory. It somehow signified more to him now than it had back then.

"I can go with you."

She removed her hands from her face. "To the gallery?"

"Yes."

"Why would you do that to yourself? As I recall, you never really liked art."

"I like art. The kind I understand. You know, the kind I can tell what I'm looking at, like yours."

She chuckled. "I wish more people like you bought my paintings. I was told to choose a different path, another technique, another style, paint with oil instead of acrylic, or do something groundbreaking," she mimicked a posh male voice and pushed her eyebrows up at that last word. "When I did, I was told that I wasn't giving it my all. I guess I just couldn't feign doing something I didn't love just because it's the current taste." She played with the straw in her smoothie then looked up at him. "That was my quitting speech, by the way."

They laughed in tandem, leaning toward each other in the process.

"Then you stormed out?"

"Nah, the gallery's door was too heavy. At the risk of sounding like a whiney 'no one understands my vision,' I just bullshitted something about how my style was so backward that it was actually groundbreakingly forward. Then *I walked myself dignifiedly out of there."*

They laughed again, and he wanted to grab and hug her right there and shut that self-deprecating mouth of hers with a kiss.

"But he was right," she said, her gaze drifting to the beach view outside.

"Give it a chance," he said. "Will you go if I go with you?"

She hesitated for a moment, bringing her eyes to his. "Okay."

"See you tomorrow?" he asked when they parted.

"You will."

He picked her up the next day, and they drove to Wayford. She wore a floral dress that tied around her neck, and her legs looked so long, and her skin so fair that he wondered if she tasted like buttercream.

"So, where's the gallery?" he asked as they walked into what looked like a depressing office space from the seventies.

"You're looking at it," she said.

"But it's an office."

"You're supposed to think that. Wait."

They passed through the space and into a bigger room that looked like a gallery with warm lights, paintings hanging on the walls, a few statues in the center.

"Why waste the room they have there?" he asked, squinting at a statue whose shape didn't

remind him of anything except an oddly-shaped, crumpled piece of paper.

Jane laughed. "Eddie's boyfriend had this idea to first get you in a certain mood, and then break it."

"Oh, I'm going to enjoy this," he said, scoffing and gazing at the well-dressed Wayforders who strolled holding wine glasses. "Do you think it's champagne?"

"Probably just sparkly white wine. They're new. I don't think they have the budget for champagne and waiters." She took him to a table covered in white at the side, and they took two glasses.

"To you," he said then clinked his glass with hers.

She introduced him to Eddie and his boyfriend, and they walked around, looking at the paintings and reaching hers at the end. She had three hanging there, among dozens of others, most of them in a completely different style.

Hers were easy to tell apart from the rest, and Finn could tell what she had depicted—the families' beach of Riviera View, the sand peeping from among a sea of colorful beach umbrellas; a balcony overlooking the ocean with an empty, rumpled bed reflecting on one of the glass doors that opened to the view; and another was of a woman floating on her back with a pink swimming cap in a vast blue ocean.

"This one is kind of sad," he said, unable to remove his eyes from her paintings, especially the one with the empty bed. He wanted to know everything about her life in San Francisco, everything about her.

"It all depends on how you look at it and how you interpret it," she said.

"How did you interpret it when you painted it? And, why is this woman floating alone?"

Jane chuckled. "I'll tell you on the way home."

"Already? Come on; let's stay. I want to hear what these people are saying," he whispered, leaning closer to her. Her hair brushed his face, and her lemony scent filled his lungs.

They moved aside as a group of four stopped to look at her work.

"You see, they like your stuff," he whispered to her after eavesdropping on the group.

When those people moved on, he went to get them both another round of wine. "Let's play a game. Every time someone says something artsy-fartsy, we drink."

She chuckled and clinked her glass with his. "Just say you want to get drunk."

He laughed, but he was already drunk. On her.

They went to stand close to another group and listened to their conversation that included a repetition of the term "avant-garde" on what looked to Finn like a beheaded panda. This group alone had them finish their glasses, so they refilled them while moving to stand behind a couple who were talking about one of the statues.

Jane and he looked at each other with muffled laughs and drank again.

He was about to take a sip when another couple commented on the statue, but Jane listened attentively. Then she looked at him, smiled mischievously, and they drank.

"I actually agreed with the second couple, but I was thirsty," she whispered to him, chuckling. Her breath on his skin made him harden in his jeans.

In another instance, she looked at him, her lips hovering over the glass, and he waited for her verdict, his eyes on her lips, his heart and cock envying the glass until she gave him a nod and a look of oh, yeah, they're full of it, *and they both drank.*

"They're playing our song," he said when an acoustic version of "Whiter Shade of Pale" played in the background.

Jane narrowed her eyes as she tried to distinguish the notes from the general buzz of the gallery space. She then nodded and smiled as she recognized it. "We have a song? And it's a jumble of unconnected sentences that no one understands?" Her smile widened, and she skimmed her eyes over his face as if she was trying to read his mind.

If she could read minds, she'd find that he wondered what she tasted like everywhere and why his heart throbbed at the thought that this evening would soon end.

Eddie approached them. "We haven't sold anything of yours yet, but there's interest."

"You see? There's interest! You might just make a fortune out of it," Finn said after Eddie left them.

"Only if I die young in some tragically embarrassing circumstance and it suddenly takes off," she muttered.

"God, I love you," he blurted out as he laughed.

She laughed, too, but he realized what he had just said. They looked at each other. The words came right out like they had been ready on his tongue. They had only met again the day before. Only exchanged one earth-shattering kiss four years ago. Only shared a friendship for one year in high school. Yet, the words he unthinkingly uttered rang true.

When they left the gallery, neither one of them was fit to drive. They giggled their way to a diner that was still open and sat there for a cup of strong coffee.

"Your work was the best there," he said.

"It was the only one you understood?" She winked at him.

"Yes." He laughed. But it was more than that— he could see her soul in those paintings; they had a heart.

His own heart hammered against his rib cage, as if it raced to understand what she was doing to it. He had read about the impressionist style earlier that day—visceral brush strokes, incredibly tactile—he could see these qualities underlying in Jane herself. He had felt that rawness in her kiss.

"I still can't drive. I need to clear my head a little more," he said when they left the diner.

"Me neither," she said, going in the opposite direction to where they'd left the car. "Let's go down to the beach." In Wayford, the beach was at level with the main street and easily accessible.

It was early November, and the moon was waxing. It wasn't too cold, and there were other people on the beach; jogging alone or in pairs, some with dogs, couples strolling. They did, too. Silently.

The crash of the waves rolled like drums in Finn's heart. He felt like he was standing on the edge of a pool, yearning to dive but, for the first time, hesitating to leap because he couldn't see the bottom.

They stopped just outside the reach of the water. Every wave that broke ceased its roll before it wet their feet. Jane slightly bent to grab the hem of her dress in case the next wave hit them. When she straightened up, she was half pivoted toward him. Their arms brushed, and their gazes locked. Her eyes, which the moonlight reflected on, were ocean-deep.

At that moment, he knew—if he dove into this unknown vastness, he'd never find his way out. And worse, he didn't want to.

He gripped her forearm and pulled her to him. She let go of the dress. His lips were on hers before he even had his arms around her. He then wrapped her in his arms and crushed her to him, bringing her as close to him as possible with their clothes on. She gripped his shoulders, and every bit of that kiss from four years ago was there again—forceful, hungry, fiery, bruising his lips and his heart. She kissed him as if the world would end tomorrow and she'd never kiss or be kissed again.

They didn't speak with words until they reached her house in Riviera View, and it was plain that he would be coming in. When the door closed behind them, she spoke first.

"Finish me off, Finn," she whispered.

And he did, right there by her front door.

Her back slammed against it when he pinned her to it and kissed her like he'd later fuck her—hard, deep, rough. He trailed his lips over her neck and his hands down her body. Then, kneeling in front of her, he dragged the dress up her long thighs, revealing the milky skin. He kissed and licked it, chafing his hands down her legs, sliding her lace panties until they pooled at her feet. He placed one of her knees on his shoulder and got full access to lick and suck at her core.

Her fingers clutched his hair, and she had no capacity for anything except moaning and gasping until she throbbed and shattered against his mouth, the muscles of her legs almost giving in.

He let her ride it to the end before he brought himself up to be at level with her. She looked like she'd fall if he didn't hold her. Her eyes were wide, her gaze almost wild. Though he was rock hard already, this made him harder.

He kissed her again, trekking his hands over her bare shoulders and the front of the dress, knowing he was seconds from tearing it all off of her.

"Fuck me, Finn" she breathed against his mouth.

"I intend to," he rasped. With his hands under her thighs, he picked her up and walked to the bedroom. In that small house, it wasn't hard to guess where it was.

He threw them both on the bed. A string of fairy lights around the vanity mirror lit the room. He rose to his knees and let her watch as he unbuttoned his shirt and took it off then unbuckled his jeans.

She reached to touch his abs and chest.

"Not yet." He caught her wrists and pinned them above her head with one hand while, with his other, he untied the dress from around her neck and tugged it down to her waist with one strong pull. She had a strapless bra under it. He caressed it with his free hand for a second before he yanked it down and exposed her breasts. He leaned in and kissed her mouth, brushing his tongue along her jawline to her

ear. *"You're so beautiful, Jane," he whispered in her ear.*

She writhed under him, looking for more contact, her wrists still gripped by him as he kissed his way down to her breasts. The wine color of her nipples peaking on the pale skin was almost his undoing. She gasped when he moved his mouth between her breasts, sucking on one, then the other, while kneading her flesh with his hand.

He pulled himself up a bit so he could pull the dress farther down when something caught his eyes. He sent his free hand to caress her left hipbone. A small replica of a Van Gogh sunflower was tattooed there. He moved his gaze to her face. A sunflower for a tall girl who wasn't friends with the sun. It was her sense of humor; he knew it was.

"It's the less famous version he painted," she said, panting, her voice hoarse, her hands still above her head. "I love the ones few notice."

"Me, too," he rasped, his eyes never leaving hers. He loosened his grip, took one of her hands, and placed it on his bare chest. His heart inside it was already hers, though she didn't know it yet.

He bent and kissed the sunflower tattoo, then licked his way up to her breasts, pushing his weight into her, his body fitting perfectly against hers.

She caressed him, chafed her hands all over his chest, arms, and back, kissed his neck, bit his shoulder, until they scorched each other in a kiss.

"Hard," she said when he thrust into her. And she didn't have to say more; he knew what and how she wanted it. Raw.

"It's always the quiet ones," his friend had commented after witnessing them kiss at the club and how dazed Finn had been after.

The living, writhing, moaning proof was under him now. Unlike her exterior implied, she wasn't delicate, or fragile, or shy, or quiet. She demanded and pleaded him to fuck her harder, deeper. She gripped his hair as he did, kissed him like she'd die if she didn't, called his name loudly when she came. She made him come so hard that it took him several minutes to gain the capacity to speak again.

But more than anything, he couldn't speak because the words he had blurted unknowingly at the gallery had become unfalteringly true from the moment he had sunk himself deep inside her for the first time.

"What are you doing for the rest of your life?" he asked, wrapping her in his arms, pressing her hard against him because he couldn't imagine being without her from that day on.

~~~~~~~~~~~~~~~~

Parking across the street from Eddie Melton's gallery, Finn looked over at the lit windows. It was late, but there were still people inside.

The place looked fancier than he remembered. Not surprising. Wayford had become more lucrative and expensive over the years, leaving Riviera View behind.

Finn turned the engine off, stepped out of his car, locked it behind him, and crossed Wayford's stylish main street toward the place where he had first said the words *I love you* to the only woman he had ever meant it with.

Chapter 7

With Wayford only a thirty-minute drive from Riviera View, and her mother pushing those flyers to anyone who had set foot at the bakery, Anne wasn't surprised to meet several of her parents' friends and the bakery's clientele at the gallery.

"It's not a solo exhibition," she had tried to warn, to no avail.

Her uncle and aunt, Darian and Fernando, were there, but luckily, their daughter didn't see fit to attend.

Bella came the day before, and she had shown her around.

"I have no idea what I'm looking at," her father said honestly when they stopped before a charcoal drawing that proclaimed it was a self-portrait. "A self-portrait of what?" Bert added, tilting his head ninety degrees.

"What's there to understand? You just make up whatever you want of it. Right, Jane?" her mother said.

She smiled at them both. "Right," was the easy answer. She worried if she started explaining, she'd have to take a sip with every other pretentious-sounding word she'd utter.

"Anne, congratulations," a female voice said behind her.

She turned around. Connie Latimer and her partner, David. She had expected they'd drop by, but she was surprised to see Libby and her fiancé, Luke Delaney, with them.

"Thank you all for coming! I know my mom made you." She chuckled.

"No, we want to support you and see this," David said, swiping his hand across the gallery's space.

"We looked around. Yours are the most beautiful here," Connie said, leaning closer to her and speaking quietly, as if she was afraid to hurt the other presenters.

"I'm here for you, but also for Eddie. He's an old friend," Libby said.

"Oh, that's true." Anne smiled. She remembered Libby and Eddie being close at some point in high school, though she had always suspected that Libby had been secretly in love with Luke. Turned out, she had been right.

Seeing Luke reminded her of his older brother, Jordan, and the rumor Bella had repeated regarding Avery. To obliterate that thought before it'd bring Finn into her mind, a place he had occupied rent-free for years and expanded since his visit to the bakery, she hurried to say, "I know Hope wanted to come, too. She texted me earlier that she's at her daughter's Model UN competition in San Francisco."

"She is," Libby said with a smile.

"Oh, sorry, I didn't mean to imply you didn't know," Anne said. After all, she had only known Hope for two years. They had become closer after

Hope had asked for unsold goods to distribute at school, and the food bank idea had been born.

"I didn't think you were implying; I was just agreeing with you." Libby put a hand on her forearm.

She wished they could stop walking on eggshells around each other, afraid that every well-intended gesture or word could and would be interpreted wrong.

Thinking of Hope, her mind leaped to Hope's unworthy ex-husband, Eric the douchebag. From Eric, it was an easy leap to thoughts of Finn. Everything led to Finn.

These small towns were too small. Cincinnati had been easier. She had lived next door to an introverted librarian, and their connection summed up in watering each other's plants when needed. Last she heard, Melanie had left for a vacation in Europe and had decided to stay.

When most of her visitors left, and she escorted her parents, uncle, and aunt to the door, Anne went back inside.

Lingering in front of a painting that had caught her imagination, the hairs at her nape suddenly bristled in anticipation as a flicker of familiar fragrance reached her. She closed her eyes.

"Jane." She had known that voice would come, even before she had heard it, yet her heart still flailed.

It nearly stopped when she thought that her parents or, worse, his former in-laws had seen him come in. How would she explain his presence?

She turned around. "What are you doing here?" she asked, trying to repress the fact that his eyes were an ocean, his face the ache in her heart, and his shoulders under the black Henley her former respite.

"I could lie and tell you that I was in the neighborhood, if it helps."

"It doesn't. I need you to leave."

He smirked. "Wow. I hope you're nicer to potential buyers." The warmth in his eyes was tinged with reminiscence.

She couldn't help but huff a chuckled breath. "No, Finn. Really, I mean it."

"I know you do. You need me to leave, and I just need you."

No. No. She was not going to let that word infiltrate her heart. She couldn't. *Need.* She hated that word.

"Do you *want* it or *need* it?" her mother used to challenge when she would ask for something precious, something that was hard to get. Needing meant you had to have it, couldn't do without it. And what was the point in needing something you couldn't possibly have? She had spent *years* trying to kill the need. At first, by being angry at him. It had been easy to do from afar, but the first time she had seen him after his marriage, she had realized that they were both in this, that he was the only one who could understand, and that it was even harder on him.

She moved her gaze left and right, ensuring no one else heard him. "It's not the time or the place."

"It never is. I've been divorced three years now, and I wanted to come to you from day one."

"Well, you shouldn't." *Kill the need.*

"You're telling me everything I already know, Jane."

"It's Anne. If you know it, then why are you here?"

"Because, Jane."

"Your in-laws were just here." *Kill the need.*

"*Former* in-laws. I saw them coming out."

"Why didn't you stop to say hi to them?" *Obliterate the need.*

"All these years, Jane. You *know* that you were always on my mind."

She knew. *The cards.*

"We're not an Elvis song." *Kill the need.*

He expelled a half-laugh at her reply. "You want to tell me that you haven't thought—"

"It was hard not to with those cards you left me every year." *Lie.* She would have thought about him with or without the cards. If only for the weekly phone calls with her mother that always included updates about Avery, and naturally about Finn and Max, too. But, mostly, because she loved him so much that he left no room in her heart for anything else, not even long-lasting anger. And yes, the cards.

The cards that she had tried at first to resent because they kept her tethered to him had become a link to the only person in the world who knew what she felt and who felt the same. It was a source of consolation and renewed pain. She didn't want him to suffer, she didn't want him to hurt. She wanted him to be happy. So, every year, on November eleventh, her birthday and his wedding anniversary, she dreaded and eagerly awaited those unsigned cards that her mother picked up from her mailbox and sent to her. She dreaded them *because* she so eagerly awaited them, as if she wanted him to be happy and forget her, but she also didn't.

Like the song that he said was theirs, it was a fucking incoherent mess.

Her mother thought they were from old school friends, but she knew only one person would choose cards with a Monet painting, a trumpet, a sunflower, a funny Abba cartoonish misquote, or Jane Austen one such as, "*It is a truth universally acknowledged that today is your birthday.*" She had never replied, returned, or made contact. He was a married man. And even when he wasn't ...

No cards had been left in the two years since she had returned to Riviera View. She knew why and thanked him for that—some things were easier and safer from afar.

"Is this yours?" he suddenly asked, pointing at her watercolor that hung by the painting that she had been perusing before he'd entered.

She didn't reply. She knew what he was doing—forcing her to admit she had thought of him, as if it wasn't clear enough.

"That swimmer over there; it's yours?" he repeated.

"The theme of this exhibition is the human body's resilience," she replied as laconically as she could. That painting wasn't him, but it also was.

He looked at her with an expression that she thought was almost pity at her inability to lie. He then pointed at the painting closer to them, which she, too, couldn't decipher what was painted on it. "You mean that *this* is also supposed to be about the human body's resilience? I'd take a sip right now, if I had a glass," he said, his smirk a clear reference to that night a gazillion years ago.

"That one actually sold." She pointed at the sticker next to it. "Anyway, it was a pleasure, Finn, but I have other guests; buyers, maybe." Since he stood in front of her, and there was a wall behind her, she swooshed past him to the side, her long, loose, forest green wrap-dress rippling behind her.

He caught her wrist, stopping her in her tracks. "Jane."

She closed her eyes for a moment then turned to him. Was the human heart resilient? Probably not because, otherwise, he wouldn't be here and she wouldn't be feeling as she did.

"What do you want, Finn? What exactly do you expect happens now? That I jump into your arms and we spend eternity together?" She looked at him in desperation. *Kill the need.* "That's not possible, so … what is it that you want?"

He wet his lips and darted his gaze to the side. There was an opening to a back corridor right beside them.

Without replying, still gripping her wrist, he pulled her to cross those few feet with him.

As soon as they turned the corner into the corridor crammed with boxes and frames, she stopped. Again, she found herself with her back against the wall, literally and figuratively.

Why was it that, every time they were in close proximity, it felt as if no time had passed? As rare as their meetings had been over the years—she could probably count them on less than ten fingers—and as little as they could talk or even be next to each other on those occasions, it always felt like they were frozen in a time capsule, just them.

His hard chest touched hers. In her high heels, they were almost the same height. Her heart pounded hard against her ribs, her gaze glued to his blues.

"First of all, yes, that's what I want. You, in my arms, for eternity," he exhaled.

She shook her head. "I don't have to tell you, Finn—"

"Jane," he said in a *cut-it-out* tone.

"Anne." From almost anyone else, it'd be an affront. Not from him. From his mouth, her old name was a declaration of love that she couldn't accept. "Let go of me, Finn."

"I'm not holding you anymore," he said.

Only then did she notice that her wrist was free.

"I know you're not seeing anyone."

She let out a dry scoff. "Do you really think that's the only thing that stands between us?" She remembered the Christmas she had brought Tom.

"I know it's not."

Maybe a reality check would help. She could use the reminder, as well, because Finn, in this proximity, made reality slip for her, too. Not only was her need for him not obliterated, it exponentially grew, which only made it imperative that she slew it.

"Do you really want to rip your son's family apart?" she asked.

He swayed back. It worked.

"Max is the only reason I didn't come to you until now. But I don't fucking know what to do anymore. I love you, Jane. I love you, *Anne*, okay? I tried to unlove you. For years, I did my fucking best to stop, to forget, to move the fuck on. But I can't. It all comes back to you."

She just stared at him. His words were hers, the ones she didn't utter.

"Do you think this is easy for me?" he asked when she kept quiet. "Do you think I don't know how messy this is? Especially with Avery. She's ... I've been in competitive sports all my life—I know healthy competition when I see one—and she's ... not it."

She felt guilty for wondering if Avery had gotten pregnant and married him just a few months after her younger brother had married his high school sweetheart because it was some sort of a win she had to exceed.

"You have more to lose than I do." She knew the moment she said it that those words gave away her weakening resolve, but he could use the reminder.

Finn pressed his lips for a moment and his gaze drifted to the wall behind her. She knew these reminders were working. He then looked at her again with steel-blue eyes and flattened one of his palms on the wall next to her shoulder, caging her in.

"Do you still love me?" he demanded.

"It doesn't matter. And it's been years, Finn."

"It matters to me. Do you love me?" His eyes pierced her.

She wet her lips, trying to stall for time. His gaze dropped to her lips, and God help her, she felt that between her legs.

"No," she lied.

"I don't believe you," he gruffed.

She could hardly hear the words because Finn leaned in, bending his elbow so his forearm was on the wall, imprisoning her. The look in his eyes, mere inches from hers, the muscle that flexed in his jaw, and the way their breaths intermixed, made her pulse so loud in her ears that it sounded like the shrieks of a truck in reverse on its path to collision.

She closed her eyes, knowing what came next, knowing that once he kissed her, she'd be lost.

Beep. Beep. Beep. Beep.

The alarm of her heartbeat kept screaming. If she was afraid of it before, knowing what it could do to her, she yearned for it now. She wanted Finn to kiss her like only he could.

When no collision hit, she opened her eyes.

Dark cobalt skies met her gaze, and in the blue, she could swear she saw her own heart reflecting.

"I thought so," Finn rasped.

She felt that low rasp in her body.

Now that he had proven his point, Finn took a step back, his arm leaving the wall, and Anne could breathe again.

"Are you punishing me, Jane? Because, trust me, it won't work. I must be a glutton for punishment. I spent too many years married to your cousin, for fuck's sake, and loving you all along."

"I'm not. I'm just trying to save us both more heartache."

"It's not working."

"Then I'm trying to spare the others." She took a deep breath. "Finn, it's a small family, just two branches, twin ones, nowhere to run or hide. But forget the grown-ups. Can you imagine the clusterfuck of your son's Christmases and Thanksgivings if we walked into a family gathering together? With his mother there, and her mother, and mine? Me, who he thinks of as an aunt, though he doesn't see me too often, and now I'd be his dad's … a clusterfuck. Avery will *never* accept me with you, and I doubt her parents will, which means that your son will be torn."

He inhaled deeply then let it out slowly, averting his gaze. She could hear the low murmur of conversation from the people who were still in the gallery, on the other side of the wall.

"Do you think I *wanted* to marry your cousin?" he asked, bringing his eyes back to her.

"I don't need you to rehash the entire history for me, Finn. I was there."

"Do you think I wanted to *stay* married to her? Maybe you need to hear this again, Jane, because I never had a chance to tell you. Do you think it was easy for me to stay away from you all those years? From the woman I love? And you know why I stayed. Let me rehash *that* and tell you a few things no one knows, not even you, because you *weren't* there."

She didn't want to hear. What if the things he told her hurt even more? What if they made her love him more and destroy what little resistance she had left in her?

"She was eight weeks pregnant when she told me. Her belly wasn't even showing," he said. "I had forgotten all about her. I didn't know she was your cousin. I did what I thought was the right thing because you said there was no option for us either way."

"There wasn't. And I know all of that."

"No, you don't. You don't know that two days after town hall, with a pregnant wife at home, I came to you … but you were already gone."

"*What?*" She was stunned but still noticed the way he had uttered the word *wife* and said *town hall* instead of *my wedding*.

"You're my drug, Jane. Two days after that wedding, I was ready to throw it all to hell just to be with you. And if you had been there, I know what I would have done if you gave me the chance. That's why I stayed away from you all these years. Because I *knew* what I was capable of."

Her mouth was agape. She knew that, to him, who suspected he was the result of an extramarital affair, this was all the more horrible. She also knew that, if he had found her then, she would have—was—capable of the same. And then they would have truly been screwed—they would have hated themselves and eventually each other.

"Yes, Jane, two days after my wedding. I wanted to be with you. I wanted to tell you that I couldn't give a damn about doing the right thing if it meant I had to be without you. That I made the biggest mistake of my life. That I was happy she wasn't feeling well so I didn't have to touch her. That I was going to divorce her, get the marriage annulled, or whatever I needed to do to get out of it so I could be with you. I was going to *make* you take me. I didn't care how messy it was going to be with your cousin about to give birth to my child. I didn't care. Not about her and not about anyone else. Just you. But you weren't home, so I went to your mother and invented some excuse about a present I needed help exchanging. She told me you went on an unplanned road trip."

"I had to make your *wedding* cake, Finn! And *attend* your wedding. All I could do later to stop myself from screaming was get in my car and just drive for three days with hardly any stops. I blew a tire in Cincinnati, so I just stayed."

The dim corridor that they stood in was the back side of a beautiful, illuminated gallery. It somehow fit their state and the look in Finn's eyes.

"We messed each other up. *I* messed us up. I hardly knew her. One miscalculated, unnecessary, forgetful ... thing ... before you and I got together ..." He drifted off.

He looked lost; drowned in a sea of guilt. But the guilt wasn't just his.

She had played a part in the way things had unfolded, too. But they had both done what they *had* to do.

"It wasn't anyone's *fault*, Finn." She wanted to reach out and touch his face. The years have sharpened the edges in them, made him rugged.

"You know what happened a week after the wedding, right?" he urged.

"Avery lost the pregnancy," she mumbled.

"Yes. And the guilt, Jane, I can't tell you ... the guilt." He shook his head. "All I could think of was that it was my fault. Because I didn't *really* want it. I wanted to be free, and here I was, but at what cost? It was my fault. Because I'm a shit human being and because I loved you so much my fucking skin hurt, and I felt that losing you was worse than losing the

…" He took a deep breath. His eyes glistened with pain, regret, guilt. "I kept thinking … if only I had waited one more week. One week, and I could have been … I wouldn't have to … I would have *you*."

"I didn't know all that." The words came out as a half-whisper. She was glad she didn't believe in fate. Fate sounded like a bitch with a cruel sense of humor.

"I couldn't exactly tell you. I didn't know where you were. And I couldn't leave a woman in that state, not even her. And the guilt … I had to make up for it. She lost another pregnancy at seven weeks sometime after. I knew that was my fault, too, because I treated it as some debt I was paying to a God I don't even believe in."

Anne looked at his face. Eyes washed in pain, features hardened. She knew what that felt like— trying to do something right and only making it worse. "You couldn't leave her in that state and even if you knew where I was, *I* wouldn't have let you abandon her then. Not even *her*. I wouldn't have taken you."

"I know." His eyes were fixed on her. "Then, she was pregnant with Max, but you didn't show up for the christening."

"Did you really expect me to be there?" Her mother had given her hell over it, but she just couldn't.

"I didn't want you there." The muscle in his jaw flexed. "I didn't want to have to see you and love you from afar at my own son's christening."

Tears prickled her throat now because the new shards in her heart weren't dulled by time like the old ones.

What a mess. No wonder "their" song was a mumbo jumbo of words that no one understood. The two of them made about as much sense as the lyrics.

"At Noah's daughter's christening the year after, you walked in, and all I could do was pretend we were relatives and old friends meeting. I hugged you, with the entire family standing there, and God help me, I wanted to throw everything away just to be with you. Weeks of guilt … months … for one hug …" He trailed off.

She remembered that event. Her mother hadn't let her dodge Noah's daughter's christening. She remembered that hug. She remembered drowning in his arms. She remembered him whispering in her ear something he knew she'd understand. "*What fresh hell is this, Jane?*" It was a quote that made them laugh when they had studied Dorothy Parker's writing years before. She remembered Avery saying, "*Anne, you've got to hold the baby.*" And she had. She had held baby Max and sworn to never let Finn touch her again, to never let this hell take over Max, him, her. She had seen in his eyes back then that Max was what kept him going.

Tears brimmed her eyes now, and she swallowed, trying to stop them from falling.

Finn reached out, cupped her face, and brushed the tears away with the pads of his thumbs. She knew what he was going to say before he said it.

He closed the distance between them, and his body touched hers again. "What fresh hell is this, Jane?" he half-whispered, this time against her lips.

The initial soft touch, that first taste, was all it took for them to be thrown right into where they had left off.

Like years ago, like no time had passed since they had last kissed, they held each other, clinging to the other's touch and taste. Finn kissed her hard and rough and deep, like only he could. They were two people knowing and rediscovering each other.

Her head floated, but her body remained anchored to his. His fingers tangled in her hair and he held her firm against him, his pelvis and chest pressed into hers, and he was hard everywhere. She held on to his forearms and slipped her palms up to his biceps and shoulders. God, to touch him again …

But when her palms landed on his chest, and she felt the thudding of Finn's heart, she pushed him. *Kill the need*.

"No. No. This is still wrong," she panted against his lips, which he refused to withdraw from hers. She turned her head to the side and pushed more. "You're Max's dad. He's my cousin. I can't stand Avery, but she's my cousin, too. And my aunt and uncle, and my parents, they're not going anywhere, and they're not *nothing*."

Finn pulled himself back from leaning into her and tilted his head back, though he still held her with his hands in her hair. His eyes were the color of crashing waves.

"And for what, Finn?" she continued before he could speak. "We only spent one week together. We bonded over two broken dreams." She swept a hand in the general direction of the gallery. "We never had a great basis from the start."

"You *know* that's not true," he said, slipping his hands out of her hair and down to his sides.

He was right; it wasn't true.

"I have to go," she said. Sweeping her back against the wall, she moved to the side, out of his reach, then turned and walked out of the dark, messy corridor, and into the luminous gallery, leaving him behind.

She faked a smile and ran a hand over her hair to smooth it back to place. Then, despite her shaky legs and the heat that flooded every part of her, she walked toward Eddie and joined him and a few lingering guests, nodding at their artistic conversation. She ignored the way Eddie's baffled gaze dropped to her lips. She knew they were probably red, raw, swollen. She smiled, or at least hoped she managed to wear a smile, to cover the ashes of her heart.

Moments later, from the corner of her eyes, she saw Finn walk out.

Her gaze and heart followed him, but her body stayed put. She couldn't complicate her life, or her family's. If she wanted to be a mother, she had to put others' needs in front of hers. Just like he'd had to do back then. And despite what it had done to them, she respected him for that. Worse … she loved him for that, for being the kind of man who could take responsibility and do the right thing in impossible situations. And for having a rare heart.

~~~~~~~~~~~~~~~

Her head rested on his chest. They were both still catching their breaths. He held her tight, and she felt his lips on her hair.

"What are you doing for the rest of your life?" Finn's voice vibrated inside her body.

Her heart skipped at least one beat. Did he guess what she felt as she listened to his heartbeats—that she would never want to be without his embrace?

Though it'd been four years from that night at the club, from the moment she turned around at Life's A Beach and saw him, it was as if no time had passed, as if years were bridged over from that kiss to the hug they shared while her smoothie was being made. And the next twenty-four hours squeezed years into them. They had their own language, inside jokes, references, history. Their kiss on the beach had sealed it for her. Though it defied every logic, she knew beyond a doubt that she was in love with Finn Brennen.

If failing in San Francisco and coming home meant this—this man and the way he made her feel— then it was well worth it. All she hoped for right now, when she was still wrapped tightly in his arms and filled with his scent, his touch, his semen, was that he had meant at least part of the "God, I love you," he had blurted earlier at the gallery. She didn't want to be just a torn page or a chapter in his book, especially not when she knew that, given the chance, he could make up all the chapters in hers.

What would she do for the rest of her life? She lifted her head, and just to be on the safe side, in case it was something he meant as a joke, she looked into his eyes and said, "You."

His laughter surprised her.

He pulled her up so that her face was at level with his and kissed her. He then looked at her, and in the deep blue, she saw he meant every word when he said, "Great, because that's what I want you to do."

When he flipped her over and sank into her again, he stilled inside her, caressed her hairline, and skimmed his eyes over her face. "Jane," he said. One word, her old name, but she knew he was claiming her for himself with it, cementing her as his own. There was nothing she wanted more.

They didn't leave her house for three days. They hardly left her bed. Even when they did, they found themselves fucking in her tiny shower or against a random wall, knocking down an easel and stumbling over scattered paint tubes, brushes, and cloths.

She excused herself from going to the bakery, telling her mother over the phone that she found a gallery to exhibit in and had to paint.

"Are you always like that?" he asked in one of those times, panting in her ear, hugging her from behind, still inside her as she was bent over the back of the sofa, and he was bent over her, his chest pressed against her back.

"Like what?" She tried to catch her breath, still riding the aftershocks of another Finntastic orgasm.

"How many were there before me?" he half-whispered in her ear, still gripping her.

"Few." She smiled, turning her head to the side so she could kiss him. "Very few." She didn't add that, even put together, the few men she had been with couldn't match him. "You?"

"A few. Not one of them kisses or fucks like you," he said right into her ear, and the aftershocks between

her legs almost hurt from the vibration that his low rasp and words sent down her body.

"How?"

"Like it's the end of the world and it's your last time." He gripped her jaw and turned her head toward him, kissing her as if they hadn't just finished. "Like you want to make sure you're still alive, and you want it just as you like it—hard and a bit rough." He kissed her again, and she felt him hardening inside of her. But then he pulled out of her, and with his hand still around her waist, he straightened up with her and spun her in his arms to face him.

He grabbed under her thighs and lifted her, kissing her again. He might have aimed for the bedroom, but they found themselves in the kitchen. He set her on the counter and pushed into her just as soon.

She wrapped her legs around his hips and her arms around his neck, and they kissed as he moved inside her, gripping her hard and thrusting even harder.

"Fuck, Jane," he groaned against her neck when she threw her head back. He cupped her breast with one hand while holding her tight against him with his other. He pushed the mound up into his mouth and sucked on the soft flesh and hardened nipple.

She gripped his neck and stabbed her fingers into his short hair.

They cupped each other's faces in a forceful kiss until they had to breathe, together, as they came hard, gazes linked, lips a centimeter apart.

Finn's pulsation inside her matched her own. He wrapped his arms around her torso and buried his face in her neck.

"I love you, Jane." His voice against her neck was muffled, but the words were clear.

Finn pulled his head back and looked into her eyes. His were a misty ocean. "I love you," he repeated.

They stood there, naked, him still inside her, as they held each other in the haven of her little house.

"I think I began a long time ago," he added, caressing her cheek.

She nestled it further into his palm and kissed his wrist. "I love you, too, Finn. I never thought I'd get to tell you."

"You have a lifetime," he said, then leaned in to kiss her.

They spent a whole week together, but it didn't feel like a week. It felt like the beginning of eternity, of a lifetime.

"I never apologized for that kiss at the club," he said when they finally bothered to put clothes on and go out for an early dinner. They sat at a window table at a half-full Life's A Beach.

She chuckled. "Who was that girl with the sequin dress you were with that night?"

"I don't remember her dress. I don't even remember her name," he said, chuckling. "I think I forgot it as soon as you and I kissed."

At another table, she saw Roni, Libby's best friend. In high school, she had been well-liked, pretty, talkative. Anne secretly admired her sarcastic remarks in class. Roni was with Don, her fiancé, her high school sweetheart. She noticed that Roni eyed her and Finn, though they didn't touch each other.

"Did you have a crush on me in high school?" he asked when they went down to the beach to watch the waves.

"Don't flatter yourself. It was such a tiny crush that even the science class equipment couldn't find it."

"I had a thing for you in your band uniform."

She laughed and smacked his arm. He caught her hand and kissed her.

A week was all they had. Because, on the eighth day, Finn showed up at her door, his face the embodiment of a whiter shade of pale.

"What happened?" she asked.

"Can I come in?"

This worried her even more because, until that point, he'd just grab her and enter with her already wrapped around him.

"What happened?" she repeated.

He took her hand and led her to the living room that, in the smallness of the brightly painted house, was a few feet from the door. With his hand on her shoulder, he made her sit on the sofa while he drooped down on the coffee table, facing her, their knees huddled together.

He turned even paler.

She threw a hand up to cover her mouth. "Oh my God, Finn, tell me. Is it your mother? What?"

He covered his face with his hands, then took a deep breath and started talking, his voice muffled by his palms. "Eight weeks ago, before you were even back in Riviera View, I ... I hooked up with someone. Once. Could barely remember it or her right after."

Her heart sank to her knees. She didn't think it could sink any lower, but his next sentence crashed it on the floor.

"She's pregnant."

When only silence followed his words, he removed his hands from his face.

She just stared at him, thinking she must be as pale as he was.

He gripped her forearm, leaning closer to her. "Jane. Say something."

"What do you want me to say?" She felt numb inside.

"I don't know. That we can work through it, that I can be involved, but you and I will be okay."

"Yeah," she mumbled. "I don't ... I guess."

"She called me an hour ago. Showed up at my house, showed me the results of ... a blood test. And the weeks. They match. My mom was there, and she told her. And..."

"She told your mother?*"*

He nodded.

Her hand shot up to cover her mouth again. "Who does something like that?" This reminded her of the more burning question. "Who is she?"

"Avery Miles."

As if a bus had hit her, she thudded against the sofa's backrest. Her heart that was already on the floor felt like the sandcastle that Avery had once stomped on because it had been bigger than hers. She didn't even see Finn's face anymore.

"Do you know her?" he asked.

She looked at him. His face was a ghastly mix of sincerity, grief, shock, and disbelief.

"You don't know?" she asked.

"Know what?" His voice almost broke. He looked like he couldn't take any more bad news.

"She's my cousin."

"What do you mean?"

"My mother and her mother are sisters. Twins." She didn't add that even their names were a continuation of the other—Linda and Darian—one name ended with the syllable the other began with. And that was just how they thought of their daughters—as sisters.

"But you never ..." He shook his head, as if trying to negate what she had just told him.

"Mention her? Talk about her? I know." She shrugged.

"And your last names ..."

"We have our fathers' last names," she said. Though, from the look on his face, she saw that he had just figured it out himself.

Having been back in town only recently after years away, he couldn't have known or remembered that she and Avery were related. With four years between them, and two years between Avery and Finn, they hadn't been in each other's circles growing up. And she didn't spend time with Avery or talk about her unless she had to.

And, as if it just struck him with a renewed force, Finn stumbled to his feet. "Fuck. Fuck. Fuck. Fuck," he mumbled as he walked away from the coffee table and just paced back and forth in the room.

"Fuuuuuuuuuuuck!" he yelled and slammed a fist into the wall. "Fuck," he then breathed out, shaking his fist and covering it with his other hand.

She got up from the sofa and went over to him. Drops of blood appeared on his knuckles, his skin was torn. She took his hand between hers. She felt his pain in her own body, as if she needed to borrow it because she couldn't feel her own. Not yet at least.

"Jane." With his free palm, he gripped both her hands that held his. "I'm so sorry. I ... if I ... I didn't know."

"I know. It's okay."

"It was before ..."

"I know."

"I'm so sorry, Jane." He looked lost. The blue of his eyes never seemed so gray, like angry winter waves. "I love you. I love you." His eyes searched for hers.

"I love you, too, Finn."

"I thought I was careful. I swear. I never ... except with you. What am I going to do?" He was twenty-five, on the verge of new beginnings, and his life had suddenly taken a sharp turn.

"I don't know," she said, but deep down, she foresaw it. Finn never knew his father. It was a gaping hole in his life. He was too good to let a child of his grow up without one if he could do anything about it. He would have been involved either way, but Avery had made sure to tell his mother. She could imagine the pressure he'd be under to do more than just be involved.

And like another truck, it hit her then—in whatever constellation this was going to play out, she and Finn couldn't be together anymore. Because she couldn't be with the father of Avery's child. It was like being with your sister's baby daddy. And it didn't even matter that the two of them didn't even like each other.

The very words—Finn, father, Avery, child— didn't make sense. She wondered if they ever would.

"I want you. Just you," he half-whispered. He then wrapped his hand around her nape, pulled her closer, and kissed her. A kiss that grew more desperate, and hard, and deep, and demanding, defying, with every second. She gave in to it, and on the sofa, where her heart had been broken, Finn made love to her for the last time.

After a week of heaven, they had a week of hell. And though it took everything in her, she made him leave her house and asked him not to come back, because they both had decisions to make.

When he banged on her door at one a.m. two days later, she buried her head under a pillow that still smelled of him. If she let him in, she'd never let him go, and he needed to go. She knew it.

She thought that going back to work would be an escape, but designing wedding cakes wasn't helpful.

Two days later, while she worked on a flowery design in the back room, her mother took up one of the cloths they used to clean the surfaces and came to wipe the counter next to her.

"You won't believe what I have to tell you," Linda said. The expression on her face was that of concern, not gossipy and amused.

Knowing what was coming, Anne pressed the leaf-shaped cutter down on the vanilla gum paste.

"Avery is pregnant. From that boy you used to tutor in high school. The swimmer. Marie Brennen's kid. Finn."

"Really?" She also grabbed a cloth and wiped it over her reflection on the shiny metal surface.

"Yes. But no one should know about this. Your aunt and uncle don't want people to know Avery is pregnant. She's not showing yet, but she will soon, so Darian is worried, what with Avery being a teacher and all."

"I won't tell." The words came out robotic. *"What is she going to do?"*

"She's keeping it, obviously. She's almost twenty-eight, you know. She told him and his mother, and now Darian and Marie are working on them both to do the right thing and get married fast before Avery shows and before anyone does the math later on."

"Is she sure it's his?"

Linda stopped wiping the counter and gave her a sharp look. *"Why are you talking about your cousin like that? Of course it's his!"*

"Avery wants to marry him?" She felt sick to her stomach just uttering the words. She wished, not for the first time since Finn had told her, that it had been her who was pregnant. But she was responsible enough to take pills.

"Why wouldn't she? He's a beautiful boy, and he's a swimming champion, and he just got a great job coaching a team in Blueshore, and they've already ... you know."

She knew. She so fucking knew. With every pained fiber in her.

Why did it have to be Avery of all people? They might have made it through this somehow, in some format, like him just being in the picture, if it wasn't Avery.

"But, do they know each other? Love each other?" she challenged futilely, trying hard to keep the bitterness from her voice, because it wasn't like her mother had taken sides. She was oblivious to the whole thing. She wondered how her mother would have reacted if she had told her.

"Love?" Her mother said it as if it was irrelevant. "They're going to have a baby! They'll learn to love each other ... with time. What matters now is the baby. And Marie is ... well, I guess you remember she was a single mother, and she wants better for her grandson."

Grandson. They were already family-terming it all while, to her, he was still her *Finn. Her Finn, who waited all night outside her house in his car and hardly let her out of his arms when she came out at six a.m. to go to the bakery to work on several orders.*

"I'm not mad at you, Finn," she had whispered against his neck that morning. "I just ... don't know what to do."

He hadn't contradicted her, just whispered, "I love you."

She threw down the cloth and took up the cutter again. "Finn turned out great," she said then immediately regretted it. No one knew about them yet, and now no one should or could ever know. "I mean, he sounds great, and he was, from what I remember. So what if his mother was single?" She didn't add the opposite example—Eric Hays had grown up with both parents and was a piece of shit.

"This generation!" her mother exclaimed, putting extra energy into polishing a surface that was now squeaky clean. "If a baby can have both parents together, why deny it of him?" Her voice then softened. "We grew up different, Janey. My brother-in-law is going to make sure they get married." She placed a hand on her daughter's shoulder, and Anne had to brace herself to not shake it off.

"You know, dear, you should go see Avery. You've been back four weeks now, and you haven't seen your cousin yet. I really wish you would be closer. She needs our support now. Who but your own family would support you? And when she marries that boy, he'll be like a brother-in-law to you."

And he was.

On November eleventh, her birthday, a little over a week after he had knocked on her door in complete shock, she went to town hall in a blue dress, with the cake her mother had asked her to make.

"It's all a bit rushed. They don't have time for niceties. Let's at least make a nice cake for them to make it a little less shabby," Linda had said.

With a numb heart, she had decorated it in pinks and blues—"because we don't know the baby's sex yet," her excited mother had said.

That entire week had been a haze. Finn came over the day before his intended marriage, and she had let him in.

"I want you*," he'd said, his face already buried in her neck and hair. "I'll never want anyone else."*

"You can't know that," she'd said.

He had pulled himself back and looked at her, his eyes ice rock.

"I want you, too, Finn. But I can't be with you. You're having a baby with my cousin. I know it was all an accident, a mistake, but I can't announce to the world that we're in love and sleeping together, and that you'd still father Avery's child."

"I don't care. I'll announce it," he'd said.

"No. Her parents will go crazy. Mine will die. My mother and aunt will be torn apart. And if she knows about me, you might not see that child of yours—trust Avery for that—and you wouldn't survive it. So, either way, we can't be together. There's no way this is going to work. You might just as well do the right thing. If it wasn't someone from my family ..." She hadn't been accusing, she'd just tried to explain.

"I can't change what happened, so tell me what to do."

"We already know what to do."

"No." He'd held her by her biceps and shaken her a little. "Tell me, Jane."

"We'll just have to unlove each other." It had felt like empty words, but she wanted them to be true.

"Fuck, I can't ever unlove you," he'd said.

At the wedding, Finn looked at her. His eyes were glazed. He had told her not to come, but her mother wouldn't let her miss it.

"If I can't have you, then I don't want you to see this," he had said.

"Congratulations. On the baby and ... everything," she said as soon as the short ceremony was over. The bride was in a baby-blue dress and held a small bouquet of pink flowers.

"It matches our cake," an excited Linda whispered to Anne. "And look, she's not even showing yet."

The groom was in black jeans, a short-sleeved, buttoned-down shirt that hung over it, and a jacket that looked like an afterthought.

"I hope he kisses her more passionately when the family isn't watching," Bert joked in a quiet aside to his wife and daughter. "He calls that peck a kiss?"

No one of the handful of guests knew that, inside, she wanted to throw up or die, whichever came first. No, that is not how Finn kisses, she wanted to scream. That is not who he loves.

"I hope we get to dance at your wedding soon," Avery said when Anne congratulated them. For once, her cousin sounded sincere. Probably the effect of happiness and having a one-up over Noah, who stood there with his beaming wife.

Finn looked at her like he wanted to throw up or die, too.

In the midst of the excited chatter, handshakes, and congratulations that surrounded them, he grabbed her hand and slipped a piece of paper into her palm. She opened it alone, outside town hall, in the unused car that she had borrowed from her parents. There were four lines handwritten on it. The first two were quoted from the only lines in their song that somehow made sense:

> And although my eyes were open,
> They might just as well have been closed.
> I love you.
> Finn

She threw it out the car's window when she drove along the coast, hoping the wind would carry and drown it in the ocean, along with her love for him.

Chapter 8

An empty house, a sleepless night. Finn lay on his back, his folded arms under his head. He almost wished Max would call to tell him that he couldn't fall asleep and ask him to pick him up from Eli's, even at three a.m., like he had done in the past. That could spare him from running everything in his head again.

So many what-ifs.

He had given up shunning the what-ifs.

What if they tried?

What if he hadn't made that single, half-drunken mistake? What if he had waited another week before marrying Avery?

What if it had been someone who wasn't closely related to Jane? That way, at least the divorce would have made a difference.

He remembered the moment when the magnitude of the impact had wrought on him—that not only he would have to leave Jane for Avery, but that he was marrying himself into her family and that they'd remain each other's perpetual, torturous reminder of what-ifs and could-have-beens.

Ironically, the knuckle of his ring finger still bore the scar from when he had slammed his fist into the wall.

He knew the answers to all these rhetorical questions, having answered them in his head a million times already.

Two years older than him, he hadn't really known Avery except by first name and looks. Her *come hither* attitude in a bar had looked promising for a one-night stand to his depressed mind. It had been mediocre, at best, and completely forgettable, but that one night had turned into years. He remembered using a condom, but maybe he hadn't.

It was only one week, Jane had said at the gallery. But it hadn't been just that. That one week had been long coming, ever since that first time he had met her at the library. Except for his son, he had never been truly happy, other than when he was with her, in that single week or even before. Not even when he had won the gold medal in the preliminary relay. That medal, his son, and that single week, which had been the first and last time he had felt what love really was, when every part of him was in love—these were the three peaks of his life.

The medal accumulated dust on a shelf next to its lesser peers; the love was lost, though he kept crashing against it like an endless tide. His son was the only happiness left. He should be satisfied with that, yet he had allowed himself to put that aside and go see her.

And now he had kissed her. He had gotten his dose. The first one in fourteen years. She was in his bloodstream. It couldn't end with that. Not just because he already needed more, craved more, would figuratively kill for more, but because that kiss had told him that she loved him, too, just as much, just like then. She had kissed him like she always had—in desperation, with abandonment, hunger, surrender, love.

Not going for her was against his very being. Zooming in on his end goal was a part of him, of his life, of who he was. She was his end goal. Yet, he couldn't be with her.

At six a.m., when he realized he wasn't going to sleep, Finn got into his car and drove to the pool. His Rav4 stood solitary in the parking lot. He locked the pool doors behind him, took his clothes off, and dove in. The cool, clear water wrapping his naked body was oblivion. An hour and a half later, he activated the robotic cleaner, opened the front doors, greeted the lifeguard who arrived for a morning shift, and got in the shower.

At nine a.m. sharp, he waited in the car outside Eli's house. A few minutes later, Eli's mom waved at him from the door as Max took the front stairs two at a time.

"Blue Jam?"

"I want the large pancakes," Max said, buckling up next to him.

"You got it. How was it?"

"Great. Kylie is really good at *Overwatch*. She beat us. His mom said we could play *Overwatch* because Kylie is older than thirteen."

"And beside Kylie and *Overwatch*?" He made a note to self to re-check what that game was. "Did you sleep well?"

"Yeah, Dad. I'm over that part. It was a long time ago."

"Last year."

"At my age, last year is a long time ago."

Finn laughed.

"You went swimming?" Max asked. Finn could never quite get rid of the chlorine smell. Avery used to say it made her sick, which worked well for him, but Max didn't seem to mind it.

"Yeah. Woke up early," he lied.

As soon as Max's pancakes and Finn's breakfast burritos were served, Max dug in. He was beginning to develop the appetite of a teenager. And the silences of one, too.

"So, what else did you do?" Finn asked.

"Kylie said that the kits I gave the swim team were really cool. She asked me to buy her one next time I'm in Riviera View, but I explained it was a popup booth and gave her mine."

"That's nice of you. You like her?" Finn forked his side salad, pretending the question was as casual as taking a bite.

Max took a moment to reply, and Finn noticed he blushed.

"She's a year older than me, and Eli doesn't always get along with her. Even if I asked her out, and even if she said yes, I don't think Eli would like that."

"It's complicated." He nodded sympathetically. He should know.

"Do you think I'm too young for her?"

"Hmm ... Like you said, at your age, a year counts, but when you're older, it won't count as much."

"Mom is two years older than you," Max said with his mouth full.

"Yeah." He didn't really know what to say. He wanted to say that their age difference never played a part, but it sort of did, because if they had been closer at age, he might have known her before he got together with her. He might have known she was Jane's cousin.

"Did you ever ... you know, date someone who was your best friend's sister?" Max asked.

"No." *But I married the love of my life's cousin.*

"How long did you and Mom date?" Max took a sip of orange juice.

"Not long." They never told Max why they had married.

"You must have really been in love to marry fast."

He just smiled, hoping the way his throat clogged didn't show on his face.

"Did you have lots of girlfriends before Mom?"

"Not lots." *Maybe lots, but only one counted.* He sipped his coffee to alleviate the desert in his throat.

"How come you don't date anyone now?"

"I don't know. Do you want me to?"

"Um ... I don't *want* you to, but I don't *don't* want you to, you know?"

Finn chuckled. "Yeah, I think I do."

"I mean, if it's someone nice, and she made you happy and all, then I don't think I would mind."

"That's good to know. Same goes for your mother?" He suspected that Avery had been dating. He didn't care, as long as she made sure any man she'd let near Max was good.

"Yeah. I mean, lots of kids in my class have half-siblings and all." Max shrugged. "It might be weird at first, but then … you know, people get used to everything."

How about half-siblings who are also second cousins? Is this something people can get used to?

"They do?" He smiled, looking at his clever, sensitive son, his heart melting.

"Yeah, like how *we* all got used to me living with you and seeing Mom on the weekends."

"Is that bothering you?"

"No. I love living with you. I …" His cheeks reddened, and he hung his head.

"What?" Finn's stomach flipped.

"… prefer it," Max finished quietly, as if he was admitting something shameful. He then brought his eyes to him. "I love Mom, but you and I, we get each other, right, Dad?"

If love could kill—and he knew it could—this moment just killed him with softness.

"Right. I feel the same." He smiled and patted Max's hand.

Max looked to both sides. "Dad," he admonished in a *you're-embarrassing-me* tone.

"Okay, okay, sorry." Finn chuckled. "I didn't like being an only child. Is *that* bothering you?"

Max seemed to ponder the question for a moment, his fork hovering above his plate. "Not really," he said, then took a bite, as if having the answer freed him to continue eating. "I mean, it could be nice, but what if we didn't get along?" he spoke while chewing. "I know of lots of brothers and sisters who don't. Mom says she and Noah didn't get along." He then lowered his voice. "I think they still don't."

That's because your mother hardly gets along with anyone. "Every family is different. Every person is different."

They took a sip from their cups in synch.

"So, anything else bothering you?" Finn asked.

"No. Why are you asking?"

"Quarterly check-in," he said. "I just want to make sure you're good, happy. Are you happy?"

"Are *you*, Dad?"

The question was nonchalantly retorted at him. From his tone, it was obvious Max wasn't expecting an answer, but Finn knew what he would reply. *You make me happy, but other than that, there's a huge void in my life, and her name is Jane. Anne. I need her to be really happy, to be complete.* But he couldn't say that to his kid, so he just looked at him and smiled.

"There's just one thing," Max said. "I'm too old for trick-or-treat."

"Too old? Why?"

"It's for little kids."

"Would you say that if you went trick-or-treating here next week?"

Max bunched his mouth to one side in displeasure. It made him look like the little boy he once was. "Here, it'd be okay because I'd go with Eli and others. In Riviera View, I go with Mom. It's humiliating at my age to go with your mother. I don't know any kids there."

"How about if we talk to your mother beforehand and ask her to check if there are kids your age in the nearby houses that you could go with?"

"That's even more embarrassing!"

"Just at first. You can meet them earlier, shoot the breeze, then go together trick-or-treating."

"No one says shoot the breeze anymore."

"Yeah, I'm uncool like that."

Max chuckled.

"You have to be at your mother's for Halloween this year. I know the holidays are still confusing, but we're all doing our best to get them right, am I right?" He smiled at his son, almost pleading with him to understand.

The first year of their divorce had been easier because they had lived in the same town, but since Avery had moved back to Riviera View, things had shifted.

"I know," Max mumbled, his shoulders stooping.

"Are you still going as that other Aquaman?"

"Namor."

"Right. Because you're not into DC anymore; you're into Marvel now," he quoted Max with a chuckle.

"You remembered!" Max raised his palm for a high-five and Finn high-fived him.

He also remembered that, on Max's recent birthday, Max had brought home leftovers of a Namor cake that his grandmother had ordered for him and which Jane had made.

"Yeah, but ..." Max seemed to remember that he was going to spend the holiday in another town.

"Think about it, going to your mom's for Halloween means no school the next day," he said with a cheerful *look at the bright side* tone. Avery had promised she'd take the day off to spend it with Max.

They had a busy week with school, work, and practice. It only partially saved him from thinking about Jane, about how, with every passing day, instead of forgetting, instead of time dulling the effect, his need for her only grew. It was a familiar burn, one he'd experienced every year.

Every goddamn year he had hoped for and dreaded the holidays. Besides rare family events, the holidays had been his only chance to get a glimpse of her, of being near her. The little he had heard of her was through Darian and Avery, and they had said she was happy. He had hoped she was. He wanted her to be. Though he dreaded being invited to her wedding one day.

Every year, a hope and a dread. Her coming had been a lottery. Most times, she had never made it home and her parents had flown to Ohio. Then, when she had shown up, the weight of their secret had been tangible, crushing. Whether she came or not, the holidays had crapped a year's worth of self-work for him.

There had been the year Avery's mom had said, "Guess what. Anne is coming, and she's bringing Tom. It's about time we met him."

Tom. The man she had lived with. The searing pain of knowing she was with someone. He didn't know if it was better than the pain of knowing she *wasn't* with anyone and he still couldn't be with her.

That year she had missed the flight, or so her mother had said. Guilt had awaited him everywhere he'd turned—because of him, she had lost time with her family. She had stayed away because of him.

Then another year, there had been the blizzard excuse.

Then the next year, she had arrived alone.

"Are you sure this Tom really exists?" Avery had asked her mother quietly, eyeing Jane from across the room.

"He exists. I've seen pictures of him," Darian had replied.

Finn had searched social media and the few family pictures that Darian had forwarded to Avery, but he'd never seen Tom in any of them. Just the face that was carved into his heart.

Jane.

~~~~~~~~~~~~~~~

He stood beside his wife and mother-in-law, looking at Jane, his Jane. The Jane he wished was his. The Jane he had spent eleven months since last year trying to get over again, although she hadn't even arrived. The Jane he had last seen from afar two years before at a funeral before she had snuck away and left.

Now, he didn't dare come close, wondering how he'd make it through the evening. Even if he did, how he'd make it through the next day, knowing she was still in the same area code as him, eluded him.

"So, Anne, how's Tom doing?" Avery spoke while strutting toward her. "He's an artist, too, right?"

Jane avoided looking in his direction. "He sketches, but he teaches Physics in college," she replied.

"And he had to grade papers over Christmas?" Avery taunted, her tone implying that she suspected he didn't exist.

"No. He flew to Connecticut to spend it with his parents. They're unwell."

"And you came here? How lucky for us!" Avery added.

"My parents need me here," Jane replied, the strain in her voice clear.

He couldn't take it anymore. Not Jane, but Avery and her poison. He crossed the room in wide strides and stopped next to them, noticing Jane's facial features hardening at his approach.

"Hey, Anne. I'm glad you came. We missed you." That was the closest he could get to the truth. That, and calling her Anne. *He quickly rubbed a hand over her bicep like he had seen her aunt do just before. That should look normal. But the way his heart clenched at it wasn't.*

"Thanks." She smiled.

The arrival of Noah and his family just then was a much-needed distraction and a place for him and Jane to guide their gazes.

Max kept him busy most of the evening and, luckily, he sat the farthest from her at the table, with the buffer of the entire Miles family.

"This is perfect. All my family together," Darian said, raising her glass soon after dinner started. "I wish your mother could have been here, too, Finn."

His mother had married a widower and moved away. She and her husband spent part of the holidays with him and part with her husband's grandkids.

"I wish dear Tom could be here," Linda said, raising her glass and looking at her daughter. "Hopefully, he will be next year. Maybe you'll make me happy before—a wedding, a grandchild, I don't care about the order anymore."

Finn's heart almost stopped. He leaned forward and glanced at Jane, who sat on the same side as him, but with people between them. She was the color of the tablecloth.

"Mom!" she said.

"At least you're embarrassing her and not me this time," Bert said jokingly to his wife, and everyone laughed.

Everyone, but Finn and Jane.

It was the first time since they had sat down that their glances crossed paths. She averted her gaze immediately after.

Max helped end the evening early by throwing up soon after dinner.

They left early, and when he made his way to the door, holding Max, who was five years old then, Jane passed by with an empty salad bowl on her way to the kitchen. With his free hand, he grabbed hers. He shouldn't have, but he couldn't stop himself. He was a selfish sonofabitch.

"Take care, Jane," he half-whispered so only she could hear him using that name.

She gave his hand a little squeeze that told him more than words ever could. It was as if she had squeezed his heart. She then freed it from his and brushed it over Max's hair, whose head rested on his shoulder. He knew what she was telling him beyond the words she uttered.

"I always do. You, too, Finn." It was her way to tell him that she knew that everything he had done was for his child's sake.

That year, he bought Jane Austen's Persuasion *and read it clandestinely, concealing it in his car like other men hide porn.*

Anne.

No blizzard saved him two years later from seeing her with Tom.

Chapter 9

"What do you think?" Anne took a step back to appreciate her work. She tilted her head to one side, then the other, as if she was examining a canvas.

"Looks great as always, Annie," Bert said, wiping his hands on his apron. "It looks just like the book's cover. And that wand and the scarf are perfect."

"I had to make the glasses twice. The first ones didn't look geeky enough." She was happy with the *Harry Potter* theme cake.

"Lucky kid," Bert said. "They'll pick it up in three hours, so I made room in the new refrigerator." That fridge was two years old, but they still called it the new one versus the one that had been there for twenty years.

They needed it for the line of theme cakes that had been born after she had returned from San Francisco and people had seen the Jane Austen books pile cake that she had designed for her mother's birthday. She had picked that work again when she returned home from Cincinnati. The years had made a difference; the designs now were more complex, but she loved doing them.

"Anne, I have the final list for Halloween." The swinging doors were pushed open, and Linda entered, her face buried in her phone. "We had four total. It's going to be a madhouse here. You'll have to start two days before."

"I was planning to. We have the special Halloween boxes for the food project, and I'm preparing those for early distribution. Everything should be finished by four, so I'll take Halloween afternoon off."

"Oh, it's beautiful! They're going to love it!" Linda finally raised her eyes and gestured toward the cake. "I forwarded you the requirements and phone numbers in case you have questions." She then snapped a picture of the cake. "For our Facebook page." She looked at her phone again. "Uch, that moron."

"A cancellation?"

"No, it's that idiot on the fan club." Linda used Facebook for the sole purposes of the bakery and engaging with other Austen fans online.

"Mom, when is it considered too old to fight with strangers on the internet?"

"Never. Not when they don't understand the first thing about what a good adaptation is."

"Okay, have fun. I'm meeting Bella." Anne wiped her hands then removed the apron.

On her way out of the bakeshop, her phone rang.

"Eddie, hi. Should I come to pick up the paintings?"

"You sold two. I want to leave the third, and could you bring the one we kept as a maybe?"

"Really? Which ones sold?"

"*The Swimmer* and *The Man in the Garden*. For the marked price."

"Five hundred each?" She stopped in her tracks on the way to her car.

"Yes. I told you we should aim for what we really want and not compromise."

"Can you tell me who bought them?"

"A couple from Wayford bought the *Garden* and *The Swimmer* was purchased by phone. He said he'd be picking it up later."

"Do you remember their names?" she asked, though she just needed the name of *The Swimmer's* piece.

Eddie mentioned the couple's name and then said, "*The Swimmer* buyer, let me see … a Freddie Wentworth."

Her heart bungee-jumped in her chest. She knew who had bought the painting even before Eddie had said that, but now she realized what he'd done—sent her yet another message.

"Anne?" Eddie said when no response came from her.

"Yeah. Thanks, Eddie. I hope we sell the third one, too, and I'll drop the *maybe* one later this week."

Frederick Wentworth and Anne Elliot, the severed lovers who got a second chance after years, despite family objections. Suddenly, her mother's choice of a middle name for her sounded like fate. A prophecy maybe.

Chapter 10

"I think you'll surprise yourself and enjoy this more than you think," Finn said when they entered Riviera View on Halloween. Max sat next to him, his costume in the backpack on the floor, between his feet.

"You liked living here, Dad?" Max changed the subject, looking at the holiday-decorated houses and streets.

"Yeah, a lot. Grandma moved here from L.A. when I was a baby. I can tell you a million stories about every street, beach, store."

"Please don't," Max said with a teenagery grunt. "I know some of those stories by heart. I used to love them when I was smaller."

"You asked, buddy."

"Yeah, I meant in general."

"I loved living here. I miss it." *I miss her.*

"Would you move back here if it wasn't for your job?"

"My job, your school." *Jane.*

"Blueshore is kinda boring, but I'm used to it. Eli's there, and the swim team," Max concluded.

"Riviera View's team is also great."

"Yeah, we compete against them. Do you cheer us or them?" Max looked at him.

"I cheer whichever team you're on. But if you weren't on it, I'd cheer Riviera's."

"I like it when you're honest," Max said.

Finn laughed. *God, this kid of mine …*

When they parked outside Avery's house, Max lingered in the car, his shoulders hunched.

"You came with such low expectations that you could only surprise yourself. Trick-or-treating can't be bad either way. You'll have tons of candy."

"Yeah. Bye, Dad. See you tomorrow," Max said in a tone that clearly said *you don't understand*. The teenage mood swings were becoming more apparent in him by the day. He wasn't the little kid he had been when his parents had divorced. He was a tween who adjusted fast.

What if …?

"Try to have fun and call me if you need to." He sighed, watching his son walk up the lane to his mother's house.

Are you happy, Dad? He remembered the question.

He drove to the bakery first. At this hour, she was probably still there.

Finding a parking space wasn't easy. Ocean Avenue was packed, as was the bakery. Everyone shopped for holiday-spirit cupcakes and cookies.

He didn't have to get to the head of the line to see she wasn't there. He had a ready excuse in case her parents asked him what he was doing there, but he didn't have to use it. They didn't even notice him. Neither did Connie Latimer.

Getting back into his car, he didn't heed to any of the reasonings his mind kept throwing at his heart. He knew this town like the palm of his hand. And despite the years, he knew *her* like the palm of his hand. And whatever the years had changed in her, he was determined to know, because enough was enough.

He needed his dose. A lifetime of it. Happiness and agony.

~~~~~~~~~~~~~~~~~

Can happiness and agony co-exist? The thought crossed his mind as he stood alone in the living room of his mother-in-law's house. Everyone else had gone to the foyer to welcome Jane and Tom, who arrived for Christmas. Even Avery. She was curious about Tom.

His stomach had been churning for two weeks, from the moment he had found out that they would be coming, and then it had flipped at the sound of the voice he would recognize anywhere. A voice that had once said, "I love you, but we could never be together." Another voice was unfamiliar; it didn't belong to Bert nor Fernando.

Happiness and agony. She came. He'd get to see her ... with another man.

He took it as his punishment—if she had to see him all these years with her cousin, then it was only fair that he would have to experience the torture of seeing her with another man. Not only seeing her but hoping she was happy with him.

Happiness and agony.

He couldn't bring himself to join the others. Remaining in the living room, his gaze was on the tree, blurred by the lights.

"Hi, Finn." The voice came from behind him.

He turned around, bracing himself. It'd been two years.

She stood there alone, beautiful in a long, red dress. Her hair was tied up, exposing her delicate neck.

Happiness and agony. His heart exploded in his chest.

"Jane," he said in a half-whisper.

She averted her eyes to the tree. "Trying to decide which gift to open first?" She tried to instill some humor.

"That obvious?" He smiled.

She stood closer to the room's entrance with the entire carpet between them. Voices came from the foyer.

"Where's Tom?"

"Probably wolfed-down by now." She turned her head back before returning her gaze to him.

"Yeah, they can do that to you," he said.

"He teaches chaos theory. Time to put that to the test."

Fuck, he missed her so much.

He watched as someone approached the living room. Excited chatter came from the foyer, where the rest were probably talking about the newcomer.

"Banana," the man said, stopping behind Jane and wrapping his arms around her waist. He was an inch shorter than her, his salt and pepper hair brushed back. He peeked at Finn, his cheek next to hers, but not touching it.

Every detail was burned into Finn's retina.

He could see her swallow before she said, "Finn, this is Tom."

Tom stepped from behind her. "Hi. Nice to meet you."

Finn crossed the carpeted floor. "Same." He shook the man's hand.

"Heard you were on the Cal Poly team. I used to swim in junior high. I sometimes go for a few laps," Tom said.

He threw a quick gaze at Jane before looking at Tom again. "You still swim? That's good."

"I like to catch the US Opens on TV from time to time."

Finn pressed his lips together and nodded. "Yeah, they're great."

"Banana, can you tell me where the bathroom is?" Tom placed his hand on the small of her back. Finn followed it with his gaze.

"Over there." She pointed.

"Sorry, long drive. Fresh from the airport, and I love my herbal tea thermos," Tom said, smiling and looking at Finn apologetically.

He just smiled.

"Banana?" he asked the moment Tom was gone.

"Anne. Anna. Anna banana. Banana." She shrugged.

He sucked in his upper lip and nodded. Jane. In my vein. Pain. *Yeah, Banana was better.*

Just then, what felt like a wave of people, but was really just six of their relatives, streamed into the living room and swayed Jane with it to admire the tree, which she properly did.

"I got you this," she said, bending toward seven-year-old Max and handing him a wrapped gift. "Sorry I couldn't come earlier and put it under your tree."

Finn watched as Max thanked her.

"Can I open it now?" Max asked Avery. "It's not under the tree," he added in a tone that indicated it made opening this one legitimate.

"Go ahead," Avery said.

For some reason, Finn felt his insides clench, as if the gift was for him, as if he was supposed to find some hidden message or meaning in it for himself. His in-laws and Jane's parents were busy whispering among themselves, probably still exchanging impressions about Tom, who was still absent.

"Aquaman!" Max called, pulling out the box with the action figure.

"Heard you loved him the most," Jane said, smiling. Finn could see the tension leaving her body, as if she was happy that her gift had been well received.

"Yeah, water is in his genes," Avery said.

Pain cut through Finn's heart, knowing how that would sound to Jane. He looked at her. She seemed absorbed in Max, but a muscle danced in her jaw.

"He already has one," Avery added. "We got one two months ago, remember?" Avery spoke to Max.

"They're not the same. They're different. This one has the Mother Box of Atlantis. I love them both," Max said, smiling at Jane.

Finn wanted to hug his son for that. Happiness and agony.

"I'm glad, because we're flying back in two days, and I wouldn't have had time to replace it," she told Max with a chuckle.

Choosing a seat at the other end of the same side as Jane and Tom spared him from seeing them throughout dinner. He hardly ate as he listened to them fielding a million questions, some of which were heavily laden with hints regarding grandkids. He sat next to Max to keep himself busy but still managed to learn more about her life in Cincinnati than he had in the years since she had moved there. She seemed content. He was happy.

Happiness and agony.

Using Max as an excuse, Finn went upstairs to put his son in bed. They were staying the night so that Max could open the gifts with his grandparents in the morning.

He stayed in the room long after Max had fallen asleep. There was a shit ton of guilt he had to deal with. Guilt over still loving Jane, over wanting her to be happy but hoping she didn't forget what they had, though it had been nine years. Guilt over keeping her away from her family, because he knew almost certainly that her rare and short visits were a result of the impossible situation he had put her in. And guilt over his willingness to do it all over again just to re-live that one week when he had loved her to sustain him forever.

When he went downstairs, he heard the TV in the living room, and from the sound of The Property Brothers, *he knew that Avery had turned it on. Excited goodbye chatter came from the foyer where his in-laws saw Jane, Tom, and her parents out.*

He turned to go back upstairs. He didn't want to see Jane again, not with everyone else. Not with Tom, who kept calling her Banana throughout dinner, which her parents and his in-laws had thought was cute. By now, his agony was greater than the happiness that the sight of her had brought.

Watching his son sleep and spending the night on a mattress on the floor of the bedroom that his child slept in was his only consolation.

His foot was on the carpeted first step when her voice came from a few feet behind him.

"Thanks for the card."

He turned around. She looked like a fairy with the lights infiltrating from the living room behind her.

"You're welcome," he said. He had left a card in her mailbox on November eleventh, hoping she'd get it. He kept leaving those cards every year, letting her know that her birthday meant more to him than his wedding anniversary. He felt like the world's biggest shit cheater, but if he hadn't let her know he thought of her, he'd feel like the world's biggest shit cheater, too. There was no way for him to win this. He had to stay true to something, and he chose her.

"Gogh for it. Clever," she said with a smile, quoting the inscription on the recent card that carried the artist's self-portrait.

"Thought you'd like it," he said, a smile rising inside him. "He seems nice."

"Vincent?"

"Tom," he said, laughing. She could make him laugh around the blade in his heart.

She looked away. "Yeah, he's nice." She then returned her gaze to him. "I have to go."

"Gogh for it." He stressed the otherwise silent gh.

She huffed a little chuckle. "Merry Christmas, Finn."

"Merry Christmas, Jane."

He watched her leave. He didn't suspect that he wouldn't see her for another five years until he'd kick down the boundary that kept him from her and enter the bakeshop on the town's fair day.

~~~~~~~~~~~~~~~~~

Parking his car in the first space he could find, Finn left it behind and crossed the street. The remnants of twilight were helped by the multitude of lights oozing from front yards that were decorated for the holiday, and trees that were covered in fairy light strings. He loved that about Riviera View—in its quaint, modest way, it was beautiful.

Her house. It almost hadn't changed. Those yellow shingles and white window frames. That mailbox that used to be his confidante every year on November eleventh. One floor, two bedrooms, and the stretch of lawn that separated it from the street were once, for a short while, his haven. The front door was tucked away on a porch that had flowerpots hanging around it.

He knocked, almost feeling her presence inside. Every nerve ending in his body, every cell that made up that thing he called his heart was stirred.

The porch shielded them from view when she opened the door and stood frozen in the doorway. Her hair was long enough to graze her shoulders. Her eyes looked huge, and her body lean under the long dress she wore.

"Finn." She looked like she needed a moment to gather herself. He saw the tendons in her neck flex. "You developed a problem with boundaries?"

"Only when it comes to you," he gruffed. He took a step forward, getting into her space. She didn't budge until his chest nearly touched hers. "I don't want to hear it, Jane."

He took another step, and she stepped back in synch. He could see that she had known this moment would come. He could practically read the inevitability of it that flitted across her face.

He caught her waist and pulled her to him as soon as they were past the threshold. *Jesus*, the feel of her under his touch. If agony would come later, it'd be well worth it.

"I don't want to hear anything except what and how you want it, and my name on your lips."

He stepped forward, his knee getting between hers. He closed the door behind them. "I love you, and I know you love me. I love you so fucking much, and I don't intend regretting more time without you than I already have."

He brought his other hand up and put it on the side of her neck, his eyes never leaving hers. He traced his palm over her nape until his fingers drowned in her hair, pushing it up, clutching it in his fist. He then crashed his mouth on hers and devoured her like a man ready to wreck and shatter anything that would come between them.

Chapter 11

She couldn't even tell herself that she had tried to resist him this time. Because she hadn't. Not beyond her pathetic little effort when she had first opened the door. But before he'd even spoken, before he had taken that first step forward, she had known she would give in. To her need, to her love, to her heart and body, and mind and soul, and everything that this man owned.

Try as hard as she might, this was Finn, *her* Finn, not Max's dad, or Avery's ex, not anyone's ex-son-in-law. No, he was hers. At least for now.

Only Finn could make her body and heart melt, congeal, and melt again, and again, and again with just a kiss. And after he had kissed her in the gallery, she knew that if he did it again, she wouldn't stand a chance against it.

She gave in to the touch that she had missed, to his strong arm that pressed her to him, to his palm that weaved into her hair and melded her mouth further to his, to his taste, to the pool in his eyes and on his skin. Her own hands came up, and she fisted the front of his shirt, pulling him closer, though there was no space between them, and her fist ended up pressed between his chest and her collarbone.

They kissed as if that single kiss encapsulated the last fourteen years in it. Their tongues battled, their hands chafed. His stubble scratched her chin, and their lips bruised.

Finn's leg was wedged between hers, and she felt him walking her back. In two steps, her back hit the wall behind them, and he pinned her against it, shoving his thigh further in.

Anne raked her hands up over his chest and shoulders, then up his neck, until she cupped his face and felt his jaw muscles move as he kissed her. She wanted to feel that kiss everywhere, even in her hands.

She knew there was no way they'd make it to a bed or even her couch, which replaced the old one that her heart had broken on all those years ago.

No, they were going to rip each other's clothes off right there, near her front door, and she had a little brain capacity left to hope no trick-or-treaters would come knocking.

There was nothing gentle about the way they demanded each other. Finn slid his hands over her body, her breasts, her waist, her hips. He gathered her dress and lifted it. He had to take a step back to create enough space between them so he could take it off her. His mouth was back on hers as soon as the dress was over her head and tossed to the floor.

"Fuck, Jane," Finn groaned as he trekked his hands over her naked skin. He traced them all the way down from her face to her thighs, then up again where he cupped her bare breasts. He didn't break their kiss, not even to slide his mouth to her breasts. It was as if they both needed to be rooted to the other's taste.

She could feel him rock-hard under his jeans. She slid her hand down and smoothed it over that hardness. Finn pushed his pelvis harder against her. She needed to feel it all.

Slipping her hands under his shirt, she glided them up his abs and chest. At thirty-nine, Finn was as sculpted as he had been at twenty-five. The hard muscles were not pumped; they were the result of hard work and dedication. They were Finn. With her hands inside his shirt, she took it off him.

She kissed his neck and collarbone, inhaling his skin, insisting on finding the faint scent of pool under the clean smell of soap. She felt him opening his jeans and traced her hands down to help him. She needed him inside her to satiate at least part of her hunger for him.

Through the blur, she noticed a tattoo on his upper left bicep, close to his shoulder. Something round was inked in blue and yellow, she couldn't tell. She wanted to know what it was but didn't have the capacity to wonder, not when Finn suddenly yanked her panties down, lifted her as if she weighed nothing, had her legs wrapped around him, and with his body caging her against the wall, he pushed hard into her. He didn't have to check or waste time on preparations, he knew she'd be soaking wet for him.

He filled her, lingered for a moment to savor the sensation, then thrust hard, deeper into her.

"Finn," she moaned. "Finn." His name. The only thing she wanted and needed to say. For far too long, it had been sealed in her heart, hardly ever uttered.

Pinned between two hard surfaces—Finn's body and the wall—she never wanted to be anywhere else.

Finn had one hand on her breast, kneading it rough, while the other cupped the side of her neck and cheek, his fingers splaying inside her hair. His mouth moved along her jawline.

"Tell me," he groaned next to her ear. "Tell me how you want me."

"You already know," she managed to expel.

Finn caught her lips with his and kissed her deep.

Fourteen years since the last time they had each other like this, but Finn knew exactly how to touch her. Except for his name on her lips, whispered and moaned into his ear, against his mouth, she didn't have to tell him or say anything. She held on to him, to his neck, and shoulders, and chest, feeling everything she had missed, everything her heart and body could only have imagined for so long.

Finn reveled in every moan that escaped her throat with every push of his body into hers. He brought her up and closer with every deep, rough thrust.

Fourteen years built up inside her; everything pooled into this moment, into every cell in her body that connected with his. She came hard, her head lulling back against the wall before she dropped her forehead against Finn's, and their eyes locked as they came together.

"God, Jane," he exhaled, pressing his weight further into her as she let the waves wash through her body. "*I missed you* doesn't even come close," he rasped, his palms nestling both sides of her head.

"I love you," she breathed the words that she hadn't said out loud since that last time. "I love you, Finn." However this was going to end, it was true, and it had to be said. She needed him to know, though he already did.

He shifted his head back and looked into her eyes. He then slanted his mouth on hers and kissed her. After the ferocious way they had just surrendered to each other, that soft kiss was them yielding to the totality of it all.

He gathered her in his arms and, pressed against him, carried her to the bedroom. She had no idea when he had managed to step out of his shoes and jeans, probably when she was too busy marveling at his body.

Her house was tiny so, a moment later, she was on her bed with Finn on top of her, his body nestled against hers. He propped himself up on his forearms and looked at her. His gaze caressed her face, along with his fingers that skimmed her hairline and jawline.

Her own eyes took him all in. The light was on because his knock on the door earlier had interrupted her putting away clean laundry in the bedroom.

From up close, she could see every new line on his face, the beginning of brackets around his mouth. He was even more beautiful to her now than he had been years ago. It defied logic, but with every passing year, she loved him more, not less. Distance, time—these things operated backward when it came to him.

She watched as his gaze slid down her body and a little smile appeared on his face when he caught a glimpse of her sunflower tattoo that was half-covered by his pelvis. He brought his eyes up, and their gazes locked.

Wordlessly, Finn leaned in and kissed her. Their kiss grew deeper, and he grew harder. He took one of her hands in his and intertwined their fingers, pinning their joint hands at the side of her head. He then sank into her and slowly, longingly, they moved in synch, their gazes anchored together, until Finn picked up the pace some and bent his head to kiss her neck and the dent at the base of her throat. From there, he kissed his way down to her breasts and took each in his mouth, sucking and licking her. She raked her fingers in his hair, and when they were both close, they looked into each other's eyes. Seeing the love and yearning reflected in Finn's eyes did her in. With their lips hovering close, breaths exhaled in unison, her eyes flickered shut only at the end when she called out his name.

Wrapped in Finn's arms, Anne rested her head on his chest.

Finn. This was Finn's heart thumping under her cheek. If this were a dream, she didn't want to wake. Though she had always tried hard not to think of him while she had been with others, there had been times when tears prickled the back of her eyes when a sudden, frightening emptiness filled her. An emptiness that she knew, deep down, would always be there as long as she wasn't with him.

But now, now it was him holding her, and the only thing scary about it was to think that she would have to let go of him again soon. It was unfathomable.

He held her tight because he, too, couldn't let go. She closed her eyes and just listened to his heartbeat. Then his voice rumbled in his chest, as if he heard her unspoken thoughts.

"We'll find the way. *I'll* find the way. Because now there's *this*. Us."

She tightened her lids, wanting to believe him, but she knew the main characters in their play. They were already present in this little haven and weren't going anywhere.

"Jane," he said when she didn't say anything. "Now there's us."

She tilted her head up, and they looked at each other.

"I don't want more regrets; I can't take them, Jane. I've already spent enough time regretting a big portion of my life. And it's hard for me to say that because it sounds like I regret everything, but I don't. I don't regret Max."

"I know."

With his forefinger and thumb gripping the sides of her chin, he held her gaze.

"I never regretted you, Finn. Despite everything. I never will," she breathed out. "I loved you too much to regret you."

"Loved?"

She lifted herself and leaned a forearm on his chest. "Love. I love you, Finn. So damn much."

He caressed the side of her face. "I waited so long to hear you say this again that once or twice isn't enough." He smiled.

"Loving you has never been the issue, Finn." She bit her lip. "Where *is* Max?"

"At Avery's. Until tomorrow."

"Good thing I live too far for him to come trick-or-treating here."

"Are you testing me?" he asked, the blue in his eyes steeling. "Because if you think you can scare me off with this ..."

"I wasn't trying to, but you *should* be scared," she said. "You know what's at stake, especially for you."

"I know, but I meant what I said—we can find a way. Max is not the problem. I *know* my kid."

"So, it's everyone else?"

"Yes."

She took a deep breath. Everyone else was still a lot—an entire family—but Max was the most important, and they couldn't be happy if it affected him.

"Right now, it's just you and me. I still can't believe I'm here, with you." Finn's gaze caressed her face. A careful smile spread on his lips. "My Jane. All this time ..."

She leaned in and kissed him. Tilting her head back, she caught a glimpse of his tattoo, and her breath almost hitched. Finn followed her gaze.

She caressed it—a yellow halo surrounding a crescent moon, drowned in blue streaks of dark blue sky. A single element from Van Gogh's Starry Night.

"I wanted to get a sunflower, but ..." he trailed off, and she heard the grin in his voice. Her eyes were stuck on that ink.

"You know the crescent is facing the wrong side," she said, her mind trying to grasp everything.

"I know. I didn't want a waning moon. I needed hope. Look closer."

She shifted her body against his. "Um, what am I looking at? I see there's a line above the moon that shouldn't be there."

"You're the art expert. You immediately noticed the differences. Try looking at it again."

Something in his voice made Anne look at his face instead of the tattoo. She then shifted to look at it again, gripping his muscular bicep and twisting it a bit so she could get a good look.

An elevator dropped in her stomach. "J. It's a J," she whispered. The extra line in the tattoo made the crescent look like the letter J. She shifted her gaze to his face.

Finn wore a soft smile. "It's a J. It was my way of wearing my heart on my sleeve."

A heart full to the brim can hurt as much as an empty one.

Her heart throbbed in her throat. If it had been hard for her, it had been harder on him. Tears pricked the back of her eyes.

"In plain sight," she mumbled. The tears welled up in her eyes, and she breathed deeply in to keep them back.

"Hey, hey," Finn said, pushing himself up, causing her to rise, too. They sat up, and he wrapped his arms around her, holding her face in his palms and swiping his thumbs under her eyes. "Loving you kept me going. It kept the pieces of my heart together. Some days ... some days I could *feel* you, you know? It was like ... like the blood that flowed between the ... shards—that was you. You kept it together."

Her own broken heart overflowed now, and the tears that she had held back spilled out and streamed over Finn's thumbs, down his hands, and along his wrists.

"No, no, it wasn't supposed to make you cry," he said, crushing her to him as if he was trying to stop the tears with the force of his body.

She burrowed further into him and let it all out against his chest, her hand pressing against it, as if she were trying to put his heart back together from the outside.

"Jane, look at me," he said. "Anne."

He never called her Anne when they were alone. That made her push herself back and look at him.

He smirked. "Now I know how to make you stop crying."

She smiled through the tears.

"I'll say it once and for all—everything that happened was my fault, so you shouldn't be shedding a single tear over me, okay? All this time, it was you who I … I'm sorry for what I've done to you—all of it—the fact that you had to be there and witness it all, the fact that you left, that you stayed away from your family, the years you thought of me as married. I was, but there are roommates with better and closer relationships. I stayed for Max, and I left for Max. And I ask you to forgive me."

"I already have. I never blamed you. I did, for five minutes, but I know it wasn't anyone's fault. It was a trainwreck of coincidences and circumstances. You did the right thing, Finn. *We* did. I played a part in that decision, too. Whatever it did to us, even in hindsight, I can't see how you could have done any different. I'm crying not just for you, but for me, too. All this love … I could have used it."

"You had it all along."

"I know. But it was out of reach."

"It's not anymore, if you let it. If you let *me*."

There was a knock on the front door. They both froze.

The knock repeated.

"Trick or treat," they heard a chorus of several squeaky voices from outside.

Anne exhaled in relief. "Every year, I bring things from the bakery. I did this time, too, but they'll have to excuse me." She cast her eyes over hers and Finn's naked bodies. Yeah, she wasn't going anywhere.

When the voices disappeared, Finn wiped her eyes with his hands, then lay back with her in his arms. She was so tired all of a sudden, as if she had just laid down the burden of years. The steady rhythm of Finn's heartbeats pacified her.

The next thing she knew, she heard Finn's voice coming from the living room.

Anne opened her eyes. She must have fallen asleep. The simple alarm clock she kept by the bed as a plan B for when she hit snooze on her phone's alarm showed that it was nine p.m.

"See? Told you it wouldn't be so bad. Keep a few Reese's Pieces for me." Finn's voice reached her.

"I'll try to remember that it's Kylie's favorite, too," he said just as she entered the living room, dressed in his shirt. She could get used to this sight. Finn, shirtless, with only a pair of dark blue briefs, sitting on the sofa's armrest and extending his arm to her.

She stopped next to him, and he wrapped it around her waist.

"Good night, Dad," she heard Max say from the other end of the line.

Her heart sped up. He was over at Avery's, and that was only a mile and a half from them. Despite everything they said, she still felt like a cheater, like she was stealing his father from him.

"Good night, kiddo," Finn said. He shut the call, put the phone down on the sofa behind him, and wrapped his other arm around her. He pressed his face to her abdomen, pressed a kiss to it, then rested his chin against it and looked up at her.

She pivoted and sat in his lap, wrapping an arm around his neck.

"I think Max is in love." He kissed her neck. "Like father, like son."

"With whom?"

"With you," he whispered against her skin.

She laughed. "No, I meant Max."

"I know." Finn shifted and looked at her. He was grinning. "A girl named Kylie. She's his best friend's older sister."

"Oh."

"The friend doesn't know. Good thing they're only twelve." He then buried his face in her neck again and just breathed her in.

She inhaled him, too. Reality was fast infiltrating their shabby little bubble in all sorts of forms and reminders.

"Hungry?" she asked.

Finn caught her face and kissed her. "Yeah."

"Hmm ... You taste like—"

"Pumpkin cupcake?" he mumbled against her lips. "Found the box in the kitchen and ate one. I hope it's okay."

"Of course it is." She chuckled.

In the kitchen, the coffee maker was warm, and two mugs awaited them next to two plates, one carrying a half-eaten pumpkin cupcake.

"Yeah, I might have eaten more than one while I was making coffee," Finn said.

She laughed. Coffee at nine p.m. She didn't mind it if it meant Finn.

They drank it, leaning their backs against the counter, side by side. She nibbled on a cupcake while Finn finished his second.

"It's good," he said, putting his plate down. "The bakery, you came back for your parents?"

"Mostly, yes. They needed help, and the cake line is doing well. I even designed the same complex cake for two different weddings of the same person."

"Who's that?"

"Cake decorator/bride confidentiality. I can't tell you."

He laughed. Short and husky. God, she had missed that sound.

Finn circled his arm around her. With her nape in the crook of his arm, he pulled her in for a kiss.

"I looked around. You paint a lot. Except for the exhibition, what else is going?"

"I sell paintings on Etsy."

"What *is* Etsy?"

She explained, and he chuckled.

"That's what Max said when I asked." He then signaled with his chin toward the living room. "I saw the painting."

"Which one?"

"The one with the ocean view and the bed."

"Oh."

"You know that I went back to Eddie's sometime after you left, after I knew you were in Cincinnati, and asked about this one? He said he shipped all three paintings to you. I know it sounds strange, but it felt like I lost another piece of you. Like you left nothing behind. This painting especially. I always wondered if somehow this was us."

"I didn't know it when I painted it." She set her empty plate down.

He circled her in his arms and, with one hand, caressed her nape.

She placed her palms on his chest. "Speaking of," she said, "you bought the *Swimmer*?"

He smirked. "What makes you think that?"

"Freddie Wentworth?"

"Oh, that." He threw his head back with a chuckle.

"You knew I'd find out."

"Actually, no. He asked for a name, and … it just came out. I didn't know he'd give you the name. It was a private joke I played on myself."

"Why?"

"You know I'm not big on books. A biography here or there, but not the classics. But I read *Persuasion* years ago, because of Anne. I wanted to know the story and where your middle name came from. And then it hit me. Frederick, it starts with an F, like my name. We're both in a line of work that involves water—he's a sea captain, and I'm always in the pool. He and Anne loved each other for years, and he almost married her relative."

"I never thought about it." If he was trying to make her fall for him even more, it was working.

He leaned his forehead against hers. "I learned from the best. Of course, the main difference was that no one got pregnant there, and Frederick didn't marry anyone else." His voice had timbered low, as if he hadn't wanted to utter the last part.

She didn't want to think about it. "Five hundred dollars, Finn? If you asked, I'd have given it to you for free."

"I'd pay a thousand if he asked for it. It's hanging in my bedroom."

"I need more of you."

"You do?" He smirked.

"I meant more buyers like you."

"That's it?" He tightened his hold around her and pressed her to him. She felt him hardening against her.

"I need more of you," she whispered, rising to her toes and drawing his bottom lip between hers.

Chapter 12

"Where's your mother taking you?"

"Drive around. We'll find something to do."

"Have fun. I'll pick you up around six."

The good thing about Max entering his teenage years was that he no longer woke him up before eight a.m. when he didn't have to get up early. At eight-thirty, when his phone had buzzed in the jeans that were thrown on the floor, Finn had gotten up and picked up his son's call. Jane had been asleep, splayed across his body, and he'd had to move gently from under her to not wake her up. Like the evening before, he had walked with the buzzing phone in hand from her bedroom to the living room whose walls had known them in all sorts of situations, good and bad. Talking to his son there had felt surreal. Then again, everything about them was.

He returned to the bedroom, put the phone on the nightstand, and turned to look at Jane. He still couldn't believe he had just woken up with her after dreaming of it for so long. Every inch of him smelled of her, every inch of her smelled of him. Her taste was still in his mouth. He slid under the blanket and pulled her to him.

She opened her eyes. "He can't know that you're coming to pick him up from within Riviera View, you know." Her voice was groggy, but she was wide awake. She said it as if she was reminding him and herself what they were facing.

"For now, yes, he won't know." He hated lying, but it was necessary until they figure out how to handle this. He thought he'd feel worse about it, but he didn't. Because being with her felt right. It *was* right. He wasn't doing anything wrong. Not even to Max. Maybe it was an illusion colored optimistically by being here with her. It painted everything in bright colors, and he really believed he could and would find a way.

"I lied to my parents, too." She sighed. "My alarm went off earlier, so I messaged my dad that I'll be taking the day off, that I think I'm coming down with something. They know how cranky I get when I'm sick, so they won't be coming here to check in on me."

He smirked. "You get cranky when you're sick?"

"Trust me, it's not cute."

"I want to know everything about you. In sickness and in health, Jane."

She swallowed. "You know a lot." Her voice came out hoarse.

"Yeah, I do." He tilted his head and kissed her. If his words scared her, then so be it. He meant them. He wanted her with every vow under the sun, and then some. But, before that, he had fourteen years to make up for. He intensified their kiss and smoothed his hands down her body.

Last night in the kitchen, he had lifted her and realized she wasn't wearing panties under his shirt. He had set her down on one of the breakfast bar chairs, slid down her body, between her legs, and made her come with his tongue.

He was going to do the same now. He kissed her breasts and lingered at the sunflower tattoo. She was his now, after so long. His sunflower girl.

He continued farther down and tasted her again. And again and again.

"I need you to fuck me, Finn," she moaned. "Now."

God, he missed this—the striking contrast between the pale, slender fragility of her thighs that his face was buried between and the feistiness of her verbalizing exactly what she needed and wanted from him.

Her fingers in his hair began pulling him up the more he sucked and licked, getting her close. She writhed against him and desperately clutched his shoulders.

He stormed up and pushed hard into her. She was so wet and so close that it took just a few thrusts before she shattered around and beneath him. Fuck, this woman could make him come so hard that he needed convalescence time.

"Tell me everything," he said later in the kitchen, scrambling eggs into an omelet.

"What do you want to know?" Jane looked up from the vegetables she was cutting. In a long-sleeved tee and a pair of shorts, her legs looked endless.

"Why did you break up with Tom?"

She focused on the tomato again. "I didn't see a future with him."

He watched her. She wasn't looking back at him; she just continued cutting the vegetable into little cubes.

"We were on and off as it was, so it wasn't a huge shock when I finally broke it off. I did it a year before I moved here." She stopped chopping for a moment. "What made you—"

"Divorce Avery?" he completed for her.

She bit her bottom lip and cast her eyes on her salad-cutting task.

"I couldn't take it anymore. I couldn't take *her* anymore. I waited that long only because I felt like I would be failing Max if I broke his home. But that wasn't the home I wanted to give him." He divided the fried eggs between two plates and put the two slices of the bread she handed him into the toaster. He kept on making breakfast because he sensed that she needed the diversion and not have him look at her when he told her all that.

"We were both stuck in a marriage we didn't want. I stayed for Max's sake, thinking I could give him what I didn't have. And Avery … I think she didn't leave because, to her, it was like admitting defeat in some competition. I don't even know who she competed against—her brother, her friends, maybe against me; who would break first?" He shrugged. "I don't know. It was always who had a bigger house, a thicker paycheck, a better position, a more accomplished child."

Jane scraped the vegetables from the cutting board and into a bowl. She reached for the olive oil that stood on the counter next to a bottle of balsamic vinegar. "Did you date after the divorce?" she asked without looking at him.

"I went on one date."

This made her raise her almond eyes and return his gaze. "Just one?"

"She was a nice woman, lovely even, but I felt bad for her. She didn't deserve to be with a man whose head and heart weren't there."

Jane dropped the wooden mixing spoon, and it clunked against the glass of the bowl. She turned to him and flung herself into his arms.

Surprised, he enveloped her in his arms and pressed her to him. He bent his head and inhaled the scent of her hair. "What happened?"

"Nothing. Everything." Her voice was muffled by his neck.

"I know," he said. He knew exactly how she felt. It shouldn't have been like that for them—trying to forge relationships with others while their hearts weren't theirs to give because they already belonged to someone. His belonged to her; hers belonged to him. She must have had that with Tom.

He breathed in the lemony scent of her skin. "Things can change for us. The past, as much as possible, we should leave in the past. We'll have a future."

She moved her eyes between his, as if she were trying to read something, to find that future or at least the path that would lead to it. She then kissed him.

They managed to eat, and then he got a text from Max.

"*I'm not feeling well. Can you pick me up earlier?*"

"*Sure. What happened?*" he texted back.

"*My head hurts.*"

"*Give me an hour.*" He could be there in ten minutes and felt like crap for lying, but he wasn't planning on keeping this up for long. He'd find a way.

They showered together and made love one more time. He then got dressed and hoped his son wouldn't notice that he was wearing the same shirt as he had the day before.

"I'm dropping Max off at Avery's on Friday afternoon, and I'm coming here after," he said before they left the bedroom, all dressed. Thankfully, Friday was just three days away.

She didn't argue. She nodded, and he kissed her before they opened the door.

The street outside seemed empty when he crossed it to his car.

When Avery opened the door, he wondered if she could see it on his face. He felt Jane was written all over him. Love was radiating inside every part of him, but she never knew how to read him anyway.

"Max," she called, turning her head back.

"What happened to him?" he asked.

"Nothing. I offered him to lie down for a while, but he said he wanted to go home."

He watched her. If Max had told him while he was in his house that he wanted to go home and meant Avery's, he'd die. However, she didn't seem to notice that, to Max, their house in Blueshore was home. He didn't remember Max ever referring to his mother's house in Riviera View as "home". It was always "Mom's."

"Did you swim in the ocean, Dad?" Max asked when he buckled up next to him.

"The ocean?" He gave Max a *what are you talking about* smile and head tilt.

"Yeah, you know, like when people come back from the beach and you can tell they've been in the sun?"

It's called happiness.

"Oh. No, it wasn't the ocean." He chuckled. "How are you feeling?"

"Better. Eli invited me to come over later. If I feel better, can I go?"

"*If* you feel better." He wondered if Max was feigning it just so he'd pick him up early. "How was today?"

"Okay."

"Care to expand?" he asked.

"No. You know, general fun." Max pulled out his phone and inserted an earbud into his ear. "Is it okay if I listen to music?"

"If it doesn't make your tummy worse."

Max grinned. "Nice try, Dad. It's my head, not my tummy."

He laughed. Caught red-handed in trying to gauge a fabrication.

Short texts held him the three days until Friday. It was as if they didn't want to waste words and exchanges over devices.

On Friday evening, he drove straight to her house after dropping Max off. He would have felt guilty, but there was no room for guilt. Not yet. He wasn't doing anything wrong.

"We can't leave the house," she said when he entered.

"I wasn't planning to." All he wanted was her. He didn't care where.

On Saturday morning, after a breakfast of protein to make up for all the energy they had spent, he stretched himself shirtless on her sofa, and she burrowed into him. He caressed her hair. "I was trying to picture your life," he said.

"I was trying not to picture yours."

He scoffed. "It wasn't a pretty picture, for the most part. Pretending in front of Max stopped working. Even an eight-year-old could see there was nothing there. I filed for divorce that year and got it by the time he turned nine. It went by quietly."

She brushed her fingers over his chest. "I had a cat," she suddenly said. "Uriel. He adopted me, but I gave him to the kids in the house next door after a few weeks. We found him together under the fence that separated the houses. They wanted him, but it took time to convince their mother, so I kept him. We visited each other a lot after."

"Uriel?"

"Yeah, he urinated all over my floors and couch."

He laughed. God, he missed her.

"And did you have friends there or …?"

"I had a neighbor in the house on the other side of mine. She was a librarian, and we both kinda kept to ourselves, but she watered my plants when I was away, and I watered hers. Melanie. There were the people I worked with, and Tom. Now I have Bella here. She's a close friend. Oh, you know her, the girl I was at the club with."

"I don't remember what she looked like." He had been too engrossed in Jane that night to notice even the friend that had broken their kiss.

Her phone on the coffee table buzzed. They both looked at it. "*Mom,*" the caller ID read.

She grabbed it and sat up. He caressed her back while she spoke to her mother.

"Yeah, I can't until tomorrow evening. I'm … I have other plans. I told you." There was a pause before she said, "No, Mom, you don't have to bring me anything. Really, I'm fine. I have tons of food, and I'm in and out of the house all the time. I'll drop by tomorrow evening or see you on Monday."

She shut the phone and put it facedown on the table. She remained seated with her back to him.

He lifted himself to a sitting position and circled his arms around her from behind.

She half-pivoted and buried her face in his neck. "I feel like we're having an affair, although we're both single," she said against his skin.

"If there's anyone I want to have an affair with, it's you," he tried to joke, but not really. He had thought of it a million times and had beat himself up over it a million and one while he had been married.

She yanked herself back. "You have no idea how many times …" She took a deep breath. "The guilt, Finn, wasn't just yours. I wanted you while you were married, though you weren't mine then. I even thought to …"

He cupped her cheek with one hand and held her gaze, making her stop. This, too, was his fault.

"I've always been yours. Even when I wasn't supposed to."

She pivoted toward him and hid her face in the nook between his shoulder and neck. He buried his face in her hair and breathed her in.

"Jane. Jane, look at me," he said, trying to unfurl her so he could see her face again. She didn't look up. "Anne."

She looked up, and it made him chuckle. It worked.

"Coming here, being with you, I want us to tell everyone. I'm not backing away from this."

"How? We just go and tell everybody?"

"Yes. But we'll do it wisely. I thought about this. I think you should tell your father first. He's the most reasonable one, the least involved. He'll be able to help with telling your mother. Then I'll tell Avery. We'll do it like that—a swift pull; rip it off. There'll be some bleeding, some pain, but then it will heal."

"What about Max?"

"That's what I've thought about the most. He's a smart, sensitive kid. He adjusted well to the divorce, to Avery moving away. We talked about this. Well, not about you, but in general. I think it will depend on how the rest behave. If we do it right, his mother might be reasonable about it."

"Good luck with that." She sighed. "I don't know how everybody will behave."

"Because of Avery being Avery?" He now knew her, too.

"Yes, especially. But her parents, as well. They're … very protective, and mine just want to keep the family together. So that swift pull you talked about? It won't be easy."

He took a deep breath. "So, we keep this a secret? Because I'm not letting go of you again, Jane. And your parents, at least, would want you to be happy."

"Did your mother know you weren't happy?"

He averted his gaze. "When everything happened, I didn't have the chance to tell her about us until it was too late. So, I never did. She thought I *could* be happy. She never said it, but I think that, deep down, my mother thought she already screwed me up, so she wanted to ensure any kid of mine would get what she didn't give me. Which was wrong, because she was a great mom and marrying Avery was a mistake."

She sighed. "Whichever way we go about this, they must never know about the past. It will make things worse."

"Okay. But we have to tell them about us at some point." He leaned back against the couch, and she leaned into him.

"I don't know, Finn … What if … what if it doesn't work?"

"Telling them?"

"Us."

For a moment there, he was too stunned to speak. But then he caught her gaze. Looking into her eyes, he understood what she was doing. "It's too late for putting up a fight, Jane. You know that we're meant to be. Don't give me the same bullshit we'll be getting from others. I know the facts. We've only had a week. We've only met maybe ten times in a decade. But you and I know that time is not a factor when it comes to us. You *know* me. I *know* you. Don't play devil's advocate."

She closed her eyes, then opened them and leaned in to kiss him.

On Sunday, they decided to risk it and leave the house. They got into his car and drove out of town. They went to the beach in Wayford then left the coastline behind and drove to a restaurant in a town farther inland. It felt great, like a date. Nothing to hide. Just be. Just the two of them, like normal people.

Things looked up even more when a text from Avery surprised him on Tuesday. She texted to tell him that she was seeing someone and that she wanted him to meet Max.

It was a glimpse of hope. Maybe she wouldn't make things harder than they should be once they told her. *Maybe.*

He wanted to meet the guy first. He knew he'd give him a fair chance, although Avery wouldn't do the same for the woman *he* was seeing.

"*I'll try to set it up and let you know,*" Avery texted when he asked.

Chapter 13

On November eleventh, which was a Friday, Anne found a card in her mailbox. The first one since she had moved back. It had "*Happy Birthday, my love*" on the front, and inside Finn had written, "*I'll see you tonight, but didn't want to break the tradition again. I love you now, then, and always*."

He wasn't afraid that anyone but her would see it now, yet she did wonder if everything was reflected on her anyway. She was in a cloud made of her and him, and everything else just echoed from the other side of it. Didn't others see that a cloud of happiness separated her from the world?

But no one seemed to notice except her father, who asked why she was absentminded.

That evening, she opened the door for the third time to find Finn standing there. She hadn't seen him since he had left her house to pick up Max on Sunday evening of the previous weekend. Texts and calls during the week didn't cut it. Seeing him there … she still couldn't get used to the idea, and her stomach clenched.

He was all dressed up. "We're going to dinner, to celebrate."

"What? Where?" She threw a quick gaze at the street. It was empty. She closed the door.

"A great place. I booked us a table. It's a bit of a drive," he said. "We'll stay at my house after. It's closer to Blueshore."

"How many times did you drive here today? You dropped the card, then drove back, then brought Max?"

"You're worth it," he gruffed right into her ear. "Did you like the card?"

"I love it. And you."

It took them almost an hour to leave her house because, when she tried to change, they had ended up ravaging each other on her dresser.

"I changed into this shirt in the car after I dropped Max off," he said, buttoning his shirt back. "I didn't want to outright lie about where I was going." He was usually in pullovers or Henleys, so a buttoned-down shirt on a Friday evening, just for driving his son, would have required an explanation.

"And I told my parents I had the weekend planned and that I could only have birthday lunch with them on Sunday." She was sitting on the bed, putting on her pumps. "I'll tell them. Promise. I'll find an opportunity and talk to my father." She sighed. "Remember when he said you were like my brother?"

Finn came over and crouched in front of her, putting his hands on her thighs. He looked at her. "Would a brother do what I just did?" he rasped.

She expelled a breathy chuckle. "We're so going to hell."

"I'll take you to heaven first."

She laughed, took his hands in hers, and got up, dragging him up with her. "Come on." From the look in his eyes, she knew that, if they didn't leave the house now, they never would. She took a small bag of clothes and, after a short hesitation, they decided to leave her car there and drive in his. He'd have to drop her off at home on Sunday before he picked up Max. All this planning did feel like they were having an affair, and she hated it.

After dinner, they drove to his house. She was nervous and excited. She couldn't even remember the last time she had been in Blueshore, though she had passed by it on the highway on the way to and from San Francisco.

"Is this where you lived with Avery?" she asked when he pulled up the driveway. All those years, she had managed to avoid any visits to her cousin's house.

"Yes." He gave her a look and a smile that said it didn't matter in the least.

She recalled the day her mother had told her that Avery and Finn had separated and filed for a divorce. Linda had blabbered on and said it was a pity, but Anne had been lost in her own thoughts, preoccupied with killing the flicker of hope that had ignited inside her.

The house looked like a semi-bachelor pad. It was functional, organized, and lacking knickknacks. The tables were bare, the car keys chucked into a chipped cereal bowl, and there were zero throw pillows or covers anywhere.

Max's room looked like a typical tween boy's room—a mix of childish and teenagerish. Nautical elements wallpaper, a desk with assembled Lego cars and figures, and a pile of textbooks and notebooks, a hook on the wall with swimming medals hanging from it, a gaming console with cords convoluting on the floor, and a black and orange gamers' chair. On the wall above his bed hung decorated wooden letters that made up his name.

Finn stood behind her at the doorway, wrapped his arms around her waist, and linked them over her belly.

"Did you try having more kids after Max?" she asked. She had always wondered.

"No." After a short pause, he answered the *why* that she couldn't bring herself to ask. "She didn't hint she wanted any, and it fit me perfectly because I felt that I fulfilled my part ... the guilt over the loss of the first ... I made up for it, and I had Max."

She nodded, leaning back into him.

"You know, I really *do* think that Max will accept this faster and better than anyone." He pressed her further to him at the word *this* to indicate he meant *them*.

"Yeah?" she scoffed. "You think he'll be glad to have me as your—"

"Wife?"

He suddenly spun her to face him. It was so quick that her breath hitched when her chest collided with his. His blue eyes were sharp, as if he were trying to penetrate her mind.

"It's too crazy." She shook her head. "If your first wedding was strange ..."

"It *will* be strange, for everyone but us," he said, holding her gaze.

She huffed a chuckle. "Maybe I should ask Avery to be my maid of honor."

"That would be bizarre, not strange." He chuckled. "But I'm fine with strange. I never meant for my kids to be half-siblings as well as second cousins, but there are worse things."

Her chest felt too tight for her heart all of a sudden. "You thought about us having kids?"

"I thought about us having *everything*, Jane."

He held her gaze as if he wanted her to see it all in the blue pools of his eyes.

She had never allowed herself to think those things, and if a thought did infiltrate, she killed it. She hadn't told him about the IUI. There wasn't much to tell. With everything going on, she hadn't done anything about it. Having Finn's children ... If only ...

"You know how many times I asked whoever is up there why it wasn't you who got pregnant?" he asked as if he read her mind.

"You don't need God for that. It's simple. I was on the pill."

"You know what I mean."

She knew. She had been willing to make a deal with whoever was up there to switch places with her cousin.

"I want it *all* for us, Jane. It's not too late."

"Me, too." Why did those true words sound like a lie? The first part was true—she wanted it all with him. But the second part ... she wasn't sure that it wasn't too late, that the past wouldn't ruin the future they wanted. She couldn't imagine their family, especially Avery, coming to terms with such a change in the family dynamics—she married to Finn, instead of Avery? Avery wouldn't let her have it.

Maybe he could read the hesitation on her face or voice. "Jane," he said in a *don't back out on me* tone. "I don't take this lightly. But I trust you, and I trust my kid. You're the only ones who matter. The rest will have to deal with it, including Avery."

"I hope so." She huffed a breath. "We'll tell them. Soon."

Finn leaned his forehead against hers. "I just want to be done with it. Waiting for the starting gun to go off is the hardest part."

She kissed him then. There wasn't a birthday present she wanted more than Finn's love. Not just a piece of his broken heart delivered once yearly through a birthday card in the mail, from a distance of miles and consequences. But his love—graspable, attainable, hopeful, heart, body, mind, and soul. She gave him hers in return.

~~~~~~~~~~~~~~~

"It looks good here, but not for five hundred," she said much later when they lay askew next to each other, naked on his rumpled bed. *The Swimmer* hung on the wall opposite them.

"Is it me?" he asked.

"No. And yes. I mean, it's not *you*, but why else would I choose a swimmer?"

"You're so obvious." Finn chuckled and rolled over to lie on top of her. Their bodies were still slick with sweat. He began kissing her.

An incoming message pinged on her phone, and her heart lurched. She shimmied from under him and reached for the device.

She read the text and texted back, which wasn't easy, given that Finn was busy kissing her shoulder. She then slid the phone onto the nightstand.

"What happened?"

"My mom just sent me a picture of a cake they made for me and wrote that it's too big for the three of us and that maybe we could invite everyone. I wrote that I had other plans for them. I don't want everyone there."

Finn looked at her. He knew who *everyone* was.

"Do you want me to talk to Avery first? I'll do whatever you think is right, Jane. I'll talk to your dad. I'll talk to the fucking town council if I have to."

Despite the situation, she laughed. "No, I'll talk to my dad. I don't know if it'll be this Sunday, but I'll find the right time."

~~~~~~~~~~~~~~~~

A dreamy weekend ended with Finn dropping her home where she could change and go to her parents' for Sunday lunch. To avoid any possibility of anyone dropping by randomly for cake, she took them out to Life's A Beach. They were so excited about her thirty-seventh birthday that she didn't find the right time to talk to her father.

But she did later in the week.

They took a break together on the bench outside the bakery. She drank coffee, and Bert drank his cranberry juice. They smiled and greeted the people that passed by. It was serene out here, yet the street was too busy for anyone to listen in on any conversation, and she thought this could be a good place to talk.

Bert looked back at the bakeshop then returned his gaze to the street. "Connie says she has someone who wants to interview for the baker position. If we like her, you'll meet with her, too. Okay?"

"Sure."

"I know you'll do well with the bakery once we retire. I plan on taking your mother to Europe, see the world, you know," he said, smiling cheekily at her.

"That would be wonderful for the both of you. You deserve it." They had barely ever taken more than two or three days off in all the years that they had owned the bakery. "Dad, there's something—"

"I'm so proud of you, Janey," Bert cut in, putting the aluminum bottle next to him on the bench. Her mother made sure he'd finish one every day. "The exhibition, the paintings you sell, the cake line is going great, your food project."

She pressed her lips together. That wasn't a good opening for what she wanted to say. "Is there anything I could do that would make you disappointed in me, Dad?"

"Disappointed in you? Never. There's nothing you could do that would disappoint me. Why? Are you planning on robbing something? A bank maybe?" He chuckled at his own joke.

She smiled. "No, not a bank."

"Bert, the oven. It's doing that thing again," Connie called from behind them.

They turned. She was wiping her hands on the logoed apron.

"Can you take a look?"

"Sure. Sorry, Janey," Bert said. He got up.

"I changed the ventilator already. I thought that was the problem," he spoke to Connie as he followed her back into the shop, his voice fading.

A gust of ocean breeze raised the hem of Anne's dress, reminding her that it was November, despite the sun.

That weekend, Finn had Max because Avery would have him the weekend after, which would be Thanksgiving. They knew they couldn't meet that weekend but made plans to spend Thanksgiving together. Anne could think of a million ways to give thanks with Finn.

Since they knew they wouldn't have the weekend, Finn showed up one afternoon when she wasn't working. He had just finished practice in San Luis Obispo and wasn't expected home before the evening. They made the best of the two hours they had.

"It became one of my favorite smells, you know?" she said, inhaling his skin. A whiff of chlorine was still there, making her visualize Finn's straining body in the pool. She smiled into his neck. He had been straining under and over her just a few minutes before.

"My favorite smell is you," he rasped.

~~~~~~~~~~~~~~~~

She met with Bella over the weekend.

"For the first time in years, I'm looking forward to Thanksgiving," she said. "Although, I'm going to talk to my dad before, so I hope it won't crap everything. I'd talk to them both, but we won't have time to break it to everyone before the holiday, and if my mom knows and sits at her sister's table for

Thanksgiving, she won't be able to enjoy it. I don't want to ruin the holiday for her."

"Your parents would want you to be happy. You have to tell them. And yeah, start with your dad. He'd know how and when to break it to the rest," Bella advised when she finally confided in her.

They went for a walk on the beach on Saturday afternoon. Bella's husband had arrived home two weeks before, and she needed some time away from the bustle.

It had taken Bella half an hour to get over the shock when Anne had told her soon after they had arrived at the beach.

"How come you never told me?"

"You and I weren't in touch back then. I was only here for a few weeks, and then it all happened, and … there was no point in talking about it after. No one knows, Bella. No one *should* know. Even if we tell everyone—"

"*If?*" Bella shifted her head to look at her. The wind blew a strand of hair into her face, and she pushed it back.

"*When. When* we tell everyone, we won't mention that we were together back then. It will only make everything worse. They don't need to know about it. They know we were friends in high school at some point, and that's it. It's enough. So, keep it to yourself."

"I have news of my own," Bella said. "I won't be here to tell anyone."

"What?"

"Dean got the role orders he wanted. It's a long-term station in Michigan, and it comes with a house on base. We'll be relocating soon."

Anne stopped and covered her mouth. "Oh my God! Bella! I'm ... happy for you, and sad for me?"

Bella laughed.

Anne hugged her. "Michigan! God, I'm gonna miss you. When?"

"In a few weeks. I just notified the school the other day, and they posted my position. Avery did, by the way. They already have resumes coming in."

"Already? Oh, wow."

"Yeah. I'm excited about having Dean at home, but nervous about the move. You can still use me as an alibi for Thanksgiving, though," Bella said with a chuckle.

Anne had asked her before to say she'd spend the holiday with her so she could be excused from attending the festive dinner at her aunt's. She and Finn planned on spending it together at his house. She had promised her parents that she'd join them for Thanksgiving Sunday lunch at Darian's. She wasn't looking forward to spending time with Avery and her parents now that she was with Finn, but she couldn't deny her parents the entire holiday.

"Thanks," Anne said. They stopped to stand next to each other, facing the ocean, their bare feet in the cold sand.

"Nothing beats this," Bella said. "I'll miss it."

They threw their heads back and closed their eyes. The sunset and the breeze caressed their closed lids. It was chilly, but they were both well-wrapped in sweaters.

"It's like nothing bad can exist if this happens daily." Anne breathed the clear air. The sound of waves was the soundtrack of her childhood. She had missed it in the years she had been away.

"Do it here," Bella said all of a sudden. They opened their eyes and looked at each other. "Bring your parents here to tell them. It's like Prozac." She gestured with her head toward the view.

"I might need to use the real thing, too. They think of Avery and Finn as the siblings I never had. They have always been so quick to adopt everyone— Libby, you, Finn, Noah's wife. Noah and his family are coming over for Thanksgiving, and that's all my parents can talk about. How can I—"

"Tell them that you and your cousin's ex-husband are together? Just tell them. Let everyone blow steam now and be done by Christmas."

"Sure, and by Christmas, we'll all be a picture-perfect family." She chuckled.

~~~~~~~~~~~~~~~~

A month of happiness, though clouded by the not-so-trivial fact that they were lying to the whole world, made her feel like she was walking on an actual cloud. Anne forced herself to crash into reality.

Two days before the holiday, while they were busy preparing the special orders at the back, she tried talking to her father again.

They stood at the two adjoined metal tables. He was icing the simpler cakes while she was finishing up a turkey-shaped one. "Who can even look at another turkey by dessert time?" she had asked when the order had come in a few days before.

She was cutting gum paste when she said, "Dad, what would you say if I told you that I'm in a new relationship and that—"

"Wait. Is that one of those *would you rather* games where I have to choose between two awful options?"

In a way. "No, it's—"

"Because your mother has been bugging me with those ever since she discovered them in her Facebook groups." Bert chuckled. His hand was so experienced with the icing that, even when he chuckled, it came out beautifully.

"It's a real—"

The door that separated the preparation room from the bakeshop swung open.

"It's final. Noah is not coming. Darian is crushed." Linda walked in and plopped her phone into her apron's pocket with such force that Anne was surprised it didn't tear right through it and land on the floor.

Bert looked at his wife. "Because of his fight with Avery?"

Anne's heart accelerated in her chest. "What fight with Avery?" she asked without raising her eyes from her work.

"They're going to Jill's parents' instead," Linda said.

"What fight?" Anne asked again.

"Noah and Jill are thinking of leaving L.A. and coming back here," Linda said.

"Thinking? They're already looking for jobs," Bert cut in. "The prices are soaring in L.A., and with the kids and all, they prefer living here."

"Yes, well, Noah can work from anywhere. Jill is looking at jobs here, and one opened at Avery's school, and Jill immediately applied, and Noah called Avery to tell her so they'd at least look at it and maybe invite her for an interview," Linda spoke fast, with no breaks to breathe, her tone indicating that she wasn't comfortable with the tale.

"And Avery said she couldn't because she's not allowing nepotism in her school, and that they pretty much already have a candidate they want," Bert finished. "But Noah wasn't asking her to give his wife preferential treatment, just to make sure her resume is considered."

"So, now Noah says he won't be coming to Thanksgiving if Avery is there." Linda sounded on the verge of tears.

"Why wouldn't Avery want Jill there? That's what I don't understand," Bert said.

Because Noah being here with his three kids means he'll compete with her on their parents' time and attention, because he'll be outshining her with his programming job and his marriage, and because his wife will be another person for her to one-sidedly compete with. Anne didn't say any of it out loud.

"Anne, honey, we'll be so few there, and the mood isn't going to be great. How about if you and Bella and her family all join us?"

"I don't think Bella can. It's not simple, and it's last minute, and she's having ..." She didn't want to lie like that, and now the lie was becoming worse. Her parents had enough holidays without their only child, but she couldn't give in to this pressure.

"So, just you," Linda said. "The more, the merrier. Family, you know, and in such times, it's truer than ever."

Having to alleviate the family's bickering was something Anne remembered her and her parents doing several times when Avery and Noah made things difficult for their parents.

"I can't. I'm sorry." She wouldn't give up her plans just because they needed a buffer.

"Give it a thought. Maybe you could join Bella after." Linda grabbed a tray of warm pretzels and turned toward the doors. "Connie is out there, alone, and there's a bit of a crowd. Think about it, dear."

"Think about it, Anne, for your mother," Bert said as soon as Linda was out of earshot.

She exhaled and looked at him. "Dad, I love you both, but—"

"I trust you, Annie. You always know what's right."

Yeah, she always did. So much so that it had become the bane of her existence.

"I have the food rounds, too, I don't know."

"*Did you know that Avery fought with Noah?*" she texted Finn.

"*Heard about it from Max. I'm not getting into this. Had enough of that shit when we were married.*"

~~~~~~~~~~~~~~~~

"You look so pretty, Janey. Your dad will be so pleased you dropped by," Linda said enthusiastically when she opened Darian and Fernando's door to Anne.

She had gotten dressed in her long, red wrap-dress before going on the food rounds so she wouldn't have to waste time changing when Finn arrived to pick her up. Passing by her aunt and uncle's house, she had decided to come in for a few minutes to lighten up the atmosphere and appease her own guilt.

Right before going in, she had texted Finn to let him know.

"Turns out Avery broke up with that man she was dating, so the mood is even worse," Linda whispered to her. "It's just the five of us until Max gets here. Please stay a little. I know it's unfair, and that your cousin can be difficult, but what is family for, Jane?"

Oh no.

She didn't have time to reply because she was immediately jumped on by her aunt.

"Anne, sweetheart, I knew you'd make it." Darian pressed her in a tight hug. The twin sisters weren't identical, and they always laughingly emphasized that Linda was ten minutes older.

"I can't stay," Anne tried reminding her.

"Nonsense. What's more important than being with your family on Thanksgiving? Avery will be so pleased."

How willfully blind could they be, she thought, while trying to squeeze in an explanation about why she couldn't stay.

"Anne! Now we have almost the whole family. Look at these two beaming." Fernando showed up, all smiles, and gestured toward his wife and her twin sister.

Now Anne had four elders in their holiday attire smothering her at the front door. This was going great. "I can only stay for a few—"

"Come on in, dear. Avery's already here," Darian said, taking her by the hand.

She plastered a smile on. *God, I'll give you thanks if you kill me now.* She hadn't seen her cousin since before she and Finn had gotten together, and she certainly didn't want to see her now. It was enough she'd have to see her on Sunday for lunch.

Her aunt drew her into the living room. "Avery, look who's here."

Through the dining room door, on the other end of the living room, Anne had a glimpse of the beautifully set table. Her aunt always loved things to be right and proper.

"Hey, Anne. Good to see you." Avery smiled at her from her place on the couch. She was in a blue dress that flattered her hair and skin tone.

"Hey, Avery. How are you?"

"Could be better, thanks for asking." Avery smoothed a hand over the skirt of her dress.

"I'm sorry to hear."

"Not your fault."

Anne could almost hear the *this time* that Avery didn't say.

"So, you're staying? I was told you were going to be at a friend's."

Oh God. The bile rose in her stomach. This was staring at the face of the secret and the lies that covered it up. "Um, yes, I'm not staying. I just stopped by."

"How lucky for us." That sounded more like the Avery she knew. "You probably heard that Noah and Jill are not coming. They blame it on me, but really, she was always looking for excuses to spend the holidays with her family."

Anne just bit the inside of her lower lip and tried to seem sympathetic. She sat down on the armrest of another couch, dying inside, thinking about Finn. She didn't want to do it here, but she had to. She withdrew her phone and typed a quick text to Finn. *"Held hostage, trying to get out. If you get home before I do, wait at the back."*

She raised her gaze from the phone and found Avery eyeing her through narrowed eyes.

"You look different," Avery said. From her mouth, it sounded like an accusation. She didn't have to bother; Anne felt guilty as it was.

Her stomach dropped. She knew she looked different. She had noticed it, too. It was the effect of being with the man she loved.

"Your hair maybe?" Avery said, running a hand over her own luscious, cascading, brown-with-highlights hair.

Anne touched hers. "Nope."

"Yeah, you're always wearing it like that. Why don't you do something about it?"

"I have to go," Anne said, getting up.

"Free as a bird, huh, Anne? I have to be here, you know, for my son. Or I would have flown to Hawaii. When you have kids, you'll understand. You should do something about it, you know. You're not getting younger."

Avery always knew how to pack a punch and aim it at the soft underbelly. She could imagine why Noah didn't want to come. At that moment, she almost wanted to shout into her face that she and Finn were together, but she knew better. It wasn't Avery she was concerned for; it was everyone else.

"Happy Thanksgiving, Avery," she said as she started heading for the kitchen. She peeked inside. "Bye, everyone. Happy Thanksgiving. Mom, Dad, I have to go."

"No, don't go. Can't we persuade you to stay?" Linda rushed over to her. She grabbed her wrists and pulled her into the kitchen.

"Mom ..." *The guilt*. The guilt would be her undoing. It always was.

"Look at this bird," Fernando said. He and Bert were busy with it. "It's a ten-pounder, and your dad was in charge of the sauce, so you know it's going to be great."

"I didn't bring anything," she tried.

"Look at all this food!" Darian said, holding the fridge door open. There's enough for an army. We can wrap some for your food rounds, too."

Kill me now.

"I really—"

"Look, she's softening already," Linda said, wrapping her arm around her waist fondly. "Come on, call your friend and tell her you'll drop by tomorrow. She'll understand. It's family."

"I think we can persuade her," Darian said, joining Linda.

Just then, the doorbell rang. *Fuck*. It had to be Max, which meant that Finn was heading to her house. And she wasn't sure she could face Max.

Darian shot toward the front door, which was right by the kitchen. Linda followed, still holding Anne's wrist and making her stand behind her.

Darian opened the door.

It wasn't just Max.

Finn stood next to him, his head lowered as he looked at his cellphone. She knew just then that he was reading her texts.

When he raised his face, and their eyes met, she saw the shock playing on his features.

"Sweetheart," Darian squealed, enveloping Max in her arms. "Come on in. Finn, you, too."

"I just dropped … I can't …" he stuttered.

"Where are you going to go from here? Your mother is in Florida. She called to wish me Happy Thanksgiving, so you're going to be home alone," Darian said, putting her free hand on Finn's arm in an effort to drag him in. "Why don't you come in and join us? Look who's here! Anne's here, and Avery won't mind, and we know Max would love for you to stay for dinner."

"I have plans," he said, but no one except Anne listened.

The sound of the commotion at the front door must have drawn Avery from the living room.

"Avery, you wouldn't mind if Finn stayed for dinner, right?" her mother asked. "Max would love having all his family here, especially since his cousins aren't here."

Guilting Avery didn't usually work, but Anne was impressed with her aunt's effort.

"Sure. Hey, Finn," Avery said flatly. "Max." She hugged her son.

"Hey, Mom," Max said, hugging her back. He then looked at Finn. "Dad, please stay." His voice was urgent.

Anne stood aghast. This was not good. Fuck good. This was a nightmare.

Finn moved his eyes from his son to her. The look in them was pleading, as if he begged her to ... what? There was nothing either of them could do.

"I got you something, Maxi," Avery said, walking Max toward the living room with her arm wrapped around his back. They were the same height.

"Dad?" Max looked back on his way to the living room.

"I'll be right there," Finn said. He then looked at her.

A chorus of "You have to stay," "It's like the whole family is here," "It's been years," and "Don't disappoint the boy," was heard from all four over seventy year old people.

"You, too, Anne. We're not giving up on you now that we're all here. You'll just have to cancel your other engagement."

"*Stay*," Finn mouthed to her above the heads of the shorter elders who were too busy clamoring around him to notice the gaze they exchanged.

She bit her lip and tilted her head in a *are you kidding?*

"*Please*," he mouthed again. "Anne, will you stay, too?" he then asked out loud when she didn't respond.

"You see, you have to! Even Finn wants you to. And how long has it been since you've seen *him*? You'll have a lot of catching up to do," Darian said victoriously.

She gave Finn an *I'm-gonna-kill-you* look then said, "Yeah, okay, but I'll have to leave early."

The moment all four cleared to the kitchen and the excited chatter between Avery and Max was heard from the living room, Finn took a step toward her. They were still at the entrance.

"Jane," he whispered. "Baby, I'm sorry. Max heard his cousins weren't coming, and that it was gonna be just him and the five of them"—he signaled with his head toward the interior of the house—"and, knowing that the mood was probably not great, he asked me to walk him in and stay for a few minutes. I just saw your texts now."

"Yeah, I figured."

He skimmed his eyes down her body. "You look …" He ate her up with his eyes. "Fuck, I can't wait to get that dress wrapped around your waist and—hey, Max, buddy, what you got there?" he suddenly called, taking a quick step back.

She turned back. Max was approaching from the living room. "Mom got me the Oculus VR I wanted," Max called enthusiastically.

"That's great. Come on, show me how it works." As he passed by her, Finn gripped her hand and brushed his palm over it from her wrist to the tips of her fingers.

Even that quick caress of his was enough to make her feel it between her legs. She had no idea how she was going to live through dinner.

She busied herself with helping in the kitchen as much as possible. She couldn't possibly love Finn more than she already did, but every time she saw him with his son, she loved him more. Which was sort of ironic, given that a child was what got them to that place.

Linda was with them in the living room, and it crushed Anne's heart to watch her mother enjoying the grandchild she never had. She looked at Avery, Finn, and Max as if they were the young family that she had hoped her own daughter would have one day. It seemed that her mother was oblivious to the fact that Avery and Finn didn't even bother to look at each other. Linda seemed gleeful to have them all in the same room.

"Janey, why are you standing there?" Linda said, catching her stalling there with a salad bowl in her hands. "This is turning out to be a great Thanksgiving after all. Of course, I wish Noah and Jill were here … It reminds me of that year you brought Tom."

Oh God. That year … Maybe she should have taken acting rather than painting because she was obviously better at hiding her feelings.

"Yeah, I remember that," Avery said. "Are you two in touch?"

"No."

"And we only got to meet him once. Your longest relationship. Such a pity." Avery said.

"Relationships end, Avery. Others begin. I don't regret anything," she said. Her eyes crossed paths with her mother's.

Did Linda really think her presence could cushion *this?* Or Finn's presence, for that matter? The two people Avery either spent a lifetime competing with or divorcing from? The only good thing that came out of it was that she felt she was ready to open her mother's eyes and tell her the truth. Maybe not the whole truth, but some of it. The present part of the truth, at least. She didn't think her mother could handle the past.

"I agree. That's the right approach," Finn said. "There's no use in looking back."

She looked at him. He was delectable in a dark pair of pants and a light blue dress shirt that his shoulders and arms filled so well. He had cuffed the sleeves and opened the top two buttons. She couldn't wait to get him home.

They managed to somehow make it until dinner was served. She helped with the serving, and Finn was called to help cut the turkey. It was heartbreaking to see how Darian and Fernando held on to him in the absence of their son. In some bizarre way, she felt like she was robbing him from them. Logically, she knew it wasn't so, but when had logic ever had anything to do with family dynamics?

Because they set two places for them at the last minute, they found themselves sitting next to each other. Given that they had hardly managed to take their hands off each other in the last month whenever they had the chance to be together, it required everything in them to not touch one another.

She felt it every time Finn's exposed forearm brushed hers.

They hardly spoke between them, and whenever they passed each other a bowl or platter, she felt like the undercurrents between them, even with the simplest, everyday words, were out there for everyone to see.

Max sat on the opposite side with his mother, closer to the head of the table.

"Anne," Max addressed her at some point, "you made a cake for a girl in my class."

She smiled. "Really? Which one?"

"She showed pictures of it at school and said it was from here, so I knew it was yours, and I told her I knew you. It was for her Bat Mitzvah."

His pride in her stung her heart. The cost. She prayed that there wouldn't be a cost to what she and Finn were doing.

"I had a few Bat Mitzvahs," she said. "What's her name?"

"Beth."

"Yeah, I remember now. I liked making it."

"I showed her the pictures of the cakes you made for my birthdays." He beamed at her.

She felt Finn's eyes boring holes into her. She then felt his right hand squeezing her left thigh. It wasn't a sexual touch. In the two years since she had come back and restarted the cake line, she had made two for Max's birthdays, at Darian's request—a superhero one he loved and a candy cake. She figured that Finn must have seen those.

Toward the end of dinner, Max asked to be excused until the desserts were brought and showed off his new VR to Linda and Bert in the living room. Avery helped her parents in the kitchen, and Anne felt Finn's hand on her thigh again. This was a different touch. Under the shelter of the tablecloth, and knowing they couldn't be seen from the living room, he ran his hand from her knee to her thigh. Agonizingly slow, he hiked her dress up, his palm caressing her bare leg. By the time he reached close to the crux of her legs, she was throbbing.

She clenched her thighs as he clasped her flesh. She had to hold back from making any sound, which was hard given that her nipples hardened, and she could feel the wetness nearly soaking her panties. It was torture. She needed his hand or, better yet, his tongue or cock right there.

"Stop," she whispered through gritted teeth.

"Or?"

"Stop." She almost moaned it.

"Or I'll make you come right here?" He leaned closer to her, his breath in her ear. "I know how wet you are right now, and it's killing me. If I have to get up, everyone will see how hard you make me."

God. He was killing *her*.

She slithered her hand under the table and removed his from her thigh. "This is dangerous. They'll be back any moment. And it's not fair."

"You're right," he rasped and leaned back. "I just want everyone to know, Jane. I want you to tell them this weekend. I'll tell Avery as soon as you give me the green light. Did you see how much Max likes you? If Avery could get herself together like she should, Max would be fine."

She looked from side to side to make sure no one could hear or notice their whispered conversation. "*Should.* She *should* be doing and *should* have done a lot of things. But we know who we're dealing with. Look at what she's done to her brother. Clusterfuck, Finn. It's going to be a clusterfuck. I believe it now more than ever."

"Maybe, but it's too late now to back out. And even if it wasn't, I don't *want* to. I *need* you. The only way is forward. I'm getting out of here first thing after dessert, and so are you. We'll meet at yours. There's no way I'll last all the way to Blueshore without fu—"

"Are you two catching up? I bet you have a lot of time to make up for," Darian said from a few feet behind them. She was carrying the cake that Anne had made. It was simply decorated.

Anne jerked away from Finn and looked at her aunt.

Darian turned her head back to look at her daughter and grandson, who were out in the living room. "It was so great having you here again, Finn. I wish ..." Darian sighed, almost to herself, without finishing her sentence.

Anne knew exactly what her aunt wished for—for Finn and Avery to get back together. Who could blame her?

Finn straightened up in his chair. Anne was sure that whatever happened under the table in his pants, her aunt's arrival had killed it.

"You made this?" he asked, looking at the cake then at her.

"Yes."

"It's beautiful."

"Thanks."

"I bet it tastes great, too."

She felt her face flushing. Why did everything he said sound like sex in her ears? She was going to hell. There was no doubt about it. But what a way to go!

It was all a fog after that. She didn't even remember eating dessert. All she remembered was excusing herself, kissing her parents goodbye, and getting into her car.

She closed the front door of her house after her, knowing that Finn would be there soon. She couldn't breathe until she would be in his arms.

Chapter 14

She was in his arms the moment her front door closed behind him. He pulled the string of her wrap dress like he had longed to do all evening, pushed his hands into her cleavage, and cupped her bra-covered breasts. He took his shirt off and had her with the dress still around her waist and her legs wrapped around him, lying on her back at the edge of the bed with him standing between her legs before she could utter more than his name. He held on to her hips and was inside her just as he fantasized all throughout dinner.

They were frantic that night. If he couldn't yet announce to the world that Jane was his, he'd make her his again, and again, and again when they were alone. It was a four-day weekend, and he had until Sunday to do it. On Sunday, they would get the ball rolling.

The next morning they planned it out over a late breakfast.

"At least, after last night, it'd be easier for me to excuse myself from attending Sunday lunch at my aunt's with everyone," Jane said, stirring her second cup of coffee while leaning against the counter. "I'll go to my parents' after they get back from Darian's and tell my dad and ask him to help with my mom. She's not going to take it well."

They decided that, on Monday, when Max would be safe in Blueshore, Finn would drive to Riviera View to talk to Avery. Let her make a scene without Max there, hoping she would have an entire week to blow off steam until she saw him again. In the meantime, he would prepare Max.

They would have to do it like that. There was no point in waiting anymore. That dinner had proven it. Throughout it, their secret had weighed like a boulder on his chest.

With the planning out of the way, the only thing left was to enjoy the quiet before the storm.

Sunday seemed far off on a Friday afternoon. It was almost as if they were a couple who didn't have to rely on a few stolen hours. They cuddled on the couch in the little house that became their cocoon. They gave up driving to Blueshore. Everything they needed was right here. They spoke for hours, cooked together, and she showed him her Etsy shop. They went through pictures on his phone and hers, glimpses into her life—Bella, the cakes, the house in Cincinnati, Uriel the cat, the kids next door, and even Tom. He showed her pictures of Max, of swim meets, of vacations he had taken him on.

He had never been happier.

On Saturday afternoon, they lay in bed on their sides, facing each other. He traced his fingers over the outline of her face, caressing the Anne of now and the Jane of then, the woman he had dreamed of for so long, and the real one who was here in his arms.

"I don't want this to end," she said, trailing her fingers along his tattoo.

He was about to say, "We won't let it," when the doorbell rang.

Jane's hand froze on his arm. Their gazes were linked, and he could see the alarm in the dark brown of her eyes.

They sat up, and she grabbed a robe. Quickly tying it, she brushed her fingers through her disheveled hair and went to the door. He closed the bedroom door and tried to recall in what state they had left the living room and kitchen.

"Sweetheart, did I wake you? I took my walk. You know, with all this food, I had to walk. Your father didn't want to come. Better yet, he's too slow for me. Anyway, I saw your car parked in the garage and figured you were home. How's Bella? I hope she's not too mad at us for stealing you on Thursday."

Linda's voice was loud and cheery. He hardly heard Jane's voice when she replied. He did hear Linda's voice again, though, when she said, "Oh, I'm sorry. I'll let you rest. We have lunch tomorrow, and you have to come. Poor Darian tried to convince Noah to come at least for that, but he declined. These kids are so stubborn. I think Fernando has to step in there. That's no way for a family to be."

Most of all, Finn felt sorry for Max. He knew that everyone was trying to make the holiday fun for him, and he had his new VR, which he had shown him over a video call, a call Finn had to answer only after finding a white wall to lean against so nothing of Jane's house would be caught on camera. But some of this must affect the atmosphere around Max. There wasn't a day Finn didn't bless the fact that he had his son growing up with him. He thought of the following weekend. He'd have to prepare Max to deal with Avery.

"Mom, I texted you, and I meant it." Jane's voice coming from the living room was unwavering. "I exchanged that lunch for dinner. And I can't be there every time she requires cushioning. I'll see you at home when you're back from lunch."

Linda murmured something, and next, he heard byes and the door closing.

He stepped out. Jane was leaning against the front door.

"I can't take this anymore," she said when she saw him. "Feeling like I'm doing something wrong, cheating."

"It'll be over soon." He took her in his arms.

On Sunday, Jane was on pins and needles, and although he was nervous, too, Finn got himself into the same mindset that he'd had before important meets. Though this was no competition, and no medals awaited, this was one of the most important things in his life, and his prize was the love of his life.

He imagined the finish line, that black mark on the touchpad at the far end of the pool, and he aimed for it. Any effort, any muscle burn, any painful breath were all part of getting there.

Jane hardly ate anything, and since they had spent a lot of energy, at noon, he went into the kitchen to make her his pasta primavera.

"Have you decided?" he called from the kitchen. He had offered to go with her to her parents' if she thought it would help, and she had only said, "Maybe." The time was getting near, so he had repeated his question while she tidied up the living room. They had knocked down a jar of dirty paintbrush water while going at it in the living room before.

He felt at home. Music played from his phone—a mixed playlist of pop, rock, and country, and the vegetables he was stir-frying hissed in the pan. He could see them bringing Max there, too.

"What?" he called when he heard Jane's voice.

She didn't reply, but the next thing she said pelted his heart against his rib cage.

"No, Avery, stop!" The catch in Jane's urgent voice was clear, even over the music and the hissing pan.

Like in slow motion, he knew what was going to happen next.

"Finn!" Avery called. "I know he's here. Nice try hiding his car in your garage," he heard her say.

He turned off the music and the stove.

"There you are." She appeared at the entrance to the kitchen. A mere wall separated it from the living room. "You son of a bitch!"

He knew this moment would come. It had been a long time coming, and he was almost glad. Only, he'd rather not be in nothing but his black boxer briefs for it.

"Your old pal, Joe, does renovations at the school, and he told me the other day that he saw your car in town. The way he said it, it sounded like you were driving *into* town. I thought it was weird because you usually just drop Max off and drive straight out." Avery advanced into the kitchen.

Finn crossed his arms and watched her. His blue Rav4 was almost non-descript, and after Linda's visit yesterday, Jane had parked her car in the street, and he parked his inside the garage.

"Then he saw you again in the middle of the week. For two years, no one's seen you. Then all of a sudden, you're touring Riviera View? Then Linda arrived at my parents' now and thought it was really funny that she confused someone else's car with yours yesterday. Then I remembered how the two of you arrived almost at the same time for dinner and left at almost the same time." She pivoted on her heel toward Jane, who had stopped at the entrance. "And *you* … you were always after what's mine."

"What are you talking about?" Jane was the color of the wall next to her.

"I know you. Always have. You might fool *him*, but not me," Avery sputtered.

Jane's eyes were wide, her hair still wet from the shower she had taken before. She gripped the doorframe. She was in one of his T-shirts that reached her thighs, and he knew she had only a pair of panties under it, a pair that he had been planning to peel off her after lunch. She opened her mouth to respond, but no sound came.

"Leave her alone, Avery," he said, unfolding his arms and taking a step forward. "She hasn't taken anything that's yours."

"You're sleeping with *my* husband!" Avery spat, still looking at Jane and ignoring him.

"I'm *not* your husband," he said sternly, holding back from grabbing her and dragging her out of the house until she relaxed.

She pivoted toward him. "And you? You're screwing *her*?"

"It's not like that, Avery," Jane said from her place at the entrance.

"It's not? You want to tell me you're not sleeping with her?" She was still talking to him.

"Oh, I definitely am," he said. "But it's not what you think. I knew her long before I knew you. We were friends and ..." He held back before he spilled what they had said they wouldn't reveal.

"You were sleeping together while we were married?" Avery's voice rose to near-hysterics.

"What? No! Never!" Jane sounded desperate.

"Protesting too much, *cousin*?"

"Avery, shut up and listen for once in your life!" He took another step and stopped in front of her. "There was nothing between Jane and me while you and I were married. There was nothing until recently."

"*Jane*?"

"I knew her as Jane, and she'll always be Jane to me."

"What, you're in love with her or something?"

"Yes."

Avery heaved a breath then turned her head to look at Jane. "You were always jealous of me."

"That's not true." Jane's voice came out hoarse, and she looked like the world had just exploded in her face for the second time.

He knew her guilt over wanting him while he had been married. His heart, which she had mended in the last month, piece by piece, broke into a million pieces all over again.

"Avery, stop it! No one went behind your back, and no one wanted what you had. You know perfectly well that you and I were never … We got along for Max." Even that was stretching the truth.

"It doesn't give you the right to go and fuck my cousin, my own flesh and blood."

He nearly laughed. "*Now* she's your flesh and blood? Where has that sentiment been all your life? Avery, come on; you know better than that." Maybe she could be reasonable once she relaxed. After all, she didn't deny his description of their marriage. She couldn't, because they both knew exactly what sham of a marriage it had been.

"Oh, I know better than that. We'll see who gets screwed now! Happy holidays, *Jane.*" Avery spat the name with such hatred that he couldn't believe that Max was somehow tied to her. She then turned around and bumped her shoulder against Jane while storming out.

The sound of the door slamming and the absolute silence that ensued were probably what the end of the world sounded like.

Jane was pale, even her lips were almost white. He approached her and wrapped her in his arms.

"Oh my God," she mumbled, her breath against his shoulder. Her lemony smell was his only comfort at that moment. "I'm so sorry," she whispered.

"Jane, I have to go after her before she breaks this to Max in the worst possible way."

"She's going to ruin everything—Max, my mother, Darian, Ferna—" She halted and grabbed his forearm. "Finn, don't let them know about then, about everything that happened then. It will only make things ten times worse."

"I won't." He held her by her shoulders, pressing her to the wall. He took a deep breath then released it slowly so that she'd breathe with him. She did.

"I'm so, so *sorry*, Finn," she said, pushing him with her palms on his chest. "Go before she—"

"It's not your fault, baby. It's mine. From start to finish."

Chapter 15

Finish.

How apt.

Her knees hardly bore her to the armrest of the couch. That same brightly painted room had seen them falling apart fourteen years ago, only to witness the same now. If walls could talk. Neighbors obviously could. Maybe the years in a large city had diminished her ability to grasp just how much people gossiped in these small towns. People knew each other, recognized cars and habits, and stuck their noses where they didn't belong.

It didn't matter. She was just looking for another address to aim her anger. It was easier than aiming it toward herself. Maybe they could have avoided this ugly scene if they had broken it to Avery before, when Finn had urged her to. Nevertheless, she knew her cousin well enough; the result would have been the same.

Or maybe they wouldn't have had to face any of this if she hadn't succumbed to her need for him. Or him to her. What were they thinking? There were rules. Social rules. Family rules. They had broken them. And when you broke the rules, you paid the price.

Finn was a blur as he emerged dressed from her bedroom and went toward the door. He stopped next to her and kissed the crown of her head before he left.

She couldn't let him pay the price alone. She got up and got dressed, not even knowing nor caring in what. She just threw on a pair of jeans and remained in the T-shirt that was already on her. She forgot to wear a bra and hardly remembered to stick her feet into a pair of sneakers when she grabbed her car keys.

Her aunt's house. Everyone would be there.

On her way there, the town looked like it did every day. The sun was out and bright, even in winter. People strolled the streets, the promenade, enjoying the long weekend. Coffee shops and beach restaurants were open. Everything was beautiful, which made the scene that awaited her and the one that preceded it appear in all its ugliness.

She left the car on the street, right behind Finn's. She was pretty sure her parents were still inside. There was no car to indicate it, but they lived close by and usually walked. Her mother and aunt couldn't live too far from each other, even in the same town.

She went inside without knocking.

Five adults and no child stood in the living room. They all looked planted on their stands, locked in some sort of a triangle. Her parents were by the couch, and a few feet from them was Finn, facing her aunt and uncle who stood at the vertex.

Her mother turned to look at her when she walked in. She caught her wrist almost in desperation. "Is it true?" Linda's voice was chapped, as if she desperately needed a drink of water.

"It depends." This was the only truth she was able to divulge without knowing what had been said before her arrival.

"Jane Anne Drecher, how *could* you?" Linda said, letting go of her wrist.

Anne's gaze zoomed in on the man who held her heart next to his in his chest. Finn's face was ghastly.

"Where's Max?" she asked.

"She took him. He's supposed to come home with me today, but she just took him. And he was ... he was too ... confused."

"You should leave," Darian spoke. "Both of you. I don't want to see either one of you in this house. You were sitting right here at my dining table, and you're ... with your own cousin's husband." She was looking at her now. Anne felt the bile rising.

"I'm *not* her husband," Finn said flatly.

"You're not, but you *were* married to my daughter, and you're my grandson's father, and now you're sleeping with your son's aunt. And who knows how long that's been going on."

"She's not his aunt. She's his cousin, once removed." Finn's voice was hard, strained, but callous, as if he'd had enough.

"Are you going to split hairs with the terminology right now, Finn?" Fernando took a step forward, as if he could physically intimidate Finn, who was a foot taller and probably twice as wide as the older man in his suspended pants that hung loose on his bony frame. A frame Anne loved dearly, as she loved her uncle. He was the opposite of her dad in looks, but they shared that same gentle kindness. It physically pained her to see this.

"Yes, I am, Fernando, because these things matter," Finn said. "I'm not Avery's husband, haven't been for the last three years. And I sure as hell am not *her* brother." He gestured with his hand toward Anne. "Fernando, I'm not going to apologize for loving someone else and being with someone who is not your daughter. I did marry her, stuck by her, had Max with her. I did everything I was supposed to do. I did everything right. But we're not married anymore, and we're both free to see others. I love Ja—Anne. I have for …"

Anne's heart stopped. He had almost spilled the truth about the past.

"I've known her for years," Finn then corrected himself, "before I ever met Avery. We were friends. We're both single now. And because no one else is going to say this, I will. They're *not* sisters, despite what you all tried to create, to believe." He looked at Linda and Bert, too. "They never thought of or treated each other as sisters. And I know whose fault—" he cut himself short. "We don't want to hurt anyone, and it might not be ideal, but I'm not going to apologize for being with Anne."

"But you *are* going to get out of my house," Darian said.

"For Max's sake, we'll see how to handle this going forward because we don't want him to suffer for your … But, right now, you'd better leave," Fernando said, putting a hand on his wife's forearm to stop her from taking this further. His voice was softer, and it seemed like Finn's words did get through to him, and that he was trying to be sensible.

"Dar, we have to talk about this," Linda said.

"You will, but not right now, honey," Bert butted in, putting a hand on his wife's forearm, almost mirroring his brother-in-law. "Everyone needs to calm down, breathe, and think. It's not the end of the world, and I'm sure we all can—"

"Yes, you *all* can leave now," Darian cut him off.

Anne caught the look on her mother's face when her twin told them to leave. "I'm sorry. I never meant to …" she began, hating that her throat choked with tears.

Her father stepped forward and put a hand on her shoulder just when Finn took a step toward her, too.

"It'll be okay. Come, Anne," Bert said, raising his palm to stop Finn from approaching her.

She walked out with her parents. Finn followed, and they stopped next to their cars.

"Do you want to come home with us, Janey? Talk it over?" her father asked.

"I was going to talk to you this afternoon before all this happened," she said. "I'm sorry, Dad. It wasn't supposed to happen like that."

Bert caressed the back of her hand. He then looked at Finn. "Finn, son, I don't think you and Anne should … for the time being at least. Let people digest. They …" Bert half-pivoted toward his sister-in-law's house. "They still see you as their son-in-law. They love you as one, and I can understand why. It's strange for me, too. I just hope you two didn't … while you were married."

"Never, Dad!" Anne heard her own voice as if it came from a distance. "Is that what you think of me?"

Her father's eyes were soft on her. "No, no, you're right. Even as I said it, I knew it couldn't be."

"Even so, I still can't … This is not how I raised you," Linda suddenly said. She was much shorter than all of them, but her voice was louder than all three at that moment.

"I didn't do anything wrong, Mom."

"So, why don't you come home with us and explain?" Linda asked.

"Can I have a moment alone with Ja—Anne?" Finn intervened.

"We'll start walking toward the house, sweetie; join us when you're done here?" Her father said softly.

She nodded.

Finn began talking the moment her parents were a few feet away. "I want to go with you, but I have to get Max, speak to him, at least. She didn't let me. When I came in, she had already coughed it up. I don't even know what she said. She stormed out with Max right after I arrived."

"Go. Talk to your son." More than anything, she wanted to disappear into his arms and bury her face in his chest. She was still in his T-shirt. It smelled like him on her skin. "I'm so sorry, Finn."

"Stop." He rubbed his hand up her bicep. "I'll talk to you later."

"Finn … I think … my father's right. Maybe we shouldn't see each other right now. Until things … until the dust settles."

"I don't think he's right. I don't want to give in to this shit, and I don't think we should."

"Let's talk about this later. I might have to tell my parents about … about then. They won't tell the others if I ask them not to, but I think they should know. It might help them understand. They always wondered why I left after your wedding. I sold them some excuse about how Avery getting married made me move faster with my plans for an alternative career, but it's as flimsy as it sounds."

She could see that he wanted to hold her, to kiss her, but they were still in front of her aunt's house. Finn palmed her cheek with one hand, and his eyes connected with hers until she could drown in the blue.

"I trust you," he said.

She pressed her cheek into his palm and kissed it.

Chapter 16

Max opened the door only after he stood there for five whole minutes, knocking and calling both Max's and Avery's cellphones.

"Hey, Dad."

He pulled him into a hug and kissed the top of his son's head. "Max, I want to explain." He saw Avery in the background, standing far inside, where the hallway opened to the living room. How much had she said? They had always blurred the truth for Max. Finn had always hoped he wouldn't have to explain to his son that the only reason he had married his mother was that he had gotten her pregnant, and that the only reason he had been born was that his father felt guilt when that pregnancy had been lost.

"That's okay. I understand."

Finn held Max by his biceps and pulled himself back so he could look at his face. "You do?"

"Not everything, but …" Max trailed off, his gaze on the coir doormat that Finn was standing on.

"I don't know what you heard, but Jane … Anne and I, we were friends a long time ago. You know she used to tutor me in high school." This was general information everyone knew. "Then I married your mother, and then we had you, but you know all that already. Your mom and I have been divorced for three years, and Anne and me … we discovered we love each other, and we wanted to give it a try." He couldn't tell him the whole truth. This would have to suffice. Even that felt like too much. "We never meant to hurt anyone, not your mother, or you. And we were going to tell everyone, so everyone would understand. I want *you* to understand most of all."

He hated that he had to hold this conversation with his son while standing in the doorway, but he didn't want to set a foot in that house. Not today.

Max nodded. "I understand." He raised his eyes, and their gazes finally met. The blue of Max's eyes had always reflected his own, and Finn could see that Max meant what he said.

"I was about to pick you up, and here I am. We're going home."

"Okay."

The moment Max turned away, Avery sailed toward the door and stopped next to her son. "Where do you think you're taking him?" she asked, putting an arm around Max's shoulders, as if he needed protection.

"Home." Finn looked her straight in the eyes.

"To your girlfriend's? Who happens to be his aunt? I don't think so."

"Avery, is this how you want to do this? Here?" He gestured with his head, first to the side, toward the street, then toward Max, who was half-pivoted from him. He was trying to make her gather herself for her son's sake. "I'm taking him home, to Blueshore, where he's lived all his life. It's my house and his. No one else is there. And, as for the rest, you and I will talk about it later."

"You can bet on that," she said.

He wanted to ask her why she was like this, what had anyone ever done to her to make her like this. He knew her family well, and except for the fact that her parents had always been indulgent of her behavior and had hardly ever criticized her, not even when their younger son hadn't come for Thanksgiving, there was absolutely no reason for her to behave as if everyone was a contender against her.

"Max, go get your things," he said, placing a comforting hand on his son's shoulder blade.

Without a word, Max sidestepped Avery and went inside.

They remained there facing each other. He had no idea if anyone was watching the scene they were making, but he was sure there was.

"I never cheated on you, Avery. I'm sorry things were the way they were, but I've always tried to do the right thing."

"Finn, we both know why we got married. But this? *Her*? Do you honestly expect me to accept this? To flaunt this in my face?"

"No one's flaunting or going to flaunt anything. We don't choose who we love. She and I … we go way back …" He stopped. "As friends," he added, almost tempted to tell her the truth, but knowing it wouldn't do any good. "Refusing to accept it won't change anything."

"Forget it, Finn. I won't have it. And I won't let my son … I won't let you …"

"What won't you let him, Avery?" His mouth tasted metallic, and his voice sounded steely in his own ears.

Max began approaching them, shouldering his big backpack and holding the paper bag that contained his VR in its box.

"In our family, she's practically your *sister-in-law* and *his* aunt," Avery said through greeted teeth.

"Don't try that bullshit on me, Avery."

"I won't have you confuse him or throw him into a family that's—"

"Hey, buddy, ready?" he cut her off, jutting his chin toward their son in a hint for her to keep it quiet in front of Max. "We'll talk," he added to her as soon as Max joined him on the other side of the threshold.

"Max, don't worry, okay? Everything will be all right," Avery said in a voice that was suitable for soothing a scared five-year-old.

Max didn't reply. He just slightly bent forward and gave his mother a short hug.

Finn seethed inside. He should remind her later that Max got quickly used to seeing his mother mostly on the weekends, so despite everything, he was better able to adjust than she gave him credit for. This wasn't about Max; this was all about *her*.

They didn't speak until they were out of Riviera View.

"You ended up not having lunch today. D'you want us to get something somewhere? Maybe at the Blue Jam?" Finn side-eyed Max.

"Um, Eli invited me to come over, if that's okay?"

"When did he manage to do that?"

"I texted him when we were at Mom's, and he invited me."

"Max, is it because …? We can talk about it. We should."

"I don't want to talk about it, Dad. I just want to go to Eli's."

His stomach clenched. Was he losing his son now, too? Maybe Max just needed time and distance to digest. It had been an ugly scene.

"Do you want me to drop you off there?"

"Yeah."

"But we *should* talk, Max."

"Dad, I'm fine, really. I just want to go to Eli's."

He knew there was no point in pushing the point further now.

They didn't say much until he pulled over in front of his friend's house.

"I'll be in touch later to come and get you," he said right before Max left the car.

A text from Jane awaited when he got home. "*How's Max?*"

"*He'll be ok. Can you talk?*"

"*Still at my parents. Are you ok?*" she typed back almost immediately.

"*If you are, then I am.*"

"*I will be.*"

He changed his clothes and went straight to the pool. Swimming had always helped him clear his mind, focus, aim.

He hoped they'd get to talk later, but when he finally got Max home, Max said he was tired and went almost straight to bed.

After Max had gone to bed, he spread out any legal document that he and Avery had ever signed onto the kitchen table. Max living with him wasn't legally documented because it had happened gradually. He emailed the lawyer who had handled his divorce and asked him to give him a call first thing in the morning.

He then called Jane. It was a short, whispered conversation and she sounded as dead tired as he felt. He couldn't believe that, only that morning, he had woken up with her in his arms.

Chapter 17

"Darian should never know. How can I face my sister, knowing this?" Linda said. "No. They can't know. I still can't believe this of you, Jane. You hiding this from us … all this time."

"What good would it have done if you knew? Would you have encouraged *me* to marry him instead, knowing that Avery expected his …" The words died on her lips. They had lived in her head for so long, but they died when she had tried to utter them again. "Could you have faced your sister *then*?" Her voice rose. "Do you think she or Avery would have reacted any differently? They wouldn't have accepted him being with me while fathering her child. They would have used the pregnancy to pressure and threaten Finn if I had stayed with him. I still hope Avery is not planning anything now. The result would have been the same. Only you would have felt sorry for me and differently about Finn and Avery, and everything, and still gone through with this. It was enough that I knew. I couldn't be with him either way."

"You could have trusted us enough to confide in us, Annie. I can't even imagine what you must have felt at that wedding. And how brave you were all these years," Bert said.

Anne sat next to the round kitchen table in the house that she had grown up in. Her left arm was thrown over the chair's back, and her right elbow rested on the oak tabletop. Linda and Bert both stood, leaning their backs against the old marble counter, facing her. Despite the concern and love she knew they had for her, she felt alone. Only Finn's shirt on her skin made her feel less so.

"What about Tom?" Linda asked.

"What about him? He had nothing to do with it. I met him much later. It ran its course, and it ended." It wasn't one hundred percent true. She felt like the world's biggest liar. Even when she told the truth, she still lied. But she didn't want them to feel sorry for her or judge her, or Finn, more than they already did. "Finn and Avery have been divorced for three years now. We realized we still love each other. It has nothing to do with anyone else."

"Couldn't you find another nice young man to fall for, except for your cousin's ex-husband?" Linda asked, almost pleading with her to relent.

"Mom!"

"Linda, we don't choose who to fall for," Bert said, palming his wife's shoulder.

"I know. I'm not *really* mad at you, Annie. I'm just … I'm just worried what it might do to our family. What it might do to you. Avery is not—"

"Not the easiest person? Not the most understanding of others? Not one to not make things less difficult than they are? Not the kind who will ever accept anyone touching what she thinks of as *hers*? Even if it's just her own brother's wife coming to work at her school? Not to mention her cousin and her ex-husband?" Bert said. He looked at Anne when he'd said it, his smile indicating that they were in this together.

Linda came over and sat next to her, hanging her head and staring at the floor. She suddenly raised her head and looked at her daughter. "The birthday cards."

Anne's heart ceased to beat.

Linda turned her gaze toward her husband. "Every year, I sent her those birthday cards. I always assumed they were from old friends here. They only said '*Jane*' on the outside, and I didn't know what was inside." She looked at Anne again. "Who were they from?"

Better be out with it in all its ugliness. "Finn."

"Oh, Janey," Linda said, shaking her head from side to side. "Had I known …"

Anne looked at her father. Bert's height and width filled the kitchen. The ironed shirt her mother had him wear for the lunch that never happened stretched across his abdomen, showing the undershirt he had on. He pressed his lips together, but she didn't see disappointment or disapproval on his face. She saw pain and compassion. Good thing they didn't remember that her birthday was also Finn and Avery's wedding anniversary.

Bert reached out his hand to her. She took it, and her father pulled up and hugged her.

"I'm sorry, Dad," she whispered, tears clogging her throat. "Nothing happened while he was married."

"I know. We're here for you, Jane," he said. He then freed one hand and pulled his wife up and added her to the hug.

She left their house soon after, intending to take the beach route home and leave her car where she had parked it. Before she walked out, her father approached her at the door. In the large T-shirt that he had worn after getting rid of the dress shirt, he looked cozy. Anne felt like hiding from the world behind him.

"I just realized," he said. "Avery had a miscarriage a week after the wedding. But even then he couldn't be free. And you would never have taken him from her when she was so down. I can't tell you how much I appreciate you, knowing this, Anne. How much it hurts me to know what you both must have gone through. Whatever your mother thinks or feels, Darian is not *my* twin, and I've always thought she enabled Avery's entitlement. I'm with you, and you can come to me with anything and everything."

"Oh, Dad." She threw herself into his hug. Only then did she burst down crying. Her father held her until everything she was holding inside came pouring out.

"I wanted to tell you, to consult with you on how to break it, and now it's … the worst possible way," she said, wiping her fingers under her nose.

"Knowing everyone, I don't think I would have had good advice for you, Annie. To be honest, I don't think there was a good way to do this. Now we just have to make sure that everyone remains reasonable. Although, I'm not so sure they all can be."

She nodded. He echoed her own thoughts.

"You're my little girl, no matter how tall or old you are," he said with a smile that was meant to cheer her up.

"I love you, Dad."

~~~~~~~~~~~~~~~~~

If she needed proof of how fast and how bad small-town gossip could get, Anne got plenty of it over the next few days. At first, she thought she was imagining Mrs. Vahler looking at her funny when she asked for pumpkin bread the Tuesday after Thanksgiving. But then two other women just mumbled a response to her 'How are you today?' when they were usually keen to chat.

A text from Bella was another proof. *"I'm assuming shit hit the fan over the weekend? People at work are talking. Apparently, Avery told one of the secretaries, who's got a mouth on her the size of the Grand Canyon and, from there, it started rolling. One thing I heard was that Finn cheated on her with you while they were married. When it reached me, I said that it was impossible because you lived in Ohio. But don't try confusing these folks with facts. They say his travels to swim meets was a cover."*

Her stomach plummeted. From the depth it had reached, Anne called her.

"Who's they?" she asked when Bella picked up.

"The general *they* of gossiping."

"You know that none of this is true, Bella."

"I know. But you should do something about it and, most of all, prepare yourself for some attitude. "

And attitude there was. Though Anne knew people liked her, it still didn't stop some from looking at her like they were searching for evidence in her features, and a few sounded like they had just swallowed a frog.

She wasn't sure if it had anything to do with it, but they had two decorated cake cancellations; one after she had begun working on it, so she finished it and put it as a surprise outside one of the doors in her food rounds that day.

"Anne, dear, check the order log," Connie Latimer said, passing from the bakeshop into the back. Bert and Connie used a book and pencil to take orders, as they had done twenty years ago. "There was a cancellation for later this week, but it's actually good. We need to plan this year's Christmas orders," Connie continued, and Anne knew she was doing her best to keep it positive.

"Who canceled?" she asked. She didn't mind cancellations, because for every cancellation, there were usually two new orders, but not that week.

"Lucile Hays, that cow," Connie muttered. "She'd let her husband choke on her brick cake on his seventieth birthday rather than spend a dollar."

Anne laughed. Lucile was Eric Hays' mother. Eric the douche who nicknamed her Plain Jane. She splurged on her son but, apparently, not on her husband. Anne guessed that Lucile was just delivering a message—she wouldn't buy from them now that it was rumored that Anne had been having an affair with her cousin's husband.

Hope Hays, Eric's ex, who didn't exactly get along with her ex-mother-in-law, came in one afternoon. Teaching at the same school as Avery, she was bound to hear about it.

"People just enjoy regurgitating these things. They did that with Jordan, too. Believed the rumors, spread them, added their own flavor." Just two months back, a story from Jordan's days as a political advisor blew up nationwide, and the Riviera View gossipers had a field week with it. "No one who knows both you and Avery believes a word of it, you know," she said, standing next to her at the bread basket display.

"Thanks, Hope. Congratulations, by the way," Anne said. "I heard about you and Jordan but didn't get to see you."

Hope's smile widened. "Thanks. But you know, I'm not Avery's favorite person these days either, with me and Jordan being together. Not that I was her favorite before," she scoffed.

It was true, then. Avery had been after Jordan Delaney, Libby's future brother-in-law.

"Does it affect you at work?" Anne asked.

"Once I showed her I'm not taking any bullshit from her, she doesn't give me any. But I keep my eyes open, especially since we have employee assessments coming up. Maybe you should talk to her."

"I tried calling her. She doesn't pick up my calls. I get that. I never meant to hurt her or her parents. That's why I …" She was going to say that was why she had kept her distance from Finn all this time, but no one was supposed to know that this thing between them wasn't new.

No one seemed to know, except one person— Roni Richards, Hope and Libby's friend, the one who had seen her and Finn at Life's A Beach all those years ago.

She came in with two of her children, which immediately stood out because she didn't normally come in unless she needed pastries to stage a house as part of her interior design business. Holding her youngest's hand, ready to leave with the box of brownies that she had bought them, she seemed to hesitate.

"Hope had a great idea. I don't know if she got to talk to you about it or not, but would you like to join us for a girls' night? We've been wanting to ask you for a while now. We get together every Monday evening, on the shittiest day of the week." She chuckled. "We eat things I don't usually allow myself to eat"—she raised the brownie box—"and laugh, and talk, and … Why don't you join us?"

It was strange coming from Roni. She had the least connection to her. Hope, she considered a sort of friend. Libby was … well, Libby was Libby. But Roni?

She thought of Bella's upcoming move. She'd lose her only friend. "Thanks, Roni. I'll think about it. It could be nice."

"Fuck nice," Roni whispered so that her kids wouldn't hear. "We're telling things as they are there. We'll tell you what we think of your cousin." She raised her brows and grinned. "You know it's not our first brush with her, given that she's Hope's semi-manager, had tried to force-date Jordan, and is supposedly educating our children. And, in return, you'll tell us the whole story." Roni's cheeky yet sympathetic smirk cued Anne that she was hinting at that past encounter.

Roni looked like one of those women who had a big mouth and a bigger heart. She could have opened that mouth after Finn's wedding and told everyone that she had seen the groom and the bride's cousin at Life's A Beach, but she never had, or it would have become common knowledge.

"I just might." She smiled back at Roni.

When Anne called Libby to verify the food rounds list for December, there was a pause right after they had finished going over it. She was used to awkward silences with Libby, but this one was more loaded than usual, and when Libby drew a breath, Anne knew what she was going to say.

"You know that those who care about you and your parents aren't buying the rumors. Everyone knows who you are and who Avery is, and some remember Finn, too. If I can help in any way …"

"Not everybody, Libby. We've had cancellations, and I have a feeling—"

"My mom told me. It's a small fraction. Probably the old busybodies who have nothing better to do." Libby would know something about it. The problems her father had caused, which had culminated in Connie selling the bakery to the Drechers, had evoked gossip. "Anyway, if you need anything …"

"Thanks, Libby."

Finn called and texted every day.

"It's quiet. Weirdly quiet," he said over a video chat at night. He looked tired and older. "Max doesn't want to talk about it beyond the little we did speak about it. Avery is behaving normally, which means that I don't hear from her. She's in touch with Max, but it seems to be the regular stuff. I won't go through his phone, but I tried to gauge from him if there was … Anyway, there wasn't. It's like nothing happened, and this worries me the most." He was leaning against his bed's headboard. She had great memories of that headboard. His dark gray T-shirt accentuated the blue of his eyes but also the dark circles around them. It stretched across his athletic chest and shoulders, and she imagined leaning her head on him and listening to his heartbeat. They shouldn't video-chat. Seeing him made it harder.

Finn looked away and swiped a hand over his ruffled hair toward his neck. "My lawyer is drafting an agreement that will formalize Max living with me. I asked him not to do anything with it for now, except prepare it. It'd be poking the bear if I bring it up now."

She sighed. "God, Finn, what have we done?"

His blue eyes pierced her through the screen. "We've done *nothing*. The more I think about it, the more I'm sure, and the more I'm beating myself over waiting and wasting three fucking years."

"Oh, sure, it would have flown great with everyone if we got together soon after your divorce."

"Okay, so not three years, but two years ago, when you came back, I should have …"

"What was was, was was."

He laughed. "What?"

God, she missed that husky sound. "I heard it somewhere."

"You have no idea how much I miss you." He skimmed his eyes over her face through the camera.

"I'm coming over this weekend. The only text I got from Avery was to ask that I bring Max earlier on Friday, right after practice."

"I don't know if it's a good idea, Finn."

"I don't give a damn, Jane. I have to see you. I'll just warn her not to poison him. And I'll tell him again that he can ask me anything, and if he needs me, he just has to call or text."

He was the best dad any child could want, and she wanted him to be the father of any child of hers. The clinic had called just that week, and she had told them that she'd be in touch if it was relevant. Experience had taught her to anticipate the bad, to be torn from him. Now, with this looming over their heads, she didn't want to completely shut that door.

On Friday afternoon, she opened her front door to a chlorine-smelling Finn, who had come straight from the pool. His dark blond hair was still somewhat wet, and the muscles under the long-sleeved Henley were even harder than usual. His mouth was on hers before she could say more than, "Hi."

"I didn't even stop to take a shower after practice. I reek," he mumbled against her mouth between kisses. He took his shirt off and threw it on the floor. Kissing her neck, he grabbed under her thighs and lifted her. With her legs wrapped around him, he walked them to her shower. Maybe they shouldn't be meeting until things cleared up, but he was her weakness and her strength, and she needed him as much as he needed her. With him here, her shredded heart felt whole again.

"My sunflower girl," he whispered against her skin as he slid down her wet body and kissed the tattoo on her hipbone.

Chapter 18

"You can't stay." She sat up in bed, searching for her shirt.

He grabbed her arm and pulled her to him. "I can't go."

"Finn …" she rebuked.

"Jane …" He shut her up with a kiss.

The sheet under them was moist from their shower-wet bodies that had crashed on it for another round as soon as they had gotten out of her bathroom.

She broke their kiss. "I don't have to remind you …" she halted. "I just don't like that silence of hers."

No, she didn't have to remind him. He had a feeling Avery was planning something, but his lawyer had promised him that she had no legal standing to take Max from him on the grounds of his relationship with Jane.

"I'm not going to live without you in my life anymore. Do you understand?" He locked her under him and watched her from above. She just stared at him. "Do you understand?"

"Just until things—"

"Things will never be easy. It will always be awkward when we're all in the same room. And we will have to be sometimes, at least for the next six years until Max turns eighteen, and even after that. If we wait for things to be easy, we might as well just …"

She brought her hand up and traced his face with her fingers. "Finn, we're in this together."

"Are we? D'you promise? Because I feel like you're slipping away."

"No, I'm in. I don't regret any of this. I'm just trying to minimize the shit storm."

He gritted his teeth. "Okay. I'll go now. But you and I … I'm not giving this up."

She raised her head from the mattress and met his lips in a deep kiss.

~~~~~~~~~~~~~~~~

And shit storm it was.

Avery didn't say much when he picked Max up on Sunday evening. Neither did Max. Finn asked if his mother had said anything that he'd want to ask him about or have him explain. Max said that all they'd done was play with the VR, watch a movie, and visit his grandparents.

Finn wished his own mother didn't live in Florida and that he could have Max spend some time with her. He planned to take Max to see her on Christmas.

On Monday, the reason for Avery's uncharacteristic silence transpired.

"She filed a change request to the physical custody order—Max's living arrangements. She wants him to live with her and visit you every other weekend. She says you had him for two years, and that it wasn't legally settled," his lawyer said.

He had just parked outside the pool. Sixteen people awaited him inside for practice toward a regional meet.

"She moved away and was fine with him living with me."

"I know. There's more. She says that, unbeknownst to her, you made sure the holidays were split so that you'd have Max at hers and be free to meet with your mistress because, to the best of her knowledge, this relationship has been going on since you two were married."

He slammed his hands down on the steering wheel. The honk went off. "What mistress? I'm not married!" He took a deep breath. "And as for the rest, it's all lies."

"I submitted the agreement we prepared as a counter offer, and I'll add the necessary rejection of all her false claims as to your relationship with her cousin," his lawyer said in a cool and calm manner. "We'll have a court hearing." He paused then added, "Something good might come out of it. It wasn't healthy to let living arrangements settle themselves without legally binding them."

Finn ran a hand over his forehead. Then, before he shifted back into gear, he texted the dad who was volunteering as his coach assistant. He then headed straight to Riviera View.

"Do you want to explain to the court how, for two years, you lived in another town, an hour away, and were okay with seeing your son only on the weekends?" he barked into Avery's face as soon as she opened the door. "Do you want to explain to the court why it's okay to move Max to another school in the middle of a school year?" His voice was loud, the car was left at the curb with the engine on, people were out, and he didn't care about the scene they were making.

"Do you want to explain to the court that you've been screwing your son's aunt under the roof he lives in?"

He scoffed. "Don't even try! She's not his aunt. She's not at my house. And we only now just got together. You're just being vindictive because it's her. None of this is for Max's sake. I'm not buying this, and neither will the court. Why don't we ask Max what *he* wants?"

"Go ahead. He can't address the court until he turns fourteen."

He had never needed this much self-restraint to not punch his fist into a wall.

"Do you really want to drag him through this? What for? Are you threatening me with all this just so I'd break it up with her?"

"You're choosing her over your son?"

"No, I don't have to choose. It's you who—"

"Then break it up with her, Finn. Find someone else to date, or fuck, or whatever it is you do with her."

"You're using Max to …? What's wrong with you?" He took a step forward, his voice rising. "What the fuck is wrong with you?"

"I won't have her flaunt this in my face," she said.

"Who's flaunting?" He had no idea what she was even on about. She was viewing the world through a straw, filtering everything through that narrow view of her own narcissistic needs. What had he done to his son? He regretted he didn't have the mental capacity to press record on his phone before he had pounded on her door.

He took a deep breath. "Avery, let's talk about this. Just you and I, quietly, calmly. I understand that it's difficult for you. None of this is against you. None of this says anything about you. It has nothing to do with you. But it has everything to do with Max, if that's how you're going about it. And you shouldn't. He's not in harm's way at all unless you do this to him."

"*I'm* doing this to him? Suits you to turn this on me. You, Noah, Jill, your precious *Jane*. You're all the same. *I'm* trying to do what's right. Now I want you to leave. This is my house, and I don't want you here."

"Avery, please, let's be reasonable."

"And, by the way, I'm not threatening you; it's you who's threatening me!" She slammed the door in his face.

He took a step back and turned toward his car. A neighbor stood next to the bin of the house next door with a trash bag in hand and looked at him.

He gave him a tight-lipped, quick smile and got into his car.

Everything in him begged him to drive further into town, to Jane. To normalcy. He needed to hold her, to inhale her. Maybe he shouldn't, but he had to. The courts wouldn't buy Avery's lies. He just didn't want Max to go through all that until the truth came out.

He drove toward the town's exit, then U-turned the car and drove back in. He hadn't seen her since Friday. They had lost the weekend. They had lost fourteen years.

He parked on the back street behind Ocean Avenue and went to the back door that was used for delivery trucks and taking the trash out of the bakery. Jane's car was parked next to it. He pulled the door. It was open.

He found himself in the room where the baked goods were prepared before they went into the ovens in the next room. She was there alone. In a short-sleeved blouse, a pair of jeans, and sneakers, she stood with her back to the door, busy decorating a two-tier cake. Her hair was tied up, her nape exposed, except for the white ribbon of the apron that she had on. Finn wanted his lips on that delicate neck. He looked at the way the apron cinched her waist.

"Jane," he said, not wanting to startle her by suddenly touching her from behind.

She pivoted, her gloved hands covered with pink icing. She expelled a surprised breath and smiled. "Finn."

He closed the distance between them, enveloped her in his arms, and inhaled her deeply. "My love," he whispered into her hair.

"Something happened. What are you doing here?" she asked, wrapping her arms around his shoulders but holding her icing-covered palms in the air.

"I'll tell you later. I'll solve it. I just had to see you," he said, placing a kiss on her neck. He pulled his head back to look at her face then kissed her lips.

"I love you, baby, so fucking much. You have no idea." He leaned his forehead against hers.

"I do, and I love you, too. You're scaring me, though." She recoiled her head. "Where's Max?"

"At home. He's fine. It'll be fine. I have to go. I'll tell you later. Don't worry."

She nodded, and they kissed again before he left his heart with her and went to his car.

~~~~~~~~~~~~~~~~

"Finn Brennen?"

"Yes." He looked at the two uniformed cops who stood in the doorway. His stomach had plummeted when he'd opened the front door of his house to find them there.

"This is an ex-parte restraining order under your name." The taller officer handed him a folded stack of papers.

If the San Andreas fault had leashed at that moment, he wouldn't have been more rattled. "*What*?" was all he managed to say.

"You'll have a court hearing where you can contest this in three weeks. Until then, you can't come within a hundred yards from Avery Miles or her house."

His pulse sped up. He could feel it everywhere. He leaned an arm against the doorframe.

"Dad, why are the police here?" Max came and stopped next to him, his head popping from under Finn's arm to peek at the officers.

"It's nothing, Max. Go back inside. I'll be there in a minute." He ruffled his son's hair.

Max stalled and looked at the men.

"Go inside, son," the older officer said. "Your dad will be there in a moment."

"What is this for?" Finn asked the moment Max was somewhat out of earshot.

"You threatened her in her home?" the younger officer asked.

"No, I tried talking to her." The blood seemed to fly through his veins, his palms went numb.

"You coached my son," the older police officer said. "The special needs program. He can swim, thanks to you. It empowered him. Listen, three weeks will get you into Christmas with this. Ask your lawyer if he can do something before that."

He nodded. "Thanks."

He had known it wouldn't be easy. He had known it wouldn't be pretty. He didn't imagine it'd be this ugly. He didn't mind ugly for himself, as long as he had Jane. He'd give up anything for her, even his ability to swim. But his son was involved, and now his hands were tied.

"Dad, what did these cops want?" Max asked as soon he closed the door. He was standing next to the dining table, the VR set dangling from his hand.

"Sit down, Max," he said. With a hand on his son's shoulder, they both took seats at the table, and he pivoted his chair to face his son. "Your mother and I had an argument. You know that she's not happy about me and Anne. I don't know what you heard, but we've never done anything wrong. We're just two people who want to be together as a couple. Your mom … she thinks it's better if you live with her and see me every other weekend. I went to talk to her. I might have raised my voice. The cops came to make sure that everything was okay, that we keep a bit of distance to cool off." Jesus, he hoped he made it sound right.

"*Live with her*?" Max asked.

He nodded.

"I want to live here, with you, like always," Max said.

He smiled. He wanted to cry, but he smiled. "I want you to live with me, too, kid. That's what I told your mom, that we can continue as we have until now."

"I'll tell her, too."

He sighed. "You know that, when people divorce, usually there are lawyers involved. Let me consult my lawyer about this. Maybe you shouldn't say anything yet. For now, we continue as usual. You're here with me, and I'll drive you to Riviera View on the weekend. I might have to drop you off at your grandparents' house, though." He didn't want to mention the restraining order.

Max nodded.

"We didn't really talk about this, Max. About Anne."

"You call her Jane," Max said.

Hearing it from Max's lips, Finn's heart made a somersault.

He huffed a chuckled breath. "I call her Jane. I've known her as Jane for many years. I can call her Anne, too—it's her middle name—but she's ... Jane to me."

"What do you want to know, Dad?" Max asked.

"If you're okay with me dating Jane." He wanted to say *being with Jane*, but *dating* was a term that would make it all sound daily, not like his life depended on his son's reply.

"When Mom came to Grandma's on Thanksgiving and shouted about it, I didn't know what to think. But I thought about it since, and I like Anne. She's a nice person." Max shrugged. "I don't mind if you date her."

"It's not too weird for you?"

Max pursed his lips, creased his chin, and shook his head. "Not really." He shrugged again.

"It makes me so happy to hear you say that." *Happy?* He would have died if the answer had been different, and what he felt now was beyond joy. It was as if Max had just reached in and placed his heart back in its place.

He hugged his son. Then, leaning back, he added, "You might be hearing a lot of things about me, about Jane, about your living arrangements, about the future and the past. I *need* you to know that any question you have, any doubt you have, you can come to me, and I'll tell you the truth." He meant it, even if it meant the truth about their past, though he hoped Avery wouldn't stoop to spreading the affair lie to their son so he wouldn't have to relay the real story to a twelve-year-old.

"Dad?"

"Yeah?"

"I love you."

"I love you, too." He hugged him again.

"Dad?" Max said from within his embrace.

"Yeah?" He pulled himself back so he could see his son's face.

"Can we have pizza for dinner?"

He laughed. "You got it!"

~~~~~~~~~~~~~~~

"She upped her game. This is getting dangerous. Courts tend to take these things very seriously. If you had a witness there who saw you yelling at her—"

"I raised my voice. I didn't yell. In fact, her neighbor might tell you that I *didn't* threaten her."

"We can't rely on that." His lawyer sounded metallic over the car's speaker. It fit the taste in Finn's mouth. "Here's what we're going to do. You keep that restraining order; don't go anywhere near her. Drop your son and pick him up at his grandparents' after you call to make sure she's not coming out of the house, and you park at a distance, you hear? We're not taking any chances here."

"I can do that." He stared at the beach that stretched from side to side in front of him. He drove there to breathe after dropping Max off at school.

"I'll try to get an earlier date for the hearing, before Christmas, but I can't promise anything."

"Max is supposed to be with me for Christmas. We're supposed to visit my mother in Florida for part of the time."

"She contested that in her filing. You can't take him out of state. You might have to let her have him for Christmas. And, right now, we don't want to get into that when we have Max's physical custody at risk. We pick our battles."

Finn closed his eyes and released a slow breath.

"Lastly, I suggest you refrain from seeing her cousin until I give you the green light. Her claims of an affair with a family member, along with the threat accusations, aren't working in your favor."

He opened his eyes at once. "Aren't we playing right into her hands?"

"You want main custody, you want your son to continue living with you, that's your end goal. Show you're squeaky clean. Stay away from her for the time being."

"How long?"

"However long it takes."

For the second time in his life, Finn felt that his single mistake from a long time ago had cost him his heart.

Chapter 19

On the second week after Thanksgiving, the decrease in special orders wasn't just her imagination. It was especially noticeable because it was close to Christmas. She had imagined all kinds of scenarios where her family would be hurt by her and Finn, but she had never considered this sort of impact. Luckily, they were able to absorb it, and they all silently expected this to blow off soon.

"Hey, Anne, something going on?" Amy Locke from The Mean Bean wiped a hand to remove the strands of bleach-blonde hair that fell into her eyes as they placed the packed food boxes in the back of her car.

"What do you mean?" she asked, her stomach plummeting because that question these days only brought bad news for her.

"I had three people call to ask if I decorate cakes for Christmas."

"Let me guess, Lucile Hays is one of them?"

"And her bridge friends. Told them I don't offer those. I buy them per need from you." Amy's hoarse chuckle ended in a cough.

"Well, you know what's going on, Amy." Anne straightened up after depositing the last box inside.

Amy Locke was nice in the chatty sort of way, and a good customer of their baked goods, but as a café owner on Ocean Avenue, she heard everything worth repeating in town, and therefore, she probably had the answer to her own question.

"Yeah, that's not true, though, right?" Amy said, verifying Anne's assumption.

"Right." She slammed the trunk shut and turned around.

"I've always wanted to put something in her salad," Amy said, chuckling. "Did you notice that the prunes and prudes of this town are the same people?"

She laughed, too. Chatting with Amy was refreshing. These days, the bakery was mostly silent. Her father and Connie concentrated on work and looking for bakers. Since she didn't have as much work at the back, Anne helped out front more. Her mother, who was usually talkative, was quiet even while they hung the Christmas decorations and dressed the display windows in greens and reds. It was the first time that Linda and Darian didn't speak. It wasn't an official thing, but they couldn't talk much around the humongous elephant in the room, and any conversation on *that* topic could lead to an argument that they both weren't interested in. So, silence it was. No joint plans for Christmas, no excitement like her parents usually showed during this time of year.

Bella was busy packing and up to her nose in moving-related stuff, and Anne seriously considered Roni's offer, which Hope had repeated. It could be better than driving along the coast and imagining movie-montages-like what Finn was doing. Maybe if she met with people, like in a movie montage, time would condense and pass quickly.

She was surprised to find him waiting on her porch just two days after he had stopped by the bakery. Their calls since then had been brief, and he only said he was handling things and that he'd tell her. He must have come to update her. It was Thursday and, despite her warnings, she did hope they'd get to see each other over the weekend.

As soon as she was on the porch, he gathered her into his arms and pressed her to him. She kissed his lips.

"Is everything okay?" she asked when she saw the look in his eyes.

"Let's get inside."

Her heart hammered in her chest as she opened the lock and let them both in.

"Let's sit over here," he said, pulling her by the hand toward the couch. Just like all those years ago, he had her sit on it while he settled on the coffee table, facing her, holding both her hands.

"Finn, you're scaring me."

"I didn't want to tell you this over the phone. She has a restraining order against me."

"Oh my fucking God!" She squeezed his hands. "What? Why?"

"She submitted a custody order change and lied through her ass there. I went to talk to her, she refused to listen, and it turned into an argument. Next thing I know, I have two cops serving me a restraining order in my house."

"Oh, Finn. Oh my God, I'm so sorry," she expelled. "I knew she'd stoop low but I didn't realize just how low."

"That's not all."

"There's more?"

"I'm not allowed to take him out of the state, so no Florida, and probably no Christmas at all because she's contesting our entire arrangement and, with the restraining order, I don't have much leverage."

"Finn, no," she called, tears making their way from her throat to her eyes. How anyone could hurt him at his softest point, she couldn't even imagine. This shouldn't be happening. She knew the cost might be too much to bear. She had known it from the beginning, from the day that mirrored this one all those years ago.

"Max wants to live with me, so I hope that will count. My mother will fly in to spend the rest of the school break with us, so there's that, too. But that's not all, Jane."

She prepared herself.

"Apparently, my lawyer agrees with your father. He thinks we shouldn't meet until this whole thing is resolved. He doesn't know how long it will take because she seems happy to drag it out."

"Nothing is worth it if you lose Max, Finn. You and I won't work if this is the cost. Neither one of us could live with that. So, we'd better—"

He shook his head. "I need you to hold on, Jane. To wait with me until this is over. Because I'm not giving it up. I'm not letting her ruin Max, me, you. I won't let her. I spoke with Max, and he's fine with us being together, so this gives me hope. It might take time, but I need to know that you're waiting it out with me."

"You know that I am."

"I came here because I needed to hear it and see you when you say that."

"I'm saying it. Finn, I love you. I've never loved anyone else. Whichever way this turns out, I just want you to be happy. I always have."

He leaned closer. "I also came here because I needed my sunflower drug one more time before—"

He didn't finish the sentence because, with those words, he had already pulled her to straddle him and kissed her hard and deep, like a man preparing for a withdrawal.

He carried her to the bedroom, and they took it long and slow, hoarding love and touch to last them as long as necessary.

"I'd do it all a thousand times over just so I could have those moments with you," he said.

"*Now* who's talking like it's over?" She chuckled, though her heart felt like it was made of gravel.

She let the tears fall only after he had left.

~~~~~~~~~~~~~~~~

"What did you expect, Annie?" Linda asked when she told her parents.

"Not this!" Anne pushed the kitchen chair back, abruptly standing up. The sound it made was like fingernails on a blackboard. "I thought she'd at least want to spare her son."

"Maybe she thinks she is."

"I bet she does, and I bet your sister doesn't tell her that she's hijacking everyone's lives. Is Noah coming for Christmas, by the way, or is his mother still giving up on him and his kids for Avery's sake?"

"It's not like that, Janey. Family is complicated. Siblings are complicated. You don't know because you don't have any, and that's our fault."

"Mom, I love you, but are you real?"

"Annie, I'm just trying to see this from all sides, but I will always be on yours."

"Good to know!"

Linda stood up and hugged her. It took Anne a moment before she hugged her back.

"Finn doesn't deserve this, and neither do you," Linda said quietly, hanging on to Anne, and not letting her out of her embrace. "Divorces are ugly. I'm not justifying what she did, but the bigger the eruption, the more time it takes for the dust to settle, for the debris to be cleared."

Bert, usually calm and pleasant, looked like atypical steam was rising inside him. "I'm of a mind to march over there and give them all a piece of my mind," he said, getting out of his chair, too.

"No, Dad, it won't help right now. Let Finn handle this the legal way." Anne extricated herself from her mother's hug. She wrapped her arm around her father's back. "But thanks, Dad."

On her way home, she called Libby.

"I need your advice as a social worker. It's confidential. Can we meet?"

Libby bit her lip when they met for coffee at Life's A Beach an hour later. She inhaled, then spoke over a sigh. "A restraining order, that's not something to trifle with. These things are taken very seriously, especially in this county after … after that shooting in Wayford in the summer." A few months back, Libby's job had her involved in a custody dispute where a man held her and his ex-wife at gunpoint. "Though the cases are nothing alike, courts tend to go with *better safe than sorry*. He'd better do what his lawyer tells him."

"So, except for attending the hearing, there's nothing he can do about any of this?"

"I'm afraid not."

But *she* could.

~~~~~~~~~~~~~~~~

"You don't have a restraining order against me yet, right?" she asked as soon as Avery opened the door the next evening. A fresh wreath had been hung over it. "I'm here because you don't answer my calls."

"I'm not used to us calling each other, and I'm not interested in speaking to you now."

"Can I come in?"

"What do you want?"

"To tell you that I'm not in touch with Finn. You can lay off the threats, the restraining order, and let him spend Christmas with his son. Even here, in California." She looked to the side to check if any of the neighbors were out.

"So, you *are* in touch with him if you know all this."

"No, he just updated me and broke it off. Don't do this, Avery."

"Don't tell me how to handle my ex-husband and how to raise my son."

Ex? That was progress.

"I'm only giving you the relevant information," she said quietly, trying to keep the conversation's volume down. They had enough people in their business as it was. "This is what started all this, right? So, I'm telling you it ended."

"You'll say anything. You were always after what's mine."

"How? How was I always after what's yours? We hardly see each other, and I wasn't even here half the time. Avery, you and I both know that we never got along. But you know what? I ignored it. I never confronted you. You know why? Because of my parents. Beside me, you and your parents, and your brother and his wife and kids, are the only family they have. So, I kept the peace, and I never told them to stop calling us sisters when we obviously weren't. You and I are not my mom and yours. They wanted us to have what they have."

"How big of you."

"It's not big. It's family."

"Exactly. Family is off limits, so don't go for your family's ex. Leave my ex-husband alone."

Good thing she didn't say *sisters before misters*, or Anne would have broken down in much-needed laughter.

She took a deep breath. "I didn't *go* for him, Avery. Not intentionally. And like I said … it's not happening anymore. I won't put him, or Max, in this situation. I'm not with him. Although, as you said, he's your *ex*-husband."

"And whose fault is that?"

An Avery punch to the gut. She didn't know about their past, yet her method was to aim in all directions, and sometimes it hit just where it hurt the most.

Anne breathed out slowly and reminded herself that Avery's relationship wasn't her fault.

"You think you know him?" Avery continued. "I've handled that man like you never will."

"What do you want, Avery? You already won. There was no competition, yet you won it anyway. You had it all. You have a son with Finn. Don't ruin that by messing up your relationship with his dad and the relationship between them. Don't."

"I don't need you to explain family to me. Unlike you, Anne, I didn't live half my life across the country."

Jaw punch. One she couldn't even defend against without revealing the truth about why she moved.

"You're right." She gritted her teeth. She wanted to throttle her, but it was easier just letting her feel she had the upper hand. It was too late to change her, and it wasn't her job. The mold had been cast wrong, and now they would have to deal with her as best as they could and with as little damage to Max as possible. "You already know what to do, Avery. I'm just reminding you not to ruin it for your son."

Anne took another deep breath. "And I realize you're hurt. I'm sorry for that part." She looked at her cousin. A head shorter than her, Avery used to be much prettier, bubblier. But she was alone. She ruined every relationship she had ever had. Anne felt sorry for her. And if Avery had ever treated her as a real sister, she would have felt more guilt over being with Finn.

"Kill me if I understand what he found in all that holier than thou thing you have going." Avery waved a hand across Anne's features.

A whole lot of unholy positions, she wanted to retort but didn't. Maybe one day, when she wasn't there to try to get a restraining order removed.

"I know you love Max more than you hate me, so do the right thing, Avery."

The cool evening air was purifying as she walked away.

~~~~~~~~~~~~~~~

To ensure their Christmas wouldn't be a lonely one, she invited Bella and her gang to join her and her parents. Linda was ecstatic when she heard they were coming.

Anne wondered how she'd make it through the holiday knowing that Finn was an hour away, all alone. The vibrant red and green decorations in the shops and streets looked gray, the fairy lights on the trees pinched her eyes.

She did everything she usually did—work, food rounds—but she couldn't paint. She picked up a paintbrush and found herself standing there, holding it ten minutes later. Painting was usually the bandage that she swathed her heart in, but now it just sat there in her chest, bleeding freely.

She didn't dare risk Finn, so despite wanting to get in touch with him, even by a simple text message, just to know he was okay, she refrained from it.

She was boxing a specially ordered Christmas cake when her phone indicated she had a message. Reading it, color returned to her world.

"*Darian invited me to spend Christmas dinner with Max at theirs. Said you talked to Avery. She lifted the injunction for the duration of the holiday.*"

"*Best news I got in a long time!! You and Max deserve this.*"

"*I know you told Avery that we were over for this.*"

"*I'll do anything for you.*" Even leave you, she thought.

As if he read her mind, and maybe he did, he texted, "*You'll need a restraining order to keep me away from you, Jane. I can't live without my sunflower.*"

"*I miss you doesn't even come close,*" she texted back, quoting him from just a few weeks back.

Anne placed the phone down, closed the cake box, and began preparing a new one.

"I thought you finished with the orders," her mother said when she came into the back.

"I did, but I thought we could send a cake to Darian. Let her know we're thinking of them."

"That's a wonderful idea, Janey. Something Christmas-related."

"Oh, yes." She was so going to hell, but she didn't care anymore. Knowing that Finn would be not an hour, but five minutes away from her, and that they couldn't meet, was fresh hell anyway.

Chapter 20

The last thing Finn wanted was to spend an entire evening with Avery and her parents. There were so many internal circuits that he had to shut down to go through with this that he wondered if it wouldn't be best for everyone if he just dropped Max off and picked him up two days later, like they did on the weekends. His son was still living with him and that was all that mattered. However, Max wanted him to come, especially when he'd heard that Noah and his family weren't coming. He'd do anything for him, even go through this holiday that was so far from how he had hoped, planned, and dreamed of celebrating it. Besides, he didn't want his son to find himself alone in the same spot others had—cushioning Avery-related family situations.

He kept the holiday spirit for Max's sake. They had bought a tree and decorated it, and he had taken him Christmas shopping. He'd bought a present for Jane, one that he had wanted to buy her long ago. He'd give it to her, even if it meant she would get it in July.

"You still need to be very careful, as if the injunction is still in place," his lawyer had said. "Don't be dragged into arguments. It's volatile, and you still have a court hearing in January, so everything we talked about is valid, and I mean *everything*."

Finn had shaken his head as he listened. Even his cool, calculated lawyer had guessed how much he wanted to go see Jane.

He had helped Max pick out a present for Avery and had internally smiled to himself when Max hadn't offered they add his name to it, like they had done the year prior.

As he dressed for dinner and checked that Max didn't slack and put on his fancier clothes, Finn gathered all the focus he usually employed before important competitions so he could survive this evening.

Knowing that Jane would be so close yet so out of his reach again was killing him. Knowing that he would be sitting across a table from the woman who used their son to keep him away from Jane was almost more than he could bear.

The tension could be cut with a knife when he entered his ex-mother-in-law's house. He thought that somewhere he should feel bad for this, but he couldn't bring himself to feel guilt over loving Jane or for going after his heart. His main worry was that Max would blame him, but he didn't.

He didn't exchange more than two words with Avery and didn't return her glares.

He felt sorry for Max. Not just because of the situation, but because none of the adults felt like talking to each other, so they all just spoke to Max. And his boy did his best to provide more than two-word answers to questions like "How's school?" that were asked at least three times.

When it was finally dessert time, Darian got up and remained standing in front of her seat. "I have something special that my sister sent for the holiday. I know things haven't been easy, but I'd like to hope that, next year, all this awkwardness will be long forgotten and we can all celebrate together again." Darian took a few steps toward the kitchen then stopped and looked at her daughter. "Linda promised me that Connie made this cake."

Max seemed excited about the promise of cake and was chatting to Fernando.

"It's very Christmas-y and so unique," Darian announced, carrying a round tray back into the dining room.

Sudden warmth exploded in Finn's heart. This was no Christmas-themed cake, though the writing around it read, "It was on a starry night." The swirling blues, yellows, and whites he knew so well were all there, painted on sugar paste. He could practically feel his tattoo throbbing on his left arm.

This was the baking equivalent of his November eleventh cards to her. His Jane.

He was probably the only one who noticed that the painted crescent moon was waxing, not waning.

Finn raised his eyes. Max was looking at him. He then moved his eyes to Finn's arm, where his tattoo was covered by the long sleeves of his buttoned-down shirt.

"Connie can't paint like that," Avery's voice suddenly came from somewhere; Finn couldn't even tell where. "This has Anne's signature all over it. Who draws such things on Christmas cakes? You'd think she'd do something in greens and reds, a

Christmas tree, snow—something. No, she has to put art on everything." She didn't seem to notice or remember that a piece of that art was tattooed on her ex-husband's arm. Finn wasn't surprised.

"Avery, it's a very nice cake and a nice gesture," Fernando said. "We can appreciate the effort that went into it."

Finn thought of the heart, love, effort, and talent that went into this message that Jane had conveyed to him. She wanted him to know that he wasn't alone in all this, and that she was thinking of him. Just like his cards were a piece of his heart, this was a piece of hers.

He watched as Darian cut it and served each a piece.

Four adults ate their cake and chatted as they did. One child didn't touch hers. She pushed the plate away from her.

"I'll be going soon, Max," Finn half-whispered to his son when their plates were empty. "I'll come back for you the day after tomorrow, okay?"

"Can I go home with you?"

"You have to stay here, but I'll be back soon. And you know I'm working on this." They kept their voices low so that Darian, who had moved between them to collect the plates, wouldn't hear.

"Avery, you're sure you don't want yours?" she asked.

"Give it to Finn. I'm sure he would love to get all her leftovers."

"Avery!" both Fernando and Darian chided in chorus.

"They broke up, Avery. Now we need to move on. Everybody can make a mistake," Darian added to her in an audible whisper.

A mistake? Every cell in Finn's body seethed. *A mistake*, she'd called him and Jane. He stifled the urge to yell that the only mistake he'd made was fourteen years ago. But his son was there, and Jane had lied for his sake. Finn pushed his chair back and got up. "Yes, pack the leftovers for me. Thanks, Darian. Max, I'll pick you up the day after tomorrow from this house."

"Dad, I wanna go with you."

He put his hand on Max's shoulder. "Day after tomorrow."

Max got out of his chair so abruptly that it fell back in a loud thud. "It's all your fault!" he yelled, looking at Avery. "No one wants to come here. Uncle Noah, Aunt Jill, and Grandma Linda and Bert, and Anne. I don't want to come here anymore either. And I don't want to go to your house! You ruin everything!"

"Max!" Avery called, her face flushing.

"Maxi," Darian whimpered.

Finn tried to catch him, but Max turned back and bolted out of the room. They heard the back door slamming. He had gone out to the backyard.

"Avery, really, you have to be careful in front of the child," Fernando said. "Any issue you have with his father—"

"Thanks for the invitation, Darian. I have to go talk to Max," Finn said.

Avery stood up. "You're not taking him anywhere."

"Let him stay here, in this house, then," he said.

"I decide what I do with him when I have him."

He looked at her. Pity and contempt. She didn't need a restraining order. He didn't want to be anywhere near her anyway.

"Is it worth it, Avery?" He watched her. "Look around you. Look at your parents, at your son. Are you trying to have a one-up on me? On your cousin? On your brother? Who?"

"*This*," she said, pointing back in the general direction of the backyard. "Don't put this on me. You think you can have your cake and eat it, too." She gestured with her chin toward the half-cut cake on the table, as if anyone could miss the irony. "It doesn't work like that."

"We'll see about that," he said, nodded to her parents, and left the dining room.

"Max." He thumped himself down next to his son on the porch swing. "It's cold out here. Let's go back inside. Your grandma and grandpa want to see you're okay, and I'm sure your mom does, too." If it wasn't for his lawyer's warning, he'd take his kid and fly to Florida right now, only stopping to pick up Jane on the way.

Max looked at him. His blue eyes and light brown hair were so much like his own.

"And I promise that this will all be okay. I'm doing *everything* to make sure of it. You hear me?" He had given up Jane for this. He couldn't see what more he could give up on. "Grandma Marie will come after the holiday, and we'll spend time with her. Disneyland, Six Flags—you choose. And … I'm working on fixing everything else."

"Can I come to the airport with you to pick Grandma up?"

"Sure." He leaned over and kissed his son's head.

Chapter 21

Thanks for the cake card. I needed it. Sorry about this one; it's all I could find.

I can't wait to hold you, kiss you, feel you, lick you, and I ran out of place to say what else.

I love you.

Finn.

Anne stood on the porch, holding the slightly crumpled auto body shop receipt on the back of which Finn had written in blue pen the note that he had slipped into her mailbox. It had been peeking out of the box so she could find it when she got home after staying late with Bella and her family at her parents.

How long could this go on? She ached, knowing he had stopped by her house.

She went inside and retrieved the small, wicker box from her bedroom closet and took out the birthday cards she had received from Finn over the years. Adding the love letter receipt, Anne wished she hadn't thrown away the note that Finn had shoved into her hand on his wedding day. But hindsight was always twenty-twenty. Back then, she hadn't imagined she would get to love him again one day.

Yet, just like then, they weren't free to be together.

She went back to work the day after Christmas with a movie montage playing in her head as she tried to imagine how things were for Finn. In her imagination, he and Max had a much-deserved good time with Marie. One day, soon, she hoped to be part of his life, an integral part, not a part that should be hidden.

It might have been the holiday spirit, but fewer people of those who had looked at her as a homewrecker just two weeks prior gave her the same look now.

She was working with Linda on the bakery's New Year's offerings when Bert came in through the back door, carrying a logoed bag from Sarah's pharmacy.

"You went to the pharmacy like that?" Linda asked, skimming her gaze over his flour-covered clothes and dusty orange crocs.

"Yes. I needed eye drops. We ran out." Though they ensured to minimize flour dust, Bert suffered from itchy eyes syndrome. "But forget that. Listen to this; I ran into Darian and Avery."

"Oh, no." Anne pivoted toward him.

"No, no, Annie, it was about time someone spoke their minds to that woman."

"Dad, I tried talking to her. She'll just issue a restraining order against you, too."

"She can try." He then looked at Linda. "Your sister is getting fed up with her daughter. Finally. Before Avery came in, Dar and I were there alone. Well, except for Sarah, of course, but she always knows how to keep herself busy. Darian told me that Max made a scene on Christmas eve and yelled at his mother. He insisted on staying at Darian's instead of going to Avery's, and she had to beg him to talk to her later."

"Did Darian say anything about Finn?" Anne asked with a racing heart. If there was a scene there … Everything was falling apart—the family, Max, him, her.

"Wait, Annie," Bert said when he noticed the expression on her face. "She didn't say anything about him. I think Max had it out with his mother. She did tell me that Finn, Max, and Marie are visiting Noah and Jill, and that this really got her thinking."

Anne bit her lip. Her heart went out to this man of hers, the man she couldn't wait to make hers again. *However long it takes*.

"I told her that *that* was an example of how you treat family and that it was about time they did something about Avery," Bert went on. "Then you know what Sarah did?" He looked at Linda as he said that. "She told Darian that holding a grudge and all this tension wasn't good for her blood pressure. And you know how seriously Darian takes every word a medical professional says." Bert chuckled. "Then Avery walked in, and Sarah locked the pharmacy. Closed the door right in the face of two women who wanted to go in, told them she was taking her lunch break." Bert chuckled. "She locked the three of us there. Maybe she was afraid there'd be a scene." Bert did a dramatic pause and looked at them.

"And …? Come on, Bert," Linda said.

Anne was thankful for that nudge because her own pulse raised with every passing minute.

"So, I told her, I told Avery, 'Listen, Avery, it was strange for us, too, for all of us, but we all came to accept it. Even your parents.'" He looked at Anne and added, "Sorry, Janey, it's true. It was a peculiar idea for us to get used to—you and Finn. But we got used to it, and we want you both to be happy, and if you're happy together, then that's what we want." He pressed his lips together and placed the pharmacy bag on a shelf. "I took a guess when I said her parents accepted it, but Darian didn't say a word."

"And, Dad, what happened then?" She was keyed up for a bad ending, though surely, her father wouldn't look so pleased with himself if it had been one.

"I gave them such a speech," Bert said, tilting his head and nodding as if saying *you missed a great spectacle*. "I told them that I'm talking to them as a parent to a parent. I said this especially for Avery, that we all want our kids to be happy, including me, and that this craziness wasn't making anyone happy, especially not Max. When I said that, Avery gave her mother such a look! She could tell that Darian told me about Christmas." He chuckled at his own doing. "I told Avery, 'You could have had a wonderful sister in my Annie. It's okay if you're not friends, but don't hurt her.'"

Anne sighed. "Oh, Dad." She hugged him. The dust from his clothes mixed with the dust on her apron, raising a little cloud.

"You see? Sometimes it's good I stick my nose into all kinds of business."

She chuckled. "Well, I don't know. We'll have to see. Did Avery say anything at all?"

"Not much. I think Max did a number on her. Sometimes children should tell their parents things as they are." He winked.

~~~~~~~~~~~~~~~~

"Don't ask how I know this," Libby began as soon as Anne picked up her call, "but there's a motion to lift Finn's restraining order and an updated request was submitted to the court."

Anne pressed the phone to her ear. She had taken the call outside the bakery's back door, but the increasing New Year's afternoon bustle from Ocean Avenue reached there, too.

"So, could this mean that Avery is backing out on this?"

"It could mean that. I couldn't get further details, but canceling the restraining order altogether is a good sign. I thought you'd want to know."

"I do. Thank you so much, Libby! I really appreciate this." Some people were just there when you needed them, she thought. Some people knew how to be a friend. She hoped she knew how to be a friend. Her early experiences hadn't helped her feel confident in that field, and it had taken time to open herself up. If she had met Libby earlier on, maybe they could have been friends. But then her parents buying Connie's bakery could have felt even stranger than it had.

"You're welcome. Let me know if I can help with anything," Libby said.

"Do you think Finn knows?"

"It just came in today. Even if he does, he'd have to respond to it, and only the court can finalize any change or update. Until then, things still stand as they are now."

This meant she still couldn't get in touch with him. And knowing Avery's volatility, she didn't want to sabotage this positive direction.

After finishing the last round of this year's food project, she returned to help at the shop. They closed late, needing the business of those who entered to buy things for New Year's Eve parties.

She wanted to head home before the celebrations on Ocean Avenue began. Despite the good news, things were still up in the air, and she didn't feel celebratory. The colorful string lights from one side of the street to the other, the general good spirits, and the Happy New Year greetings that filled the air in the bakeshop and on the street made her feel like going home, drinking a glass of bubbly alone, and maybe paint, if she could find it in herself. Bella was away with her family, getting the new house ready. And really, there was only one person she wanted to be with tonight—Finn. She didn't even know if he was back home from visiting.

As she made her way from the bakery to her house by foot, the coffee shops, the beach restaurants, and the streets were buzzing with people. She bumped against two men whom she imagined for a second were Finn, but they didn't have his height, his feel. It was just her imagination playing wicked games on her. What if he were here? What if she could kiss him now, under these fireworks that began tearing the sky in color and light, yielding excited cries from spectators?

What if he was waiting on her porch like he had done in the past, or making his way toward her from among the crowd and he would lift her and swirl her around like in the movies?

But life wasn't a movie.

A text lit up her screen when she reached her street.

"*He will hear about it from his lawyer,*" Avery wrote.

Her heart halted, and then her legs did. "*What do you mean?*"

"*I love my son more than I hate you.*"

She was about to type a reply when another message came in.

"*Don't compliment yourself, by the way. I don't hate you. I'm indifferent to you. That's why I'm texting you. You can have him and choke on him, too.*"

She knew the pattern. Avery finally did the right thing, but now she was baiting her so she could blame her later.

"*Happy New Year, Avery,*" she texted.

When no reply came, she texted Finn and tried to call, but he didn't pick up.

Instead of going home, she crossed town again to get to her car that she had left behind the bakery. The streets were even more condensed now, but the music, and light, and the happy faces she passed by found an echo inside her.

It took her almost an hour to get out of Riviera View. Ocean Avenue was closed for traffic, and the beach promenade was congested. A torchlight parade made its way down to the beach.

The highway was relatively empty. Anne drove along the coastline. It was a dryer, warmer December. The scattered raindrops on her windshield were like tears. Happy ones, she hoped. The wipers drove them away but they kept falling.

Blueshore seemed sleepy in comparison to Riviera View. Lights and music spilled from houses and into the otherwise quiet streets, and the town center didn't seem as busy.

With guarded hope in her heart, she parked outside his house. The drizzle of rain stopped.

One window was lit—the living room—but no one answered when she knocked. She tried again. Maybe he wasn't back yet. She couldn't see his car anywhere.

She was about to turn away when Marie opened the door.

"Oh. Jane, is it?"

"Yes."

"I haven't seen you in so many years. We never seemed to attend the same family gatherings. I think it was a wedding. Or a funeral? Anyway, it was years ago."

Anne smiled. "Yes, many years."

"Finn told me everything. I'm sorry things turned so bitter. I hope you can work it out with your family, for Finn's sake, for Max's sake. You know, back then, I thought—if I couldn't give him a family—because it was just him and I—maybe Avery's family could be his family. I didn't know about you. In a way, that family was his family, but not the way it could have been. I hope you can still sort it out." Marie leaned against the doorframe, looking lost in her own thoughts.

"Is he here?" Anne asked.

Marie seemed to snap out of some internal reverie and realize they were standing at the door and that it was cold. "He's not. I'm sorry." She ran a hand through her short, coiffed hair that was dyed the color it had been originally—Finn's dark blond or light brown. "Would you like to come in? Max and I were watching TV, but I guess we both fell asleep. We just got back today."

"That's okay. Can you tell me where he is?"

"Where *can* my son be?"

Anne looked at her. "The pool?" She dropped her gaze to her cellphone. Almost eleven p.m.

"The pool," Marie confirmed. She then smiled. "Always the pool for that kid."

"Thanks, Marie." Anne patted the woman's forearm. "Happy New Year." She then rushed to her car, hearing Marie call, "Happy New Year," after her.

She didn't know where the pool was, but Google Maps led her there.

The parking lot was almost empty. There was only one car there. Her heart melted, as if she had seen Finn himself.

Silence draped the large building, and only the distant sound and blaze of fireworks from the far beach reminded her that it was New Year's Eve.

Even in the cold night air, she could smell the familiar pool smell as she neared the entrance.

She climbed the few stairs and pulled open the heavy metal door. A wave of heat, humidity, and chlorine hit her. And the sound of rippling water echoing in the large, empty space. It was fully lit, the lights shimmering on the blue, sparkling surface.

She went inside.

He was swimming. Of course he was. He had just begun a new twenty-five-yard freestyle lap. He couldn't hear or see her come in. The noise of the water and his concentration kept her arrival a surprise. His body was fully immersed in the water, every muscle working, straining.

He was naked.

She noticed his clothes, car keys, and cellphone in a heap on one of the benches next to a white towel.

Circling the pool, she went to the other end, the one he was aiming for. She removed her jacket and crouched. The water was warm when she dipped her fingers in it.

She watched him. Here it was—the resilience of the human body, this beautiful human body, and she knew the resilient, beautiful heart that resided inside it.

Her own heart flooded with love.

He touched the pool's wall and was about to turn, his head completely underwater, when he noticed her.

Anne smiled when Finn emerged, panting, looking at her with surprise, water dripping from his hair, his face, and his corded shoulders.

"Jane." A surprised smile lit up his features. He ran both hands up his face to drive the water away, ruffling his hair. Standing in the pool, he was tall enough for it to reach just beneath his pecs. "Baby," he said, lifting himself a bit, his abs against the pool's edge, so he could reach her. He cupped her face.

She leaned forward but steadied herself on the tips of her feet.

A wet kiss. His warm mouth. Strong palms that Anne placed her dry ones on top of.

"You didn't even ask why I'm here," she said, chuckling when they broke their kiss. He still cupped her face and leaned his forehead against hers. Water dripped from his chest and shoulders and onto her bent knees, pooling at her feet. His forearms wet her shirt, and his touch wet her everywhere else as she thought of his naked body still in the water.

"I just know you're here," he graveled.

"I tried calling. Have you seen any texts or calls today?"

"Not in the last few hours." He seemed fully engrossed by her presence. "Another year begins, and I just … came here."

She shifted her head back a bit so she could look at him. "Avery submitted a request to lift your restraining order and an update to her court filing. I don't know what the filing says, but she texted to tell me that … basically, she's not going to act against you because of me."

"Are you sure?" He suddenly seemed fully alert.

"As much as one can be sure with Avery. I'll get your phone."

"No. Wait." He moved his hands to grasp her forearms and stop her from going. "If it's not the good news you think it is, then let me have this. Let's have this moment at least."

"I don't want to go through another year without you, Finn."

"Then you won't."

He caught her by her waist and pulled her toward him, half-lifting her.

"Finn!" she managed to call out, her voice echoing in the large space, before the echo of the splash she made followed. She was submerged up to her chest in the warm water, fully clothed, wrapped in Finn's arms.

"Oh my God, Finn!" She laughed. Her back was against the pool's wall and Finn's mouth was already on her neck.

"That's how I love you, sunflower," he whispered into her ear. "All wet."

He pressed himself further into her, catching her mouth in a deep kiss. He was already hard under the water even before their kiss became fevered, which it soon did.

It wasn't easy to remove soaking wet winter clothes, but they managed it together, kissing and licking slick, wet skin. The water made her light as she wrapped her legs around him, leaning against the pool's wall, as Finn pushed into her.

She wasn't afraid anyone would walk in on them and wasn't aware of the fireworks that exploded in the sky far above them. All she could feel was Finn's hard, wet body against hers, inside her.

"Harder," she breathed into his neck as he thrust into her. She needed to feel him even more than usual. He slipped his arm under her knee and lifted her leg higher, granting himself better access and leverage, and the moans this drew out of her reverberated around them.

"I missed hearing you come," he groaned. "Let it all out. Come for me, Jane."

And she did, making him come right after and pulsate into her clenching walls.

"Damn," he hissed, his face resting against hers, as her head lulled back on the edge.

They breathed together, the water lapping against their naked and still-entwined bodies.

Only then did the sounds of multiple explosions reach her. The main show.

"Fireworks," she said, still trying to catch her breath. "It must be midnight." She couldn't think of a better way to start the new year.

Finn tilted his head back a bit, and their gazes linked. He took her hand and put it on his chest. "I have all the fireworks I need right here. Happy New Year, my love."

"Happy New Year, Finn," she returned, lifting her head to meet him in a kiss.

~~~~~~~~~~~~~~~

"Are you sure no one will walk in?" she asked when they climbed out of the pool, fully naked.

"Too late to ask about that, but I'm sure." Finn chuckled. He helped her collect her wet clothes and shoes from the floor, where they landed when he had thrown them out.

"Take this." He handed her the large towel.

She wrapped herself in it and sat on the bench.

Finn put on his clothes, straight on his dripping skin. "Used to it," he said with a smile when she looked at him.

"To having sex in the pool?"

He laughed. "No. To put my clothes back on without toweling off." He then sat on the bench next to her. "That was actually my first time."

She pivoted toward him all at once. "You don't have to lie for my benefit, Finn Brennen." She chuckled.

"No, seriously. I sometimes swim naked when there's no one around, but I've never had sex in the pool before. Who would I have it with?"

She pressed her lips together and raised her eyebrows in a *I'm-impressed* expression. "Not even in college?"

"Especially not in college. We were always practicing, everyone together, not a moment to lose. It was all about breaking records, making times, getting to the next level."

"Oh, wow! I'm … honored to be your first."

"Wouldn't want it to be anyone else."

His phone was on the bench behind her. She handed it to him. "Do you want to check?"

Finn nodded once, inhaled deeply, then took it from her.

She watched as he swiped and read over a few messages. Her heart thumped in anticipation. She wiped her wet face and absorbed the droplets from her hair as she nervously waited for his update.

Finn raised his gaze from the device and looked at her. He then smiled wide. "My lawyer texted, too. Three hours ago. Said I'll pay double for having him work on New Year's Eve."

"What else did he say?"

"She motioned for mediation instead of battling this. And the best thing—she withdrew her request to change Max's physical custody. He can continue living with me. She just wants mediation to ensure she can have him not just on weekends, as if this wasn't the case until now anyway."

"Oh, Finn! I'm so relieved! And happy!" She hugged him, and he enveloped her in his arms, rubbing his palms on her towel-covered back.

"*Now* I can start the new year, with you," he said into her neck.

Finn scooped her up and sat her on his lap, circling his arms around her.

She raked her fingers through his wet hair. "I'm sorry Max had to go through this. We heard from Darian that they had an argument on Christmas."

"Yeah. It was rough, but she brought it on herself. I only wish she didn't bring it on him, too. It was good we had plans right after. Max was so happy these last few days. And he loved visiting Noah and Jill."

"Yeah, I heard you took him to see them. That was so good of you."

He locked his eyes on her. "Because I want a family, Jane, and I want it with you."

"I want it all, too."

He kissed her. They both smelled of chlorine now.

"We should start working on one soon," he half-whispered against her lips.

She smiled, still not grasping this happiness. "Don't you think we should take it slow?"

"Slower than fourteen years?"

Chapter 22

"These robots will have to work harder tonight," Finn said as he activated the pool's cleaning system. "I'll let it run all night. And let's get you into dry clothes. I always have something in my locker."

"Quite a boutique you're running here." Jane peeked into the locker in his office at the back. She grabbed a pair of gray sweats, a hoodie, and his sneakers. She drowned in his garments and laughed as she put them on.

Her laughter. He fucking missed seeing her like this—unencumbered.

He wrapped an arm around her, squeezed her to him, and kissed the crown of her head. She smelled like him now—chlorine instead of citrus.

"Sorry about your clothes," he said, lifting the bag that he had shoved them into.

"Are you kidding? It was so worth it."

Everything was worth it. Everything was worth reaching this night, this hour, this minute with her. He didn't want to look back at all the regrets that had led them here, promising himself to only look forward. They still had hurdles and hoops to jump through, but they had each other.

"Texted my mother. She'll probably only see it in the morning. Told her I'll be at yours and be back to drive her to the airport tomorrow night," he said when Jane stepped back into the office after a quick stop in the bathroom.

They drove to Riviera View in his car.

This was the best beginning of a new year that he'd ever had. In Jane's little house, with her in the shower, then holding her in bed with candles lighting the room.

He sat up, leaning against the headboard. She was curled up against him. Holding both sides of her chin, Finn lifted her face to his. "Jane, I meant what I said before. I don't want to waste time. Marry me."

She exhaled and smiled. Her beautiful almond eyes smiled. "You know I want to. So much! Shouldn't we ensure everything is settled between you and Avery regarding Max first? And give Max a chance to get used to this?"

"Are you saying yes?"

"Of course I am!"

"That's all I need to know. Leave the rest to me." He placed a kiss on her lips.

When they had gotten back and taken their clothes off, he had made sure to leave his jeans close to the bed. Now he stretched and retrieved something from the tiny watch pocket. "This is something I bought you for Christmas. I knew I couldn't give it to you then, but I had to buy it for my own sanity, to have something to look forward to."

"Oh, no. I didn't buy you anything," she mumbled, and this almost made him laugh.

"It was wrapped, but I wanted to carry it with me everywhere, so I took it out of its box. I hope it's okay."

He opened his palm.

Her breath visibly caught as her gaze fell on the starry round diamond on the white gold ring. When the salesman had asked which color of gold he'd wanted, he didn't even have to think. "*White gold*."

He watched her. He wanted to register the way she looked now to his memory. She moved her glance to his face and fixed her eyes on him.

"Let's make it official. Will you marry me, Jane Anne Sunflower Trumpet Player Tutor Painter Cake Decorator Who Owns My Heart Drecher?"

"Abso-fucking-lutely, Finn Brennen."

He breathed out a relieved chuckle. "That's my Jane! Delicate fingers and a beautiful, dirty mouth." He slid the ring onto her finger. "I bought the smallest size." He kissed her ringed finger.

She took his hand in hers, caressed his knuckles, then kissed the scar on his ring finger. She then placed a kiss on the left side of his chest before she kissed his lips.

He could taste her tears.

"No crying, Anne."

She smiled at the name. "I love you doesn't even come close."

Nothing did, but he had to stop those tears that filled her eyes.

"You know what song they'll be playing at our wedding, right?" he asked.

She laughed through the tears. "I need to learn the Fandango?"

"And cartwheels."

When they made love on the bed later, Finn stilled and brought their entwined hands between them. He kissed her hand with the ring that gleamed through their interweaved fingers without taking his eyes from Jane's. He then kissed her lips and buried himself deeper inside her.

Chapter 23

On January first, she took Finn to her parents' to share their news. Bert and Linda were excited, each in their own way.

"Well, son, I've always wanted someone like you for my Anne," Bert said, tapping his palm on Finn's shoulder. "I never thought I'd get the actual you."

Finn's short, husky laughter told Anne that he was enjoying the irony.

"I'm happy for you both. I'm happy for me and Bert," her mother said. "The rest will … the rest will be okay. When do you plan on getting married?"

"As soon as possible," Finn said. "Jane wants to ensure everything's airtight regarding Max, and after everything that's happened, I can't argue with that."

Anne smiled to herself. *"I'd take you to Las Vegas right now if you let me,"* he had said the night before.

"You call her Jane," Linda said, her smile wide and warm.

Anne chuckled. "That's all you heard from what he said, Mom?"

"I heard it all. And I know what you want to say next, and I agree with you, Janey. We won't announce it until you confirm the legal part is completed," Linda said.

They told his mother later that day, and she hugged them both. "I just want you to finally be happy, Finn."

"I am. You have no idea how much."

Finn asked Marie to keep it to herself. Not trusting Avery, he couldn't tell Max and burden him with keeping it a secret until the court finalized everything.

Finn had the mediation session with Avery later that month, and the court verified their agreement soon after. With everything legally sealed, he sat Max down for a talk, while Anne let her parents decide if, and when, and how to tell her aunt and uncle.

"How did it go?" she asked Finn later.

"Word for word, this is what he said, 'I told you, Dad; I like her. I prefer her over some other lady I don't know. Or someone who's a mom from my school, like those two kids I know whose parents got married and now they have to live together.' Then he asked if he'd have to wear a tuxedo when we get married."

"The kid has his priorities right."

"Avery guessed, you know. I didn't say anything, but she hissed something about how she never believed you and that we deserve each other."

"We do. Sometimes she gets it right." She laughed.

Anne wore the ring. While she wasn't going to confirm, announce, or flaunt it in anyone's face, she wasn't going to hide it to please anyone either. Just like years ago, when she had stopped wearing flats just so that shorter men, like Tom, would feel comfortable with her towering above them, now she was done with peace-keeping just for peace's sake. Not at all costs. Not when it hid this much toxicity behind it. She had done enough of that. It was time others shouldered the burden or learned to deal with it.

Her worst fears regarding Finn were over—Avery couldn't threaten or take Max from him anymore, and Max himself seemed to accept her as his dad's fiancée. The only other fear she'd had was her family falling apart, and in a way, it did.

Her mother and Darian weren't back to their normal connection. No joint Sunday lunches, no daily calls. If they spoke, it was mundane chit-chat that was reduced to the weather. In their usual pattern, they continued to avoid conflict, though it sat there and fermented. They would have to deal with it one day, Anne knew.

She felt bad for her mother, but she was done with getting herself into the midst of it and feeling guilty. She couldn't avoid some guilt, though. After all, she'd been trained in it all her life, but guilt wasn't the same as remorse, and she could live with it.

She came over for dinner with Max one evening. All this time, she and Finn spent only the weekends together after he had dropped Max off at Avery's. They had years of catching up to do outside of bed, too—going away together, eating out, market days, strolling the beach.

"Hey, Max." She gave him a careful smile. If this was strange for her, how strange would it be for a kid, she couldn't imagine. "I hope it's okay that I'm joining you for dinner."

"Yeah," Max said with a shy smile. "But should I call you Anne or Jane now?"

She chuckled. Of all the questions she thought he might ask her, that wasn't one she would have guessed.

"Whichever one you choose. The people closest to me call me by both names."

"Maybe that's what I'll do, because my dad calls you Jane, and I know you as Anne. Don't you get confused?"

"No." She smiled. "I'm used to it. And people can be more than one thing. I'm a painter, but I also decorate cakes. Here, I brought one." She pointed at the box that she had left on Finn's kitchen table." She decided to put the cards on the table, and added, "And I'm your cousin once removed but also your dad's fiancée. Is that weird for you?" She scrunched her nose, letting him know that she'd understand if it was.

Max looked like he was pondering her question. "All families are weird."

"That's true." She chuckled. This kid surprised her every time.

She felt Finn's eyes on them and looked over at him.

He closed his lids for a moment and smiled with an expression that told her that his heart was full.

She didn't spend the night that time.

When Finn walked her to her car, he hugged her and leaned her against the car's closed door. "Am I two things, too?" he rasped against her skin.

"Let's see. You're the love of my life but also my cousin's ex. Oh, and a swim coach and my red-hot sex?"

He laughed. "You better believe it," he then graveled before kissing her in a way that was bound to leave them both all worked up.

For too long, they had been two separate things to each other. Now they were one with each other and, in time, she hoped everything else would merge.

After another joint dinner, and another, she stayed the night. The hardest part was keeping it quiet and inside the bedroom.

It was late February, and they had decided on a late April wedding. A small one, just close family and friends. They were well aware that the term *close family* was still undefined in her case. All they needed was each other and Max, anyway.

"How about if we make a baby now?" Finn whispered that night. She was still straddling him as he leaned against the headboard, their breaths were not even fully regained yet. "Let's add fuel to this family fire. Show up pregnant at our wedding."

"Marrying a pregnant woman once wasn't enough for you?" she teased, brushing her lips over his. She had told him about the IUI before, to which he had responded, "All we need now is I, you, and I."

"I want to do everything for the first time with you. And I never have enough of you."

She had her IUD removed a few days after, agreeing to let nature take its course, which she hoped would be a quick one.

~~~~~~~~~~~~~~~~~

"I went over to talk to my sister, to invite her to the wedding. She said she came to accept this, but they didn't know if they'd attend," Linda said over Sunday lunch with Anne and Finn.

"Which is basically saying that they won't," Anne said. "I'm sorry, Mom, I know it saddens you, but there's nothing I can do about it. I don't want anyone there who isn't genuinely happy for us. And I understand Darian, to some extent."

"Linda," Bert put his fork down and turned toward his wife. "Let's face it. Things won't be the same. They will be different—holidays, birthdays, everything. Your niece will never voluntarily be in the same room with Anne and Finn as a couple. And she'll make it hard for her parents to do so, too. So, unless they tell her to stick it, this is how it's going to be. It's their choice. They're the ones who lose, not us. And Avery will have to face this—when Max graduates, when he gets married. Right, Finn?" He turned to Finn, who sat opposite him, next to Anne.

"Pretty much," Finn said. "Even his middle school graduation."

"Hopefully, by then, she'll find other things to be mad at the world about." Bert chuckled at his own joke. Then, with a serious expression, he turned to his wife again. "So, instead of the whole family gathering—which, by the way, didn't happen regardless because Avery fought with her brother— you and your sister will each have the holidays with your own kids. She with hers; you with yours. And we'll have Finn, and *we'll* have Max and *they'll* have Max. And I'm sure these two will bring us more Maxes. Right, kids?" He winked at them. "You'll still see your sister and spend time with her, Linda. And me and Fernando, we'll make sure all four of us get together. To be honest, it's even better like that."

"It's not all or nothing, Mom. I have come to realize that." Anne reached over the table and put her palm over Linda's.

"Your dad is wonderful," Finn said when they walked back to her house after lunch. "The kind I always wished I had."

"He already adopted you a long time ago." She smiled and leaned her head on his shoulder.

~~~~~~~~~~~~~~~~~

She spent at least two nights a week in Blueshore, letting Max adjust to the idea that she'd be moving in with them after the wedding. Max visited her house and even asked that she'd bring an easel and supplies to his house, which she did. He watched her finish a painting, and she let him take the picture that they uploaded together to her Etsy shop.

"You painted all these?" Max asked, looking around her living room.

"Yes."

"You also painted the one in my dad's room. It's the same style."

She smiled. "It's called Impressionism."

"I like the ones with the houses and the gardens. It's … relaxing," he said. "The colors are strong, but it still looks … soft."

She looked at him, surprised. "It is. It's a relaxed form of reality. That's why I like it." It had gotten her through a lot when her reality wasn't.

"Do you recognize these places?" she asked.

"That's the beach here, in Riviera View." He pointed at the one that had hung in a gallery years ago.

~~~~~~~~~~~~~~~~~~~

"All three of you? Maybe I could go for a coffee with each instead?" Anne asked, chuckling.

"Come on, it'll be fun. I promise," Hope said, handing her credit card. "You already know the food will be good." She tilted her head in the direction of the bakery's boxes inside the bag Anne handed her. "And Libby's is just down the street, so when you're off work, just get over there."

She smiled. "Okay."

Since Bella had moved away, and with Hope, Libby, and Roni being supportive, she couldn't say no. She didn't *want* to say no. She wanted to go for the things she craved—love, family, friendship.

Love, she had. Beyond measure. The ring around her finger was the embodiment of it, in plain sight.

Family, she had. Finn. Max. Her parents. And the members of her aunt's family who wanted her in their lives. She was fine with that.

Friendship could be next.

Since she and Finn still officially lived in two separate towns, not all her Monday evenings were busy.

A few hours, a decorated cake, and a short walk after, Anne climbed the stairs to Libby and Luke's apartment in early March. It was right above Books And More on Ocean Avenue. She always wondered what it looked like.

The door was flung open before she could finish knocking.

"There she is!" Roni announced to the room. She was already chewing on a cookie, half of which was still in her hand. "Come in. I'm glad you came. It's a great way to spend Monday evenings."

She followed Roni in and was immediately hugged by both Hope and Libby, who were arranging food on plates in the kitchen.

"So glad you're here," Hope said, brushing her auburn bangs from her eyes.

"Hey, you," Libby said. "Finally." She chuckled.

"So, how does it feel to be here after you two pretty much grew up in the bakery but never really connected?" Roni asked.

"That's Roni for you," Hope said. "Doesn't shy away from uncomfortable topics."

Anne laughed. "I brought these." She handed Libby an assorted box of cupcakes. "Everyone's favorite flavors."

"Thank you!" Libby said.

"As to your question," Anne said, turning to Roni with a smile. "We can kick that elephant out of the room. I love the bakery, and I knew Libby loved it, so seeing her every day at school and knowing my parents owned it instead of her mother ... it might be stupid, but it made me uncomfortable. And I'm not super great at starting conversations." She smiled as a warm recollection zoomed through her. The only person she had no problem striking up a conversation with was the least likely one. Finn Brennen.

"Your parents saved my mom by buying it and keeping her as an employee. I resented my dad for putting us in that situation, not you." Libby then turned to Roni. "There, elephant kicked. Anything else?"

"Yes. We want to know it all. And how's Avery?" Roni smirked.

Anne chuckled. This was not going to be easy.

"Ignore her. We eat first," Hope said, picking up plates to carry to the living room.

They all helped, and Anne noticed they seemed to have permanent seats. Roni slumped herself horizontally on an armchair, her smooth, black hair dangling off one end while her legs off the other. Libby sat on one side of the couch, with her legs folded under her, and Hope sat on the rug, leaning against the other side of the couch and stretching her legs under the coffee table. It was a warm and cozy apartment, with framed pictures of Luke and Libby. She sat on the armchair opposite Roni.

Except for a few inside jokes that she didn't get and they hurried to explain, they made sure she felt comfortable and included. She hadn't had that kind of girls' night since college, and she was enjoying it so far.

"Can we get to the interesting part now?" Roni asked when the coffee table had only leftovers and dirty plates on it. "One thing you can count on, Anne, is that everything that is said between us remains between us. And no one here can stand that cousin of yours, so feel free."

"Um, she's dating someone," Anne said. "And I hope it goes well, for everyone's sake." The week before, Linda had come into the preparation room and excitedly whispered to Anne, "Allison at Flowerelle just told me that she had a delivery for Avery. A dozen red roses. From that boyfriend she had a few months back."

"Yeah, I saw them being all touchy-feely on the promenade the other night," Roni said. "The things you see when you take your kid out for a late ice cream—her school's vice-principal shoving her tongue down some guy's throat."

Hope sprayed out the water she had just sipped. She covered her mouth and stopped the rest from spilling out. "Roni!" She exclaimed as soon as she could speak.

"Yeah, you should tell Jordan that he missed out big time, Hope," Roni said, laughing. "Finn probably knows he's not missing out on anything, right?" she then said, smirking at Anne.

"Veronica!" Libby rebuked, though she couldn't stop laughing.

"What? Too soon?" Roni said, looking between Libby and Anne.

Anne laughed. "Not too soon, and yeah, he knows. I think he's … fine." She smirked at Roni.

Roni measured her through narrowed eyes, tilting her head to the side. She then nodded. "You know, I look at you, and I have a feeling"—she waved a hand across Anne's features as Avery had done before Christmas, but Roni's conclusion was different than Avery's—"that he's more than fine. It's always the quiet ones," Roni said with a cheeky smile. "Am I right, Anne?"

"My God, Roni! Anne, I'm so sorry," Libby hurried to say, placing a hand on Anne's arm and glaring at Roni amusedly.

"She won't join us again," Hope said, hardly able to stifle a chuckle.

"No, no," Anne said, laughing. "That's okay. I like this take-no-prisoners attitude. I've had to walk on eggshells much too often. And, Roni, all I can say is … you're not wrong." She smirked back at her.

"Welcome, Anne." Roni tilted her wine glass with a warm smile.

She then agreed to tell them the history, trusting this small circle of friends to safeguard her and Finn's story that only three other people knew—her parents and Bella.

"Wow," Hope said when Anne was finished. "I didn't know."

"No one did."

"No, that he roughed up Eric in high school!" Hope said, a gleeful smile spreading on her face, knowing that someone had stood up to that ex-husband of hers when he had been at his nastiest.

They all laughed. It was a burst of releasing laughter, which was better than the pitying expressions that they'd had on throughout her narration.

"I can't believe this. You look at someone and think you have them all figured out while, inside, they're different, and you have no idea what they've been through. So, Avery doesn't know?" Roni said.

"No. And she shouldn't know. It was, and still is, a very sensitive issue for everyone, and knowing this will only cause more harm."

"Yeah, I can't even imagine," Libby said, brushing her fingers pensively through her brown hair. "I don't know what's worse—being in love with a man who only loves you as a friend, like Luke and I were, or having a man love you just as much and not being able to be with him."

"There are no winners in this competition, Libby," Anne said, scoffing and patting Libby on the shoulder.

"Damn right," Hope said.

"To long-lost and new-found love," Roni said, surprising everyone with a heartfelt toast. "Come on, don't look at me like that," she said, getting out of the armchair and leaning forward, glass in hand, toward them. "Cheers, ladies."

They all got up, leaned forward from their side of the coffee table, and clinked their glasses together.

Chapter 24

His Jane. She wasn't just two things; she was a rainbow—his lover, his best friend, his secret that—even now when she was his in plain sight love—only they knew how deeply they loved. His sunflower, delicate and calm outwardly, yet fiery if you knew how to kindle her flame. His soon-to-be wife and mother of his second child.

They were attending Max's swim meet two weeks before the wedding. She arrived straight from work and missed the beginning, but it wasn't Max's turn in the water yet. Since this was a school meet, Finn wasn't on deck as a coach. He sat with her on the benches among the other parents and did his best not to analyze the swimmers' tactics and their coaches' strategies.

"I'm late," Jane said when she took the seat next to him.

"You were on time. It's not his turn yet."

"No, Finn, I'm late."

He turned to look at her. She was smiling.

"Two weeks now. I didn't want to say anything before, but I'm never this late."

"You're peeing on a stick as soon as we get home," he said before cupping her face and kissing her, just when everybody around them jumped up to cheer the heat that had just finished.

And she did, and she was, and he couldn't be happier.

He'd always wanted it all with her, and now he had it. He wanted them to have everything that they had been deprived of for so long by that bitch—fate.

Jane was his, and he was hers. And that was all that mattered.

And that's what he said when they each read their vows in San Luis Obispo's City Hall. They didn't want to see the inside of Riviera View's town hall again.

Her parents; his mother and her husband; Noah and his family; Jane's three new friends and their loved ones; Bella, who arrived alone, happy to leave her husband to handle the kids for a few days; Connie Latimer and her partner; and even Sarah Latimer from the pharmacy, who felt she had contributed to it all, were there. And the four of them in front of the judge—him in a white dress shirt and tie, Jane, beautiful in a long, pearl dress, Max not in a tux, and the peanut no one except him and Jane knew about.

The wedding cake that awaited at the beautiful garden restaurant that they took everyone to dinner to had been made by the bride—a tall, plain, white cake with delicate pool-blue flowers. They laughed as they slow danced, holding each other way too close and whispering their song's incomprehensible lyrics between them as if they were sweet nothings.

His mother and her husband stayed with Max for a few days while he and Jane spent their honeymoon in a cabin in Lake Tahoe.

"Too cold to swim, but we'll have a waterfront view," Jane said.

"All I need is a private cabin and you."

He held Jane's face in his hands, his fingers tangled in her hair, absorbing how pretty she was all flushed from exertion and the warm glow of the fireplace. "Promise you'll keep kissing me as if it's your last time every time," he rasped when they were devouring each other during another round on the bed. He loved the remoteness of their cabin. She could make all the noise she wanted, all the sounds he could get out of her.

With her eyes locked on his, she breathed, "I'm just making you mine one kiss at a time."

He drew her even closer and kissed her as he loved her—hard, deep, and all-consuming.

Playlist

Songs mentioned or ones I thought of while writing:
Whiter Shade Of Pale – Procol Harum
Black – Pearl Jam
Dancing Queen – Abba
Lovesong – The Cure
Running Up That Hill – Kate Bush (which I loved decades before Stranger Things ;))
The Winner Takes It All – Abba

Author's Notes:

The idea to write Anne came to me years ago from a combination of a single sentence in Gabriel Garcia Marquez' *Love In The Time Of Cholera* and Jane Austen's *Persuasion* (and if you watched Netflix *Persuasion* – please know that this is not Austen's Anne). Marquez's sentence about the fire that burns behind quiet façades and Austen's internally broken though externally quaint, cool, and collected heroine both inspired my Anne. I hope you loved her and her story.

A little Easter egg: Melanie, Anne's neighbor in Cincinnati, is the heroine of *Of All Places*. I had fun connecting them in some way, ha-ha.

Read the other books in the 'Riviera View' series:

Visit Lily's website, sign up to her newsletter, and get
a bonus epilogue: www.lilybaines.com
Don't miss updates, follow her on:
www.facebook.com/lilybainesauthor
www.instagram.com/lily_baines_author/

The 'Of All Hearts' Series – finding love in an
unexpected place, time, and person:

Acknowledgments

Writing my heart out on a page is a lonely experience until it reaches the eyes and hearts of others, so thank you for being on this journey with me.

Thanks Brooke Burton and Devin Sloane for being the first set of eyes and hearts that glimpsed into mine and provided valuable feedback. To Leigh Ann Jordan (@read_pair_share), Lissete Aberg (@lissthebooklover), and Demi Abrahamson for beta reading and lending me their insight and reader hearts to let me know I was on the right path.

Thank you to those who encouraged me throughout in a million ways – Joscelyn, Kau, Alexandra, Susanne, Nalani, Marla, Brenda, Caroline, Debbie, Sionna, Louise, and many others who dm'd, commented, shared, and helped spread the word. Thank you to every single reader on my ARC team, some are with me from the start!

Thanks to Kristin, my editor, who weeds out my grammatical mistakes and run-on sentences.

Thanks to M.O. who let me use her beautiful apartment during the day – I couldn't finish writing this book if it wasn't for her help!

And as always, thanks to Roy, who proves that love transcends dirty dishes and piles of unfolded laundry and every other aspect of routine and does his best to enable my writing, and to the three grumpy sunshines of my life who are growing into amazing, intelligent, and sensitive people, and make me so proud.

Printed in Great Britain
by Amazon